Pants On Fire

By Lacey Black

Lacey Black

Pants On Fire

Lacey Black

Index

Lacey Black

Also by Lacey Black

Rivers Edge series
Trust Me, Rivers Edge book 1 (Maddox and Avery) – FREE at
all retailers   ~ *#1 Bestseller in Contemporary Romance*
Fight Me, Rivers Edge book 2 (Jake and Erin)
Expect Me, Rivers Edge book 3 (Travis and Josselyn)
Promise Me: A Novella, Rivers Edge book 3.5 (Jase and Holly)
Protect Me, Rivers Edge book 4 (Nate and Lia)
Boss Me, Rivers Edge book 5 (Will and Carmen)
Trust Us: A Rivers Edge Christmas Novella (Maddox and
Avery)
       ~ *This novella was originally part of the Christmas
       Miracles Anthology*
With Me, a Rivers Edge Christmas Novella
BOX SET – contains all 5 novels, 2 novellas, and a BONUS
short story

Bound Together series
Submerged, Bound Together book 1 (Blake and Carly)
       ~ *An International Bestseller*
Profited, Bound Together book 2 (Reid and Dani)
       ~*A Bestseller, reaching Top 100 on 2 e-retailers*
Entwined, Bound Together book 3 (Luke and Sidney)

Summer Sisters series
My Kinda Kisses, Summer Sisters book 1 (Jaime and Ryan)
       ~*A Bestseller, reaching Top 100 on 2 e-retailers*
My Kinda Night, Summer Sisters book 2 (Payton and Dean)
My Kinda Song, Summer Sisters book 3 (Abby and Levi)
My Kinda Mess, Summer Sisters book 4 (Lexi and Linkin)
My Kinda Player, Summer Sisters book 5 (AJ and Sawyer)
My Kinda Player, Summer Sisters book 6 (Meghan and Nick)

My Kinda Wedding, A Summer Sisters Novella book 7
(Meghan and Nick)

Rockland Falls series
Love and Pancakes, Rockland Falls book 1
Love and Lingerie, Rockland Falls book 2
Love and Landscape, Rockland Falls book 3

Standalone
Music Notes, a sexy contemporary romance standalone
A Place To Call Home, a Memorial Day novella
Exes and Ho Ho Ho's, a sexy contemporary romance
standalone novella

Co-Written with *NYT Bestselling* Author, Kaylee Ryan
It's Not Over
Just Getting Started

*Coming Soon from Lacey Black
Love and Neckties, Book 4 in the Rockland Falls series
Can't Fight It, Fair Lakes Book 3 with Kaylee Ryan

Prologue

Cricket

10 years ago

They say that nothing can bring you down on the happiest day of your life, right? Well, that's total crap. Truth be told, a cocky playboy with a charming smile and twinkling blue eyes can bring you down faster than a lead balloon any day of the week, especially on your happiest. All it takes is a few ill-fated words and everything comes crashing down. Those plans you spent countless hours making? Ruined. The money you've already shelled out for an overpriced studio apartment in a neighborhood you can't afford? Gone. The stupid cocky playboy that you want to punch in the face for dropping a bomb in your well-planned, happy little life?

You see where this is going, right?

We need to talk.

My happiest day started with a text as I was getting ready for my college graduation. My entire family was in town, anxious to see the first Hill go to college and actually finish with a degree instead of a baby. Three generations of Hill women, all knocked up before their expected graduation day. My older sister barely made it through her first semester before she was with child. My mom? Pregnant with my sister her sophomore year. And my grandma was expecting sometime during her third year of school and didn't finish.

But not me. I was determined not to fall into the same young mama rut that my sister, mom, and grandma all fell into. Sure, they're all happy with their decisions for early motherhood, but I knew I didn't want that. I wanted to get out of Carbondale. I wanted out of

Illinois. Away from the brutal midwestern winters. The moment I was handed my diploma, Danny and I were loading up the car and heading for California.

At least that's what I thought.

My fingers fly over the phone screen.

Me: *What's up?*

Danny: *I think we should break up.*

I stare down at the screen, waiting for the LOL or the JK. But neither appear. Instead, the bouncing bubbles on the phone reveal his next piece of word vomit.

Danny: *I just don't see us going anywhere.*

Me: *Don't see us going anywhere? We're leaving tomorrow for California, Danny!*

Danny: *I'm still going, but alone. I need to find myself. I need to set out on my own path of self-discovery, Cricket.*

I blink down at his words. Self-discovery? Are you freaking kidding me right now? The man can't even cook mac and cheese from a box without needing adult supervision. *I'm* the one who landed him the interview with *Good Morning, San Francisco. I'm* the one who found and secured our tiny studio apartment, footing the entire first and last month's rent, mind you. *I'm* the one who bought and ironed the clothes he's wearing right now, God knows where, while he tries to break up with me via text message.

Me: *Danny, where are you?*

I set the phone down on the counter, hair completely forgotten and eyes glued to the screen.

Danny: *It doesn't matter. I'm gone.*

My heart skids to a stop in my chest.

Me: *Gone?*

Danny: *I left this morning.*

Me: *For Cali? With my fucking car?*

Danny: *Our car, darling.*

Me: *Don't you darling me, Daniel James Ohara. You know damn good and well that I paid every fucking payment on that fucking car. You bring it back right now!*

Danny: *Can't. I'll wire you the money when I start my new job.*

Are you fucking kidding me right now? This is seriously my life?

Me: *Danny, explain to me how I'm supposed to get to California to start MY new job if you've already left with the car?*

Danny: *You're starting to cut out.*

Me: *We're not on the phone, asshole. Get back here now with my car!*

Danny: *You're breaking up. I better let you go.*

I pick back up the phone, my fingers flying over the screen.

Me: *Danny!*

Me: *Daniel!*

Me: *Motherfucking jerkward!*

No response. Typical.

Danny Ohara was, as my grandma called him, the big man on campus. The boy with the pretty smile and the charming personality, who played college football and received straight A's. Everybody wanted to date him, even if it was only for a night or two. His reputation for being a playboy preceded him, and the last thing I wanted was to be anywhere near his radar.

I was, however, the one he zeroed in on at the beginning of our junior year. I went to one football game. One. And that was only because his roommate, Rueben, begged me. We had a math class together, both of us needing that single semester credit to finish our respective degrees. Rueben was sweet and maybe even a little shy, with his wire-rimmed glasses and his straight, white smile. I finally agreed to go and did something I'd swore I'd never do.

Swoon over a damn football player.

Danny was spectacular. He was quick, catching almost every ball thrown at him, including the game-winning touchdown. After the game, he came running up to his friend for a victory bro-hug, and the moment his eyes met mine, I was a goner. Of course, I didn't agree to go out with him right away. No, I played hard to get. After a few weeks though, I was putty in his hands, just like the rest of the female population at Southern Illinois University. We dated straight through junior year, and when it came time to set up housing for my final year at Southern, I agreed to live with him.

Over the last year, we planned everything. His job as a television news anchor for a small station in San Francisco, and mine behind the scenes in the production studio. We both landed a job at the same station, which I never expected to happen, but since it's small, apparently everyone uses it as a stepping stone until they can land their dream job at a bigger network. Positions open up all the time.

And now what? I'm just supposed to drive myself out to San Francisco, in the car I no longer have, and work right next to the man who pretty much just threw our future in the trash with yesterday's takeout?

Fuck that.

Fuck him.

There's a pounding at the door that pulls my attention. Anger sweeps through me like a tsunami as I stomp toward the doorway, praying it's the jerk of all jerks on the other side. I disengage the lock and throw open the door, mouth open and ready to let my anger fly, when I find Rueben standing at the threshold.

"Hey, Crick," he says, giving me a sheepish grin. If I wasn't so pissed off, I'd find it a little comforting. But I don't.

"Did you know? Did he tell you he was planning this?" I demand, my hands flying around like jet airplanes as I talk. I've always been a talker with my hands, which is a big reason why I've never really wanted to be on-screen. Behind the scenes is more my thing.

He holds up his hands in surrender. "He didn't, I swear."

"Liar. You'd do anything for him," I mumble, taking a step back and allowing him to enter the apartment. There are boxes everywhere, pretty much all of our earthly possessions ready for the trek out west.

The door slams behind him, though I don't think it's intentional. "Not true. I'd never purposely hurt you to protect him." I stop in the kitchen and turn to face him. Rueben pushes his familiar glasses back up his nose, a motion I'm pretty sure he does without even realizing, and focuses those dark brown eyes on me. "I had no clue, I swear. He just called me from Kansas City, asked me to come over and, uh, well, get his stuff."

Rage burns the tips of my ears. "Get his stuff? Tell that thoughtless jerk I want my damn car!" I huff, crossing my arms over my chest and glaring at his best friend.

Rueben clears his throat, his eyes dropping to where my arms are crossed. He quickly averts them, focusing on the floor in front of him like it's the most interesting floor in the world. "You look nice, by the way," he mumbles.

Glancing down, I see what our friend is seeing for the first time. Well, besides the fact that I'm pushing my boobs up and almost out of the V neckline of my navy-blue dress. It hits just below the knee, the satiny material wrapping around my abdomen like a second skin. For someone who doesn't usually wear many dresses, it was a no-brainer, perfect for my graduation ceremony.

Rueben is wearing black slacks with a dark gray button-down and black tie. The only spot of color on his entire body is the small American flag tie tack he received for Christmas last year from his older brother who serves in the Army. His entire family is here, including his older brother, to watch him receive his computer engineering degree. We're supposed to all have dinner after the ceremony to celebrate today's accomplishments. My family, Rueben's family, and Danny's.

I feel the weight of my anger dissipate, my shoulders sagging where I stand. "What am I supposed to do?" I whisper to no one in particular.

The next thing I know, I'm engulfed in strong arms, surrounded by the familiar scent of Abercrombie & Fitch cologne, and pressed against a warm chest. It's familiar, yet so very foreign at the same time. All I know is he's offering me comfort at a time when my entire world is turned upside down.

Everything has changed.

Decisions need to be made, and quick. I'm supposed to start my new job a week from Monday. Our apartment is ready, the keys waiting in San Francisco. We're supposed to leave tomorrow to start our new life. There's no way I'll get any of my money back on the apartment and finding a new job, either in Carbondale or a surrounding town will be hard this late in the game. All of the post-graduation jobs were scooped up months ago. Never mind the fact that I don't have a car. My entire life is in shambles, but now isn't the time to fall apart. Now, I have a graduation ceremony to get through and a dinner with my family. With Danny's family, as awkward as that will be.

I can do this. I just need to take it step by step.

"I don't know, Crick. I just don't know." He places his warm lips against my forehead in an act of kindness and support and adds, "I'm sure you'll figure it out."

Chapter One

Cricket

Present Day

"This is Cricket Hill for *Good Morning, San Francisco*, reminding you all to have a safe weekend," I say, smiling at the camera in front of me. The moment the red light turns off, I sag in my seat, relieved to be done with the craziness of this workweek.

"And we're off," our producer, Cory, says. "Great job, everyone."

The usual round of chatter fills the studio as we finish this morning's news broadcast. I sigh deeply and relax in my chair, anxious to get my earpiece out and this makeup off my face.

"Great job, Cricket," Todd, my co-host coos beside me. Todd is your typical pretty boy who thinks all women fall at his feet in orgasmic joy.

"Thanks," I mumble, ready to get away from Todd and his advances. I know what's coming next, and I always do my best to heed it before it happens.

"Big plans this weekend?" he asks, jumping up and essentially blocking my exit, as he leans a hip against the desk.

"Yep. Catching a flight home," I remind him, removing my mic and battery pack from my suit and setting it on the desktop.

"Oh, that's right. I almost forgot you're heading home. Homecoming, right?" He offers me a big smile, one that says he knows more than I offered him last week. I had merely told him I was heading home for a visit. How he found out it's homecoming weekend is beyond me. Actually, no that's not true. The only person I'd classify

16

a friend at work is the makeup artist, Penny, and she probably told him. One smile thrown her way and she's practically dropping to her knees or peeling off her panties. Penny has a weakness for my cocky co-host, and all it would take is a few smiles or maybe a late-night sexcapade promise and my friend would accidentally spill all the details about my trip.

Blinded by the promise of penis.

Exhaling, I give him a tight smile. "Yep, homecoming weekend."

"That'll be fun, right? You show up and remind everyone of how much of a success you are," he croons, brushing a strand of long, dark hair off my shoulder. "Do you know what would make it even better?" he asks, taking a step forward and into my personal space.

Reflexively, I step back. "No, but I'm sure you're going to tell me," I mumble, already knowing I'm not going to like his suggestion.

"If you showed up with a boyfriend. You know, one who's a little more famous and more well-known than you?"

I have to fight the eye roll hard. It's right there, ready to be unleashed, but I somehow manage to reel it in. "Uh, no thanks, Todd," I reply, stepping around him and heading toward my dressing room.

"Hear me out, Cricket," he says, catching up with me and escorting me down the hall. "Ratings are through the roof right now, and there's that big online group on social media who are pushing for us to be together."

Probably started by him…

"Anyway, you show up with me on your arm and you'll be the bell of the homecoming ball. Plus, think of the photo op," he adds, grinning from ear to ear. "If you play your cards right, I might even kiss you goodnight." Then, he waggles his eyebrows suggestively, and my coffee from before the broadcast almost comes back up.

"Oh, uh, yeah, that's not necessary," I assure him as I reach my door. Todd stands there, anxiously awaiting the invitation to come in, but it never comes. "Anyway, I need to get going. I have a flight to catch," I add quickly before slipping through my doorway like a ninja on speed, and exhale loudly when I'm bathed in the blissful silence of my closet-sized dressing room.

Until…

"The offer stands, Cricket," Todd says through the door. "If you get there and realize you need me, I'm just a call away. I'm sure Cory would give me some time off to come rescue you, especially if there's paparazzi nearby to catch our exchanges. Ratings galore!"

"No thanks, Todd. I'm good," I state loudly. Then, I reach for the lock and make sure my can't-take-a-hint co-host doesn't come barging in.

Finally, I'm alone and drop into my chair. Todd is a nice guy and all, even though he's slept with nearly every woman in the building, but he's not my type. I don't want the egotistical man who finds photo ops around every corner. Not the guy who "accidentally" lets his penis fall into other vaginas when he's working late. (I've heard all about his late-night booty calls.) Not the one who sees women as arm candy to help boost ratings when you're seen at a mayoral luncheon or a charity dinner.

If I wanted that, I'd date Harris again.

Or worse, Danny.

Shaking off the images of both exes, I head over to my luggage and double-check that I have everything. I grab the small bag from my counter that Penny left me and shove it in the open suitcase. I'd been fine with just a swipe of a hazelnut eye shadow and mascara, but when Penny heard about it, she threw a fit. Five minutes later, I had a small travel bag filled with enough product to keep me dolled up for the next three years. As she was applying my makeup for today's show, she even taught me how to do it myself.

I've never been a big one for wearing it. In college, sure, but since then, I was always the girl behind the scenes. You don't need makeup to stare at television monitors at six in the morning and talk to the producer through the headset. Even when the co-host position was thrown in my lap, I didn't see the need for all that makeup. I leave it to Penny for the show and stick to the basics outside of it. It's how I like it.

Simple.

I shove the rest of my stuff that's making the trip to Illinois into the suitcase and zip it closed. My anxiety starts to climb as thoughts of this weekend's festivities parade through my head. The game, the dinner, the brunch. I haven't attended a homecoming game since I left Southern, but here I am, getting ready to fly home, the invitation practically burning a hole in my purse.

When the invite arrived, I was prepared to throw it in the trash. In fact, I did. Then I read the accompanying letter and realized this was more than just an alumni event. This was so much bigger. This was an invitation to give one of two keynote addresses at the Sunday brunch. The alumni are celebrating my graduating class, as well as that of the twenty-five year class. Being invited to speak is a huge deal—one I'm not sure I was really qualified for, or wanted, for that matter. But I couldn't ignore it.

Believe me, I tried.

Two days later, I found myself emailing the alumni foundation and accepting the offer to give one of the keynote addresses.

No going back now.

Even though, again, I tried.

I've talked myself out of it a thousand times. Everything from a random bout with the flu to a plane crash has crossed my mind, though that last one can't be corroborated with facts. Every time a new excuse would pop into my head, I'd see my parents. They're so excited I'm finally coming home. It's been three years, and even then, it was a short weekend visit. At the end of the day, I just don't want to hear the disappointment in their voices when I tell them I've changed my mind.

That's why I zip up my luggage and set it beside the door. That's why I verify I have my travel documents and my wallet ready in my purse. That's why I wave goodbye to my co-workers (grateful that Todd isn't anywhere to be found) and make my way out to my awaiting Uber ride. That's why I tuck in my big girl panties and prepare for a weekend of handshakes and fake smiles.

Of seeing former classmates.

Of dealing with Danny for the first time in a decade.

FML.

***

"Welcome to St. Louis Lambert International Airport. We hope you enjoy your visit."

I watch for my luggage as the carousel slowly moves, suitcases thrown haphazardly on the belt. Mine, of course, is on the bottom of a pyramid, and the moment I pull at my handle, they all tumble down. A woman comes barreling toward me, speaking in a foreign tongue, as she gathers up one of the fallen bags. I'm pretty sure she's cursing me out right now if the side-eye is any indication.

"That one's yours," I hear over my shoulder. The hairs on the back of my neck stand up as familiarity washes through me.

I spin around and come face to face with a smiling one from my past. He's still wearing glasses, though these are a black frame that, for some crazy reason, only make him hotter. He's a little beefier than he was in college, though mostly in the shoulders and chest. You can tell he puts a little effort into his appearance now, especially with his designer jeans and pressed button-down shirt.

"Rueben!" Before I even realize what I'm doing, I throw myself against his chest. He catches me easily, barely stumbling under my unexpected body slam, and pulls me tightly against him.

Against his chest.

His very nice, muscular, toned chest.

I gasp at how nice it feels, and the fact that I'm enjoying this hug a little too much.

"Hey, Crick. Long time no see," he whispers against my ear, sending little shivers of something I don't want to think about racing through my body. I've never had this sort of reaction to Rueben, and I can't start now. He's a friend, plain and simple.

I pull myself off his body and take a step back. Awkwardly, I pat his upper arm, only to find that just as defined as the chest I was just plastered against. "It's so great to see you. It's been...a long time."

Ten years, to be exact. Even though there were a few text exchanges, I haven't seen Rueben since the day after our college graduation. He showed up to get Danny's things and helped me load my stuff in a rental the following day. He offered to drive out with me, but I refused. My dad was ready to make the trip. At that point, I was determined to do it myself, to prove to Danny he didn't break me. We parted ways on the front step of my former apartment with a hug and a wave, and bid each other luck in the future.

Now, he's standing directly in front of me.

And hotter than ever.

I run my hand along my hair, wishing I had done something a little different with it. After the broadcast and my bags were packed, I just pulled it up with a hair tie I found on my dressing table. With all the hairspray and goop in it, at last look, it resembled something

21

of a football helmet rather than a ponytail. And that was before a four-and-a-half-hour flight, sandwiched between an elderly woman and a businessman who claimed the armrest as his own, in which I power-napped for a good two hours of the air travel, thanks to my trusty earbuds and old school Paula Abdul.

I probably have sleep crusties in my eyes and drool marks on my chin.

Typical.

"It has been," he replies, pulling me back to the now. Rueben rocks back on his heels and shoves his hands in his pockets. His dark chocolate brown eyes do a quick head-to-toe scan, probably noting all the not-too-flattering things wrong with my sudden appearance in the airport. Finally, after a few seconds, he adds, "You look good, Crick."

I clear my throat, thankful that he's still polite and isn't calling me on my sleep-head, racoon eyes look, and reply, "Thanks. You do too."

And he does.

Real good.

Rueben grabs the remaining bag that toppled at my feet. "This one yours?" he asks, taking my well-worn suitcase in his other hand.

"It is. But I can carry it," I quickly assure him, making sure I have my computer bag and purse secured on my shoulder before I reach for my bag. His bag is half the size of mine and doesn't appear to be bursting at the seams the way mine does. He tosses a garment bag over the top of his and gives both suitcases a pull.

"I can help. I don't mind." And then he offers me a smile. A smile that makes my heart tap dance in my chest and the air in my lungs evaporate. Then, he turns around and gives me a view of his ass. His perfectly defined, round ass in a pair of dark jeans. Apparently, dark jeans and a firm ass are my kryptonite.

Quickly sidestepping and walking around him, I head toward the car rental counter. I can feel his eyes burning into my back. Well, specifically, my ass. My suspicions are confirmed when I glance behind me and find Rueben's eyes locked on my rear. Apparently, black leggings are a guy's kryptonite.

As I approach the counter and get in line, I tell him, "You can leave my suitcase. I can take it from here."

He sets it down, and his bag as well. "I'm actually waiting to get a car too."

We stand in awkward silence for a few seconds. There're so many questions I want to ask him, but then, I know he'll want me to spill all the details of my life in the last decade too. And frankly, I'm just not that interesting. Sure, I can brag about my career, but won't I be doing that Sunday at the brunch? And heaven knows my social life has been a bit lacking these last few years, so it's not like I want to offer up any of those boring details.

Fortunately, the line moves quickly, and when it's finally my turn, I set my bags aside and pull my wallet from my purse. "Reservation for Cricket Hill," I offer politely.

The young woman taps away on her keyboard, pulling up the information. Her smile faulters though as she reads the screen. "I'm sorry, Miss Hill, but it appears there was an issue with your reservation."

"Issue? What type of issue?" I ask, feeling the eyes of everyone waiting behind me in line.

"Apparently, your card was declined after the reservation was made. You should have received an email to update the card information," she says, the sad look on her face replacing her earlier smile.

"Email? I didn't get an email. I haven't had any card issues," I start, but then stop in my tracks. My card. It was compromised a month or so back, probably around the time I booked my rental car. Someone in New York went on a shopping spree with my hard-earned money, and the bank cancelled the card and reissued another. I didn't even think about the possibility of my rental car transaction not going through.

"There was an issue with my card," I confirm. "I have my new one though. We can put it on that," I add, pulling my newer debit card from my wallet.

"I'm sorry, ma'am, but the reservation was cancelled completely. We don't have any vehicles available today to rent. If you can wait until tomorrow, we have a few that will be coming back, and I'd gladly rent you one tomorrow," she offers, tapping away on her keyboard.

"Actually, that's not necessary. I have a reservation. Miss Hill can ride with me."

I glance over my shoulder at Rueben. My face burns with mortification, but he doesn't seem to notice. Instead, he produces his reservation number and hands the lady his credit card. "That's not necessary," I stammer as he steps up beside me.

"No? You're going to wait until tomorrow to drive up? And miss the game?" he asks, searching my face with a raised eyebrow. It's as if he knows he's got me.

And he does.

Exhaling, I shove my own card back in my wallet and toss my purse over my shoulder. "Fine. But I'll pay for half of the rental."

"Not necessary, Crick."

"Maybe not, but that's the only way I'll accept the offer," I tell him, standing my ground.

"Fine. You can pay for half," he says, shoving his own card back in his wallet after they swipe it. "As long as you let me buy dinner."

That makes me stutter a breath. "What? No."

Rueben grabs his bag and the car keys the rental attendant offers him and gives me a shrug. "Fine. Then I guess I'll see you sometime tomorrow? Whenever you'll be able to get a car and drive the two hours to Carbondale."

Huffing out a breath, I go to grab my own bag, yet find it already in his hand. It's as if he knows he's got me right where he wants me. Jerk. "Fine. But dinner isn't necessary."

"It is. I'm a growing boy and need nourishment," he replies with a grin and a wink.

I'm left standing there, watching him go, rolling my bag in his capable hand and his butt flexing behind snug denim.

And there go my panties.

Chapter Two

Rueben

I know she's behind me. I can feel it. It's like her presence envelopes me, wrapping around me like a hug and refusing to let go.

I noticed her in the airport way before I spoke to her. She was standing there, her hair all crazy from her flight, and staring at her cell phone. Long, nimble fingers flew over the screen, her teeth nibbling at her plump bottom lip as she read whatever was displayed. It was the first time in nearly a decade that I saw her, and I wasn't prepared for my body's response. First, the sexual desire that struck like lightning, and then the overwhelming sense of right. It was as if I were finally home.

And that's crazy talk, considering I never saw Cricket like that before.

Sure, she's always been gorgeous with her long, dark hair and hypnotizing green eyes. Hell, you might say she's always been a step above gorgeous, not that I ever said it aloud. In fact, I never said anything at all. She was my friend. My friend, Crick.

And she was dating my buddy.

I never so much as felt a stir in my pants around her before today. Well, hell. That's not entirely true. The day I helped her load up her shit into the rental car to drive to San Francisco, I felt something—something strong (and hard, if you know what I mean)—but I blamed the emotions of goodbye. She was leaving. Danny had already left, and Cricket was off too. I was left behind, anxious to start my new career in computer forensics and melancholy that my friends were off to parts of the world I'd probably never see.

Now here I am, headed to my rental car with Cricket just a few steps behind me. I slow down and let her pass, but that doesn't help the substantial erection concealed in my pants. Her ass is framed by a pair of sexy black leggings. My eyes seem to be glued to it as if the key to world peace is hidden there.

Shit, don't get me started on finding peace with Cricket's ass.

I glance back up just in time to see her head swinging back around. Great. Now she just caught me staring at her delectable ass and is probably ready to run screaming from the parking garage. No doubt she'll be more comfortable catching a ride to Carbondale tomorrow. She never really did care about the football games anyway. Cricket only went because of Danny.

Danny.

Another wild card in this weekend's festivities.

I've talked to my former roommate a few times over the years, but this'll be the first time I've seen him in a decade. You know, after he sent me a text that he left town and asked me to go get what was left of his shit from the place he shared with Cricket? He begged me to drive it out to him too, which I ended up doing. Why, I'll never know. Especially since he never actually went to San Francisco and ended up in LA instead. Los Angeles really wasn't my thing, which is why I've never went back. Part of me wanted to tell the asshole that if he would have stayed and broken up with his girlfriend the right way, he would have been able to collect his shit himself. But no, the dumbass grabbed a few things, the keys to the car they shared, and sent texts when he was a state away.

I double click the unlock button on the keyfob, lighting up a new model SUV. No, I don't need it for the luggage space, clearly, but more for the body space. No way was I interested in cramming my six-foot-two inch body into a compact. Instead, I spent the extra hundred bucks for a more comfortable ride.

Cricket's already at the hatch, popping it open and setting her laptop bag inside. When I get to where she's standing, I catch a trace of something fruity with a hint of floral. It's familiar, yet so foreign at the same time. All I know is it's very Cricket, and I only want to smell more. Fuck, do I want to run my nose along her neck and inhale.

Assuming the request to whiff her will probably freak her the fuck out, I toss my bags and hers into the SUV and shut the hatch. "Let's roll," I holler, heading over to the passenger door.

Cricket looks at me like I've grown a second head as I pull it open for her. Her eyebrows shoot skyward in question. "What's this?"

"What? I've always been polite," I state as she climbs into the seat.

"Polite, yes, but I believe the last time you held the door open for me, you intentionally closed it on my ass."

"You were taking too long," I tease, recalling exactly when she's referring to. One night, the three of us were going to grab a burger. Danny was driving their car and I refused to get in the back seat for fear that I'd never be able to climb out again without extraction assistance. Cricket was whining about having to sit in back and taking her sweet-ass time, so when she was bent over and crawling behind the front seat, I pushed the door so that it whacked her in the butt. She went flying into the back seat and the profanity spewed like hot lava, but I smiled the entire way to the burger joint.

"It wasn't easy getting into the back seat of that two-door."

"And you wonder why I never wanted to ride back there?" I ask, propping my forearm on the roof of the vehicle and leaning in just a bit. Again, I catch her scent and it makes me a little dizzy.

"Not my fault you're giant-sized."

"Nope, that would be my dad's fault," I say, shutting her door and heading around to the driver's side. I take a deep, cleansing breath before opening my door and sliding into the seat. I buckle up quickly before pushing the button and starting the SUV. We're silent as I pull out of the garage and head toward the highway. It's been a while, but I've made the trip from St. Louis to Carbondale and back a few times, so finding my way shouldn't be too hard.

When I finally merge onto I-64 East, Cricket cuts through the silence. "How is your family?"

"They're good. Mom and Royce moved to Tennessee a few years back."

"To be close to you?" she asks. I can feel her smile from here.

"Yeah. Royce is working for some zipline company in Gatlinburg and Mom works at a bakery." Royce is four years older than me and has been out of the Army for some time now. He manages one of those tourist zipline companies, which is right up his thrill-seeking alley. And Mom? Well, she's happy anywhere she can bake cookies and breads. They're a stone's throw away from Pittman Center, a small town of about five hundred, and the place I call home. Of course, home to me is a fifteen hundred square foot cabin in the Smoky Mountains with only a single access road to get there.

"And your dad?" she asks, though I can tell by the way her hesitation is infused with the words that she already knows there isn't a happy ending to this story.

"Passed away." I keep my eyes on the road.

"When?" she asks quietly.

"Two years ago. Right after Royce returned home."

"I'm so sorry, Rueben." I hear her words, but it's the delicate hand on my forearm that has my full attention. Not good, considering I'm driving down the interstate at seventy miles per hour.

Clearing my throat, I reply, "Thank you. Mom took it hard, and that's when they moved to Tennessee."

We're quiet for a few minutes, both of us lost in thought. My mind replays that horrible late-night phone call. Mom's wails that I couldn't understand. My brother getting on the phone and telling me of the massive heart attack. The return home and the days that followed were dark, filled with sadness and grief, and ones I wouldn't want to repeat anytime soon.

"Are you still working for that insurance company?" she asks. Her question makes me cringe, considering I haven't worked for that company for six years. It's a not-so-subtle reminder of the huge disconnect in our friendship over the years.

"Uh, no, not anymore. I actually work for a company based in Chicago now."

"Insurance?" she asks, turning slightly in her seat to give me her full attention.

"No, not insurance." I rub the back of my neck and adjust my glasses. It's a nervous habit I've had pretty much my entire adult life. "It's a security company that monitors cyber threats for large corporations around the world."

Silence fills the SUV and after a few long seconds, I glance her way.

"That sounds…cool."

Shrugging, I reply, "It can be. Something different all the time. You'd be surprised by how many ways a company's online security can be threatened."

"And you get to work from home?"

I nod my reply. "I work remotely. That's the cool part about the job. I can work anywhere I have my computer and a secured internet connection."

"Very cool, Ruby."

I instantly groan. "No, not that again."

"What?" She frets innocence.

"You know what. Don't play dumb."

Finally, she busts out laughing. "Fine, Ruby, I won't use the nickname, Ruby, that you hate so much."

One time. One time I took Danny and Cricket home for a long weekend and made the mistake of visiting my grandparents. Grandma has always called me Ruby, much to my complete and utter dismay, and used the term of endearment a handful of times. Even though neither of them said a word while we were there, the moment we returned to school, Cricket would throw the nickname at me just to get a rise.

"How are your grandparents, by the way," she asks hesitantly; probably fearful that I'll share another detail of family who's passed.

"Fine. Moved to an assisted living place in Marion. Mom gets there a few times a year for a visit, but I haven't in a while. I'm hoping to swing by and see them while I'm here," I tell her.

"I'll go with you." Again, I glance her way, ready to tell her it's not necessary, but the look on her face has my mouth stapled shut. It's of friendship, of support, and of peace.

So instead of waving off her offer, I find myself saying, "Thanks. I'm sure they'd love to visit with you."

We're both silent for a while as we head east, Carbondale drawing closer and closer with each passing minute. Cricket checks her phone, her fingers flying across the screen as she replies to whatever text or email she received. A few times she adjusts the radio, bouncing between a top forty station and a classic country one. It's actually a pretty good mix of her style of music and mine. She knows I'm a country fan, while she prefers the upbeat tunes of Taylor Swift and Maroon 5.

Cricket glances up just as I'm exiting off 64 and merging onto IL-127. I've already noticed the sign for Nashville, Illinois, but it's then that she seems to realize where we are. She turns in her seat, a smile playing on her plump lips. "Do you think they're still there?" she asks. I know exactly what she's referring to.

"I don't know, but I hope so."

It only takes a few minutes to drive into the small town and find what we're both eagerly looking for. The welcome sign in the window of the small café is lit and my mouth starts to water instantly.

"Oh my God, it's still here!" Cricket proclaims happily as I pull into the lot and park. There're only a few cars now, but I know as we approach dinnertime shortly, the café will fill up with locals.

The moment I shut down the vehicle, Cricket jumps out and throws her hands in the air. She's stretching, twisting from side to side and working out the stiff and tight muscles that plague her body from hours of air and vehicle travel. What I notice is the way her shirt rides up, giving me a peek of smooth, creamy flesh and the cutest little belly button. The problem I had in my pants earlier starts to transpire once more, and I have to look away to keep from getting a full-blown hard-on in the middle of the parking lot, while lusting after my friend and picturing all the dirty things I want to do to her.

Hopping out of the SUV, I take a second to stretch myself and meet her in front of the car. She's practically vibrating with excitement as she reaches for my hand and pulls me toward the front door. Her hand is warm and soft in mine, and it's hard to ignore the zaps of electricity that zip through my blood.

Cricket grabs the door, but I quickly take the handle and pull, all while her other hand is still nestled securely within mine. It feels good—too good, to be honest—yet, I still don't drop said hand, even when we approach an empty table.

A smiling older woman approaches the table and delivers two menus. "Can I get you something to drink?"

"I'll take an ice water, no lemon," Cricket orders.

"Same," I add when the woman turns her hazel eyes my way.

"I'll go grab those and give ya a minute to look over the menu."

Cricket quickly opens the menu, scanning for the one entrée I know she's after. "Yes! They still have it," she whispers with glee, her green eyes sparkling like emeralds under the sun.

I don't even bother opening my menu. Instead, I set it aside and wait for our waitress to return for our order. "Then I know what I'm having."

The moment the older lady returns, Cricket practically blurts out her order. "I'll have the meatloaf sandwich."

"And I'll have the same, please," I add. The waitress smiles knowingly as she writes down our order and heads toward the kitchen.

"Do you remember when we found this place?" she asks, glancing around at the familiar décor. It's hard to believe, it was nearly eleven years ago when we found this little hole in the wall café that serves the best meatloaf sandwiches in the world.

"Of course, I do. No meatloaf sandwich has ever lived up to this place," I confirm, taking a sip of my ice water.

"Very true," she confirms. Cricket glances down at the table as she adds, "I remember Danny being a total diva that day. He almost missed his flight."

I snort as the memory comes back. "I was five seconds away from throwing his ass out of my car, onto the road."

"But then that security guard would have seen. You remember him, right? The one who made us drive around until Danny was ready to get out for his departure."

"That rent-a-cop had a serious hard-on for his badge that day," I recall, smiling as I picture that young guy who loved to show is authority to those dropping off at the departures entrance.

"I believe you asked him if it was his first day on the job," she giggles that familiar laugh that sends my blood pumping through my veins.

"He was quoting the rule book."

Cricket laughs. Hard. "That he did. And Danny was being a total wanker, not wanting to get out until he was ready." She shakes her head. "It was a much better ride back home than it was taking him to the airport."

I nod, recalling how comfortable we were after dropping Danny off. Two friends talking and enjoying each other's company for a two-hour road trip. My roommate was on his way to the east coast for a long weekend with his family. It was a long-ass drive there, considering Danny did everything he could to pick a fight with Cricket, and then dragged his feet when we finally arrived.

Afterward, Cricket and I got hungry and stumbled upon this little café. We were able to come back once more, senior year, and brought Danny with us. He complained about the hour-long drive to get there, the small menu, and then made gagging noises when our meatloaf sandwiches arrived. The jerk basically ruined our meal and the experience of returning to the little restaurant.

Cricket is lost in thought when I glance her way; most likely remembering the ordeal that surrounded our last visit here. When her eyes connect with mine, she lifts her water glass and holds it up. "To making new memories."

Reaching for my glass, I clink it against hers. "To making new memories." Then I chug a little bit of water, the ice-cold liquid sliding down my throat and cooling my overheated body.

So far, that toast is proving very true.

Chapter Three

Cricket

I take a sip of my water and swear I see the hint of a blush through his dark stubbled cheeks. Rueben averts his eyes for a moment, but when they lock back on mine, something shifts in the open room. The air thickens with a sexual awareness, and I'm not really sure what to do with it. Thankfully, our food is delivered at that moment and I'm saved from any unfamiliar, and slightly uncomfortable, feelings that have decided to rear their heads since landing in St. Louis and reconnecting with Rueben.

"Two meatloaf sandwiches for you," the waitress says as she slides two piping hot plates on our table.

"Thank you," I tell her as I reach for my sandwich, ready to dive in.

"Wait," Rueben says, stopping me before I can bring that first bite up to my watering mouth.

"What?"

"I think that this is a big moment, and maybe we should, you know, do it. Together."

My mouth is suddenly Sahara dry as his words run naked through my mind. Naked, because all of a sudden, all I can think about is getting naked with my friend. You know, *Do it. Together*, as he said. "Ummm," I finally spit out, not really sure where he's going with this.

I watch as he grabs his own sandwich and brings it up to his mouth. "Ready? On three, okay?" he asks, and I nod, suddenly realizing what he was talking about doing together. "One, two, three…"

My taste buds explode as I take that first succulent bite of hot meat, tangy ketchup and barbecue sauce, and gooey cheese between a warm Kaiser bun. "This is heaven in my mouth," I mumble over my food. When I glance across the table, I see Rueben chewing slowly and smiling. "What?" I ask.

He swallows and shakes his head. "Nothing. I'm just happy that you're enjoying it."

"What can I say? Meatloaf sandwiches are all I need in life," I say as I dip a fry in my ketchup.

"Well, maybe not *all* you need in life." He arches his eyebrow and pushes his glasses farther up his nose, and suddenly, it's *my* face that's blushing. I don't know why. I'm sure he didn't mean it sexually, yet that's all I can think about. Apparently, my brain is so far in the gutter everything he says teeters that dirty innuendo line.

So, I decide to take the conversation a different direction. "Well, let's not forget bubble baths."

The way his eyes dilate and then darken, I don't think my casual statement was taken as such. In fact, if the look on his face was any indication, I'd wager a bet to guess my dear friend here was actually thinking about that bubble bath…and maybe me in it.

Interesting.

When our eyes connect once more, he whispers, "Definitely bubble baths. We can never forget those."

We eat in silence, both enjoying our food and watching the locals come in for a cup of coffee and a meal. A few offer greetings as they enter, occasionally stealing glances our way, as if to check out the out-of-towners.

When the check comes, Rueben grabs it before I have the chance. "Hey, I can get that," I tell him, reaching for my purse to pull out a few bills.

"I got it," he insists, sticking a twenty with the check and pushing it to the edge of the table. "My treat, remember?"

"Well, thank you. And I'll get the tip." I don't leave any room for argument. I pull a ten from my billfold and slide it between the ketchup and mustard bottles.

After a quick stop at the restrooms, we're out the door and back in the rental. Rueben pulls back onto the highway, next stop Carbondale. I find a classic rock station, one that I remember from my college days, and instantly smile as John Cougar Mellencamp pumps from the speakers. When I glance over, he appears at ease and comfortable behind the wheel. His long limbs cause him to push the seat back quite a bit, and I'm pretty sure if I were to try to drive right now, my feet wouldn't even come close to the pedals. He casually taps his thumb against the steering wheel to the beat of the song and his plump lips move ever-so-slightly, as if singing along. His dark hair is cut shorter on the sides, and long enough on top to run your fingers through.

And those glasses? Well, I've never really found them on the sexy side before, but here I am, enjoying the hell out of how they look perched on Rueben's straight nose.

Suddenly, the song changes. The familiar song starts to play, and I whip my head to look at the driver. His excited eyes lock on mine as he says, "Do it."

I'm already shaking my head before he even says the second word. I know what he wants, and it's not happening. "No way."

"Come on, Crick. You have to do it! I dare you," he says, glancing from the road back to me.

"You dare me? What are we twelve?" I scoff, crossing my arms and glancing out the windshield.

"No, we're thirty-two and some change. If you want, I'm sure I could find a dart board at one of these bars and we could bet on it," he says with a shrug.

I know where he's going with this. Back in college, we made a friendly wager over a game of darts at our favorite pub. I was pretty good and cocky as hell, thinking there was no way my book-nerd friend was going to beat me. Apparently, I was wrong. It took him a few throws to find his the groove, but once he did, he started scoring more than me. It didn't take long before I was losing the game, and basically my pride.

The wager, you ask?

I had to sing karaoke.

I fucking hate karaoke—not because I couldn't carry a tune, because I could. I hate everyone watching me, judging me. I hate their drunken criticism because everyone knows they can sing better than the person with the microphone when there's enough booze involved. And at that point in the night, there wasn't enough booze flowing through my veins for my liking.

But I did it.

I took the stage and sang "Time for Me to Fly" by REO Speedwagon with Rueben smiling widely the entire time, much like he's doing right now from the driver's seat. I'm about to tell him I'm not singing, but the familiar lyrics catch in my throat and nostalgia sweeps through my blood. Suddenly, I'm belting out the song like I'm Kevin Cronin on stage at Madison Square Garden.

Closing my eyes, I sing the sad words about letting go and moving on, getting slightly choked up on how incredibly accurate they are in regards to breakups. I'm saved from getting too tangled up in my bubbling emotions when this horribly awful and incredibly off-key noise sounds from the opposite side of the vehicle. I look his way, shocked silent as I watch the train wreck that is Rueben singing.

He must realize he's giving a solo performance and stops to look my way. "What?" he asks, a knowing grin on his face.

"What the hell is that?" I gape.

"Singing?" he replies with a shrug. All I can do is stare at him, the song on the radio all but forgotten.

"That was *not* singing. That was like a crying dog having a coughing fit."

Rueben bursts out laughing. "Can dogs have coughing fits?"

"Of course, they can, silly man. Anyway, you're distracting me from my subtle insult. How did I not know you couldn't carry a tune?" I ask, turning down the radio and adjusting myself in my seat to angle toward him.

"I can sing," he insists, though it's a losing fight. He bursts into fits of laughter a moment later, unable to continue with his lie. "Oh, it wasn't that bad."

I can't help but ogle at the way his entire face lights up with laughter.

"Why are you staring at me?"

I shake my head and giggle. "It really was that bad. I'm sorry to break it to you, but there is no future for you on the road, singing in stadiums around the world."

He exhales dramatically. "I can't believe you'd say that, hopes and dreams killer." Rueben turns back my way, the sparkle in his chocolate brown eyes the very definition of teasing.

The familiar song ends and rolls into another one, but we both remain quiet for a bit. It's easy to get caught up in the familiar sights of the area, while they seem brand new all the same. I guess that's what happens after a decade without returning to the place that helped shape your future.

"How is your family?" he finally asks, breaking the silence.

"Oh, uh, they're fine. Mom and Dad are still in Decatur and Amber got married several years ago. She's expecting her third baby in a few months. I thought maybe the impending arrival of another grandchild would curb their well-meant comments about me settling down, getting married, and popping out a few kids of my own, but that would be a lie. It actually has only seemed to fuel the argument. Wait, argument might be too harsh of a word. Concern, maybe? Yeah, that's probably better. They're concerned I'm letting my life slip by, missing the boat to have a family of my own."

I feel his eyes on me. "You're only thirty-two. Still plenty of time for that."

"I agree, but tell that to my mom. I know she just wants the best for me, and her idea of that is married with babies."

"You don't want that?"

I can't help it, I turn and look at Rueben. Something in his tone draws my eyes to his. It's as if he understands my position, yet is still afraid of the answer to his question. So, I answer him honestly, hoping that he gets it. "I think I do, but I guess I just haven't found the right person to make me really stop and truly consider it. To me, it's something that's down the road, off in the future."

He shakes his head, keeping his eyes on the road. "Totally get that. I guess I feel the same," he adds with a shrug.

"So why are you still single?" I ask, not really sure if I want to know the answer to this question or not. Something pulls deep in my gut, a foreign feeling that burns of hesitation and jealousy. Just the thought of Rueben with a woman suddenly makes me a little unsettled, maybe even a little ragey. I shake that thought from my head, refusing to go there.

He shrugs. "I've dated," he says, but doesn't continue. I start to think he's not going to elaborate, when he finally continues. "It can be a little difficult to find that special someone when you live so remotely and really only go to town for groceries. Plus, the background on the last one I was seeing didn't come back so great."

Wait. What?

"Excuse me, did you just say background? You do background checks on the women you date?" I couldn't fight the smile if I wanted to.

He glances my way for a second, a look of shock on his handsome face. "Don't you?"

"Uhh, no, no I don't. I wouldn't even know how to do a background check."

"It's easy, actually. With a little computer work, you can find out just about anything about anyone." He makes it sound so easy, and it probably is for a man who spends fourteen hours a day in front of a computer screen. "Just say the word and I'll run checks on any future suitors."

"Suitors?" I ask with a chuckle. "Is this the 1950s?"

Again, he shrugs, keeping his eyes on the road and a subtle smile on his lips. "The offer stands."

We drive a few more miles before a question pops into my head, and even though I probably shouldn't ask it, I can't help but want to know the answer. No, I *need* to know the answer. Now. "So, what was in her background that made you run for the hills?"

He laughs and shakes his head.

"You can't leave me hanging, Rueben."

"I can, Crick. In fact, it's probably a violation of her privacy to share the information with you."

"*That's* a violation of her privacy? You're kidding me, right? You run a check on her background without her consent, and now you're worried about protecting her? Give up the goods, Rigsby. Now."

"Fine, fine. Just hold your horses, Hill." Rueben has always called me Crick, yet sometimes he'd throw my last name at me, mostly after I use his. Just the way he says Hill has me blushing and a little tingle hits me between my legs. "We had dinner at this little barbecue joint and had a nice time, so we agreed to meet up again later that week. She had mentioned being between jobs, but didn't really say what she did."

"You could have just asked her during your next date, Creepy McCreeperson."

He rolled his eyes. "But I doubt she would have told me she was in the process of going to court for an assault charge."

I stop and look his way, my eyes practically as wide as the wheels on the SUV. "Seriously? Assault for what?"

"For throwing a pie at her boss." Even though he says it with such a straight face, I'm having a hard time believing him.

"Umm...what?"

"Apparently, she was a waitress at a café and when her boss asked her to stay later to help after a particularly busy lunch rush, she quit."

"And the pie?"

"I believe she was carrying it out to the display case when she tendered her immediate resignation."

"And it somehow landed on the boss."

"His face."

Shock mixes with humor and I can't help but laugh. I feel a little guilty, but still, that's funny. "He filed assault charges?"

"Well, not right away. Apparently, she was proud of her pie-throwing abilities until the cops showed up the next day. Then, she screamed it was an accident."

"Let me guess, she tripped?"

Rueben taps the tip of his nose. "Heard this one before, have ya?"

"Well, no, but that seems like the obvious choice when backpedaling your way out of a possible assault charge." He snickers from the driver's seat. "So, what you're saying is pie is a hard limit for you? No pie in the bedroom?"

He doesn't say anything for a few seconds, and I start to worry that I might have overstepped with my sexual reference, which is stupid of me anyway. Rueben is my friend and never in the history of our friendship have either of us taken it anywhere outside of that neat little friendship box. So when he finally speaks, I'm both happy that he's talking to me again and a little turned on myself. "Actually, pie is disgusting. It's mushy on the inside and the crust is always dry. So, yes, pie is a hard limit for me. Now, whipped cream is another story..."

And just like that, my face is burning with embarrassment and my panties are wet.

Clearing my throat, I find myself saying, "I'll remember that."

The truth is, I probably *will* remember that. Every time I see a can of whipped cream, I'll forever associate it with Rueben, specifically what he'd do with it in the bedroom. My overactive imagination, mixed with my underused lady bits, is working overtime now, picturing Rueben spreading me out on top of soft sheets, my body completely under his spell. He pushes my legs apart, exposing my bare core. The can of whipped cream isn't the only noise filling the room as he shakes it and squirts a dollop under my belly button. My breathing is labored, a mix of excitement and nerves. The dessert draws a downward line to my clit, a welcome cold hits against my overheated flesh. Then, his mouth descends, gently sucking and licking...

"Earth to Cricket," he says, pulling me from the fantasy that was just starting to get good.

"What?" I ask, adjusting myself in my seat. If I were a guy, I'd have the biggest case of blue balls known to man.

"I asked if you need to stop anywhere before we hit the hotel," he says.

I notice we're approaching our exit, our destination within reach. That's good because I'm in need of a cold shower and maybe a nap. Hopefully, I'll wake up as the same ol' Cricket who sees her friend as just that and not someone she'd love to get tangled up in the sheets with. Because those images, oh, those images aren't ones I should be picturing right now, or ever. "Uh, no. I'm good. Just the hotel," I confirm.

"Are you sure? You're looking a little flushed. Are you feeling okay?" he asks, his eyes assessing me. I'm terrified of what he'll see. Maybe a note across my forehead that says "I was picturing you eating whipped cream off my pussy?" Yeah, nothing about that screams "we're friends."

"No, no, just a little flushed. It's hot in here," I insist. It's not, of course, but Rueben doesn't call me on my blatant lie.

"You're staying at the Marriott, right?"

I nod my reply. There are several hotels in the area, but the alumni association offers a group rate deal at the Marriott.

We're both silent the rest of our trip, and before I know it, we're pulling up in front of the hotel. It's busy with guests coming and going, and I instantly start to scour the faces for anyone familiar. Part of me is hoping to connect with someone from school, yet the other part is worried about who that might be. I know Danny is coming this weekend. In fact, he's the other speaker at the alumni brunch on Sunday. I didn't, however, know this when I accepted my invitation to speak, and it seemed a little rude to withdrawal after finding out.

Plus, I don't want him to see me sweat. That means he wins.

Rueben pulls up at the valet and gets out. He comes around to the passenger door as I'm gathering up my things, holding it open for me, which is completely unnecessary, but I don't say that. I just relish the fact that there are a few polite, good guys with manners left out there. When I'm standing on the sidewalk, he goes to the back of the SUV and starts to retrieve our bags. I join him, reaching for the handle of my suitcase, but he won't have it. He takes his suitcase in one hand, throws his garment bag over it, and reaches for my suitcase with the other.

"I can get that," I tell him, adjusting my shoulder bag and ready to grab my handle.

"I got it, Crick. Let's go," he maintains, waiting for me to lead the way to the hotel entrance.

The Valet attendant stops and hands him a piece of paper, Rueben slipping him a few bills in the process, before picking back up his handle and meeting me at the door. I once dated this guy, Harris, in San Francisco who refused to tip the bellhop or valet attendant. We took a weekend trip to a vineyard in northern California, and I was shocked by his lack of decorum. I ended up slipping tips to everyone the entire trip, which went completely unnoticed by him. He was too busy checking out the hotel clerk and the restaurant hostess.

"I'll pay for half the tips," I tell him as we enter the hotel.

He snorts a reply, not very manly, yet so incredibly cute at the same time. "I got it."

Rolling my eyes, I glance back at him. He's pulling all of our luggage, yet doesn't seem to be affected by the extra weight a bit. In fact, I can see the slightest outline of the muscles in his shoulders as he pulls the suitcases toward the desk. The shirt is pulled tautly against the hard plains of muscle, and I can't help but want just one little peek…

"Excuse me!" a woman says right before I run into her.

"Oh!" I reply, looking forward to the woman I just bumped into. She's tall and slender, a picture-perfect image of well put-together. She's also a harsh reminder of the struggles I had in one of my history classes. "Ellen. Hi."

Ellen Montgomery rolls her beautifully done-up eyes. "Cricket Hill. Of course you wouldn't be paying attention to where you were going."

"I'm sorry," I stammer, wishing the ground would open up and swallow me whole. "I didn't mean to bump into you." And that's exactly what it was. It wasn't like I barreled into her at full speed. It was a tap of my torso into her arm, yet she's making it sound like I just tried to knock her off her feet.

Ellen was my arch nemesis in college. We took many of the same classes together, and while I was a good student, she had always one-upped me. She was better at tests, at public speaking, at reviewing the material on the fly for group discussions. She also always let me know how easy it was for her to be one step ahead of me the entire time.

Lucky for me, she's the first person I run into when I get to Carbondale.

"And who is this?" she asks, her ocean blue eyes fixed over my shoulder as a gorgeous smile spreads across her face.

Glancing over my shoulder, I see she's talking about Rueben. She leaves her bags in place in line but moves around me and sticks her manicured hand out for him to shake. "Ellen Montgomery," she coos, each word dipped in sugar and sex.

"Uh, Rueben Rigsby. We had history together," he reminds, shaking her offered hand. I watch their interaction, the hairs on the back of my neck standing at full attention but am shocked when he doesn't seem as affected by her charms. In fact, he kinda just drops her hand and turns to me.

"Oh, yes! I totally remember you," she adds, stepping into his personal space and touching his forearm. Her nails practically dig into his flesh in a predatory and asserting way.

But when his eyes connect with mine, it's a hint of panic that I see etched in those dark brown orbs. He's uncomfortable, as if her touching him makes him a little nervous.

Ellen turns her eyes to me, and I don't miss the way they narrow just the slightest. "Are you two..." she starts, leaving her question wide open.

I'm just about to go into my "we're friends" spiel, when Rueben shocks the shit out of me with his own statement. "Yes. We're together. Isn't that right, snookums?"

My wide eyes meet his. There's a plea there, an unwritten desperate cry for help, and I'm pretty sure my brain does a little pop and drop at the idea of "winning" Rueben over Ellen. "Oh, yes. Together. You're right, sweet pea." I almost choke on the endearment and have to fight the smile. Rueben smirks at me, as if unable to control his own laughter.

"Together, together, together," I find myself adding. "We're definitely...together."

Now I'm just stammering like an idiot.

"Look at that, Ellen. I think you're up next in line," Rueben says, nodding to the hotel clerk.

"Yes, of course. Well, I'm sure I'll be seeing both of you around," she says, a little dumbfounded. It's as if the idea of someone not being interested in her is completely out of the realm of possibility. Or maybe it's just that it's *me* he's with. I mean, I did date Danny through the second half of college. Everyone wanted him, Ellen included. She was one who publicly stated on many occasions that she couldn't understand what he saw in me.

In fact, she wasn't the only one who thought that. I, myself, had wondered a time or two why he picked me out of all the females at Southern. Actually, I'm pretty sure there were a handful of guys standing in line too, even though he wasn't gay.

After Ellen checks in, it's my turn. The process is quick, and I'm handed a room key. Thankfully, I had used my new card to reserve my hotel room, so there wasn't the same mix-up as at the car rental counter. That would have been embarrassing.

I hang around, off to the side, as Rueben checks in. He gives the clerk a friendly smile that makes her stutter over her own tongue. I totally get what she sees. He's gorgeous, for sure. As he heads over to where I'm standing, the elevators just off to the left, he seems a little distracted. "Everything okay?" I ask, wheeling my own suitcase to the bank of elevators.

"Uh, yeah," he says, shoving something in his pocket.

"What's that? A phone number?" I tease, grinning from ear to ear as I watch the elevator numbers drop in descent.

"Yeah."

That causes me to pause. When I turn around, he seems embarrassed again. "Seriously? That clerk gave you her number?" I'm not surprised, actually. He's totally sexy and hot, and he did just check in to a hotel room alone.

He rubs the back of his neck, nervously, as the elevator chimes its arrival. "No, not her."

I'm stumped as I look at him in confusion. "Then who?" I find myself asking as the last person exits the car.

48

"Ellen." That one word brings all sorts of feelings bubbling to the surface. The first one is anger. Even though it was a lie, we told her we were together. Yet, here she is, giving him her phone number, as if that didn't matter.

"Wow," I reply, slipping inside the elevator and turning to face the doorway.

Just as he goes to follow me into the awaiting car, a loud voice makes him stop in his tracks. "Rueben Rigsby! Dude, it's been years!"

I know that voice. I've had dreams of it, usually totally false dreams of him begging me to take him back. I don't, of course, because, well, it's my dream. But I'll never forget that voice.

Danny Ohara.

My eyes clash with Rueben's, and I picture my shocked and fearful ones mirror his. No, I'm not afraid of Danny, per se, but more of the actually running into him part. First off, there's the fact that I have day-old hairspray hair that's probably sticking up in a billion directions. Then, the fact that I'm not wearing something sexy that would remind him of what he lost that day, but instead wearing comfy leggings. I'm in no way prepared to run into my ex-boyfriend for the first time in a decade right now, so I do the only thing I can think of to get myself out of this situation.

I push the close button on the elevator wall and watch Rueben disappear behind the door.

Yes, I totally just left him to deal with Danny alone, but they're friends, he'll survive. And I realize the only way I'm going to survive this weekend is to tuck in my big girl panties and face him head-on. Of course, if I were wearing the short gold sequins dress in my luggage and the totally hot black stilettos, then so be it.

Oh, and booze.

It's definitely going to take a lot of that to get me through this too.

Chapter Four

Rueben

I watch the elevator door close, wishing I was on it with her. Not that I'm not excited to see my old friend, Danny, but that I'd rather be with Cricket, even if only for a few more seconds. Weird, right?

"Hey, Danny, how are you?" I ask, pasting on a smile, as he approaches.

"Fan-fucking-tabulous, dude. Can you believe it's been ten years since we've been out of school?" he asks, throwing his arm around me and patting me on the back. Danny is a little shorter than my six-foot two frame, but has more bulk. Though, is that a little belly in his midsection? Hard to tell, but he's looking a little soft in the gut, which surprises me completely because Danny has always been the most vain male I've ever met.

"Hard to believe it's been ten years," I confirm, though it hasn't been nearly that long since we'd last spoken. Although, it has been a while, Danny and I have always kept in touch, due mostly on my part. I've always been the one to initiate the text exchanges or the phone calls.

"So big plans tonight? I think a few of us are gonna hit the bars, like ol' times. Oh, did you hear I'm giving one of the two addresses Sunday morning at brunch?" he asks as another elevator arrives on the lobby floor. I slip on, Danny hot on my heels. He doesn't have any luggage, which tells me he's been here a while already.

"I did hear that," I say as I hit the button for the fourth floor. I didn't even get a chance to ask Cricket where her room was before

50

she darted away without having to face Danny. "And I'm not sure about tonight. I'll have to let you know," I add casually.

Truth be told, I'd be fine with just hanging out in my room and catching up on a little work. I'll be behind after today's travels, but nothing that I can't wrap up quickly with a little computer time tonight. Of course, if I were to run into Cricket, I wouldn't mind hanging out with her a bit either. Maybe grab a late night snack or hang out and catch up a little more. There's still so much I'd like to know about the last decade, especially what led her to sitting in front of the camera instead of behind it.

"You listening?" he asks, pulling me back to the now.

"Oh, yeah. Sorry." The elevator arrives on the fourth floor and I'm surprised when Danny follows me off. "You're on this floor?" I ask.

"Yep, just down hall," he says when I stop in front of my room. "Well, I'll let you get settled. Don't think you're going to spend your entire weekend working in your room. We're hanging out like ol' times," he adds, the look he gives me leaves no room for argument.

"I'll see if I can get my work done tonight and let you know. If not, I mean, we'll always have the game tomorrow," I remind him.

Danny's tanned face lights up. "True that. I'm sure there'll be tons of people at that game. Lots of hotties too," he adds with a cocky smirk.

I laugh at his comment, but more out of habit because if there's one thing that Danny is good at, it's women watching. And flirting. And sex. Though, as far as I know, he stopped the last part when he was with Cricket. Flirting, however, was a different kettle of fish. Danny was a born flirt and did so shamelessly, even when he dated Cricket. She didn't seem to mind, though, at least that I ever noticed. She usually just rolled her eyes and smarted off to him.

He heads to a room five or six doors down, on the opposite side of the hall, as I slip into my room. There's a large bed that takes up the majority of the room, one that I'll be sleeping in alone. Never has the thought of someone accompanying me into bed ever been so strong in my life. Maybe it's the reminder it's been a while since anyone has joined me in any bed, let alone mine, or possibly after spending the last couple of hours with Cricket. I've never been attracted to her, not like this. Sure, I've noticed she was pretty. Sexy, even. But now? Now, my wayward cock is practically ripping itself out of my pants, doing anything it can to get closer to her.

That has definitely never happened before, where she's concerned.

Adding Danny to the mix only seems to make it more complicated.

That's exactly why I'm going to stay in my room and catch up on work tonight. Sleep it off, if you will. Wake up tomorrow and not embarrass myself by sporting a woody in her presence. You know, things a *friend* shouldn't do.

My cell phone chimes an alert, and I find a text message waiting.

From Cricket.

Cricket: *I'm hoping you have the same number. This is Cricket, in case I'm not programmed in your phone anymore.*

Cricket: *Plans tonight? I'm thinking I need some mozzarella sticks from Slim's. Maybe a draft beer. You know, one obtained legally and not through a fake ID.*

I'm automatically smiling that she didn't get rid of my number from her phone. It makes me feel good she didn't ditch my contact after we lost touch.

Me: *I see your cheese sticks and beer and raise you one game of darts.*

There. Sent.

That's me not embarrassing myself in her presence by staying away from her.

I pretend to not be obsessed with seeing those bubbles appear on the screen and head over to unzip my garment bag and hang my suit. It's basic black and my go-to for when I have to travel to meetings for work, which only happens once a year or so. I've paired it with a tan button-down and black matte tie with satin stripes.

The moment it's hanging in the closet, I head over to my phone, you know, to casually check and see if Crick replied. Totally. Casual. And. Completely. Laid. Back.

That's me.

Grabbing the device, I tap on her name.

Crick: *We'll see. Maybe if I'm plied with enough beer, I'll subject myself to a darts beatdown. You've probably been practicing, haven't you?*

Me: *I cannot confirm nor deny that. Cheese sticks, lots of beer, and darts.*

My fingers hover over the text. I almost add "It's a date" but don't want to make things more awkward than they already are. Instead, I just click send.

Crick: *Meet you in the lobby at 8?*

I check the clock on the nightstand beside the bed. It's six thirty. That gives me time to get a little work done and a shower before I head down to meet Cricket.

Me: *Sounds good.*

I set my phone on the small desk and grab my suitcase. My laptop is secured inside, so after I quickly unload the clothes into the small dresser, I power up my laptop and secured portable network. Time to put Cricket and her tight black leggings out of my mind. Time to forget about the awkwardness surrounding Danny and his ex and the way my cock hardens in my pants every time I think about her.

Time to get to work.

***

And hour and a half later, I'm shoving my wallet into the back pocket of a clean pair of jeans and grabbing the rental keys. Cricket didn't specify if we're walking or driving to Slim's, but honestly, it doesn't matter to me either way. The familiar hangout is about a ten-minute walk from here, which is doable. Plus, that would give me more time with her, right?

Shaking my head, I make my way to the door, grabbing my keycard off the dresser as I go by. In the hallway, I glance behind me when another door closes heavily. I'm sure it's probably Danny, considering my luck isn't that great lately, but I'm pleasantly surprised to see Cricket emerge. I actually stop in my tracks. Did she just come from Danny's hotel room?

"Hey! I didn't realize you were on this floor," she says, a warm smile on her coral colored lips that makes my dick twitch in my pants. I'm a horrible friend, because all I can wonder right now is if that color will stay on her plump lips or rub off and leave a ring around my cock.

Shit! Now I'm getting hard. In the hallway. Right in front of her.

Grandma, Grandma, Grandma, Grandma.
Grandma having sex.
Yep. That does it.

Consider my erection squashed, probably for life.

"Oh, uh, yeah," I finally spit out when she's standing directly in front of me. "Room 410."

She smiles again, seeming to find my stumbling and stammering charming, or at the very least, entertaining. Great. She probably thinks I'm cute. You know, like a puppy. A friendly puppy.

My eyes do a quick scan of her outfit, my brain short circuiting and stopping on her top. Then, they do another perusal, this time a much slower one, taking her in as if for the first time. Cricket is wearing tight, dark skinny jeans that hug her perfect ass, a black top that dips down low in the front, giving just a hint of cleavage, and a pair of black heels. Not too tall, but with just enough to add a few inches of height. She's carrying a black clutch thingy and her long brown hair hangs down in big waves. It looks soft and silky and makes me want to run my fingers through it.

Now is definitely not the time though.

Glancing over her shoulder, I try to mentally count the doors, trying to remember which one Danny went into. Was it five down or six? Cricket glances back, trying to figure out what I'm looking at. "Is everything okay?"

"Oh! Yeah, sure. You're…down the hall?"

She nods. "421."

I'm sure he went down five doors, which would mean he's in 419. He's right next door to Cricket. Should I tell her? Probably. That's definitely not a surprise she'd enjoy. I nod toward the elevators, ready to get the hell out of this hallway and away from the possibility of Danny coming out and finding us. It only takes a few seconds before a car arrives to take us down to the lobby. When we're inside, I decide to go ahead and let her know of her neighbor.

"So, I know you probably figured out who stopped me in the lobby."

"Uh, yeah. Sorry to just bail on ya, but I wasn't hanging around for that reunion. I mean, I know I'll have to see him eventually, but I'd rather it not be today. Not looking like I just spent four hours on a plane and another two in a car."

I glance her way, struck by her comment. Does she not know how incredibly beautiful she looks? Right now, all dolled up, sure, but even before that. Earlier, when she was sort of messy from work and the flight, she was the most stunning woman I'd ever seen. And I know I wasn't the only one to notice either. At least two guys waiting behind us at the car rental counter had their eyes on her. It made me a little crazy.

The car arrives in the lobby and we step out to a slew of guests waiting to be whisked away to their floors. We make our way through the crowd and head toward the front doors of the hotel. "Do you want us to drive over?" I ask, ready to head over to the valet desk.

Cricket shakes her head. "No, let's walk," she says as she heads off in the direction of Slim's.

It doesn't take me long to catch up, my legs considerably longer than hers. "Are you sure? You're wearing heels."

I don't miss the way she rolls her eyes under the night sky. "I wear heels every day, Rueben. I'll be fine," she reassures.

Still, I make sure to walk at a slower pace than normal just so she doesn't have to walk fast in those shoes to keep up. Shoving my hands into my pockets, I jump back to the conversation we started earlier in the elevator. "Anyway, so after you went up to your room, Danny and I got on the elevator together. He ended up getting off on our floor too."

"Your floor…as in the fourth floor," she says a little slowly, as if catching where I'm going with my statement.

"Yep, *our* floor."

"Okay," she replies casually, though I can hear a hint of uneasiness in her tone.

We stop at the intersection and wait for the cross walk to change. "I'm pretty sure he's in room 419," I blurt out just as the light changes to walk.

I start to move, but realize Cricket hasn't. I glance back and find her standing on the curb, her eyes closed. Before I can say a word, those beautiful green eyes open and lock on mine. I feel the earth tremor beneath my shoes, a wave of longing sweeping through my body. I almost rush back to the curb and take her in my arms, but before I can do that, she steps off and approaches. "Well, that's par for the course," she says as she walks past me, leaving me standing in the middle of the street.

The light changes and a horn honks. I turn around and rush to the opposite side to where Cricket is waiting, and we continue our slow walk toward Slim's. "Sorry to have to tell you that, but I didn't want you to be surprised."

"No, I appreciate it, really," she says, reaching over and resting her hand on my arm. It's meant as a comforting and appreciative gesture, one given by friends, for friends, but her touch does something to me. It's like a shock of electricity and bourbon at the same time. Cricket pulls her hand away quickly, and I can't help but wonder if she felt something too.

We're silent as we make our way the last few blocks to Slim's. The sidewalk starts to fill up the closer we get to campus, but I'm pleasantly surprised to find our old hangout not as packed as expected. Of course, it's still a little early for the late night drinking scene. As we enter, Cricket makes a beeline for an open pub table in the corner, smiling when she scores us a great table.

"Nice," I say as I slide onto the chair across from her.

"Right?" she replies, reaching for the menu in the middle of the table. "We used to never get an open table right away."

I glance over to the left, spying the familiar board on the wall, and smile. "And so close to our dart board," I state.

Cricket groans and shakes her head. "Of course. I haven't had anything to drink yet to willing subject myself to that humiliation a second time."

Just then, a waitress arrives at our table and sets two pub napkins down in front of us. She's young, probably barely a day over twenty-one, and offers us a warm smile. "Let me guess, here for the alumni reunion?"

"Do we look that out of place here?" Cricket asks with a laugh.

"No, of course not," she backpedals. "We've had a few tables in tonight talking about the reunion."

Cricket seems appeased by her reply and gives her a smile. "I'll have a Stella draft and mozzarella sticks."

"I'll have the same, plus an order of onion rings," I add, sticking my menu back in the holder in the middle of the table as the waitress heads off to place our order.

"Not planning on kissing anyone tonight, I see," Cricket says casually as she returns her menu to the stand.

My brain, of course, goes straight to kissing her. Our lips locked, the sweet taste of her skin against mine. The slide of my tongue along the seam of her lips, begging for entrance. And my hands, oh the things I could do with my hands while my lips are busy. But I won't do them. I *can't* do them. None of the dirty things my mind conjures up.

"No, no kissing tonight," I reply, clearing my throat as I go. It feels thick and scratchy, like I swallowed gravel.

Our beers are delivered a few moments later, our waitress assuring us our food will be out shortly. I glance around, anxious and nervous at the same time to spy someone I know. Like Danny, who made it clear he's going out tonight. This was one of our hangouts back in the day, and all I can do is pray he decided to venture to one of the other places we used to hang at.

I take a long pull from my glass, watching Cricket do the same out of my peripheral vision. She sets her glass down and licks the beer froth off her top lip, and I have to close my eyes before I do something really stupid like climb over the table and ravish that sweet mouth.

"So," I say, clearing my throat and glancing around the pub. "How exactly did you move from behind the camera to in front of it? You always hated being center attention in school."

Cricket glances down and starts ripping apart the corner of her napkin. "Funny story," she says, fidgeting more than usual. She doesn't continue right away, so I take another drink of my beer and wait her out. "I was a production director for the morning and noon newscast. It didn't take me too long to move up from assistant to director. I had always loved that aspect in school. I wanted to produce the news, you know?"

She glances over at me, as if seeking verification, so I nod in return. Cricket was brilliant behind the camera, in the production room. She knew which angles to hit, where to make edits to optimize airtime, and was always exact in her timing. But she's beautiful, and even back in school, the instructor was always trying to get her in front of the camera.

"Well, about four years ago, our morning co-host quit. No notice, just walked in and said she was done. Turns out she was offered a position over at a station in LA, like most do. We're the small station, so many use us as a stepping stone or a resume builder." Cricket stops tearing apart her napkin and glances over at me.

"Anyway, the GM came to me and asked for a favor. He wanted me to co-host until they found a replacement. A week or two tops." She takes another long drink from her glass, her eyes still locked on mine.

"And let me guess, a week or two tops is well past."

"He had no intention of finding a replacement. He wanted me for on-air pretty much from the moment I started a decade ago. Well, once he had me there, it was harder for me to step back. There was no co-host replacement in sight, and they promoted one of my assistants to fill my spot."

"That sucks, Crick. I'm sorry."

She shrugs as our food is delivered. The fried mozzarella sticks are still steaming, which makes my mouth water. "I'll bring you both another round. Can I get you anything else?" the waitress asks.

"No, thank you," Cricket replies, as I give a quick shake of my head.

My friend smothers her first mozzarella stick with marinara sauce and brings it up to her mouth. "No reason for you to apologize. It's not a horrible gig, and the money is definitely better." She eats half the cheese stick in one bite, double dipping in her sauce for the second bite. "Plus, last I was told, our ratings are so good the competition has been knocking on my door."

I have an onion ring halfway to my mouth when I consider her statement. "The competition, as in…"

"Yep. Apparently, they think Danny and I 'would make a great team.'" She uses air quotes and rolls her eyes, sighing dramatically.

My stomach lurches at the thought of Cricket and Danny together again. Jealousy? Hell yes, it is. I've never really been jealous of Danny. He was more athletic and had an easier time talking to girls, but I never held it against him, mostly because he was my friend and I didn't really want the attention like he did.

Our waitress delivers two more draft beers and leaves us to eat and visit. I notice it's starting to get a little louder in here, and I find myself leaning forward to hear her talk. With each inch I move in her direction, I can smell the fruitiness of her shampoo and the cleanliness of her body wash. It's intoxicating.

I think about her statement, about the job offers on the table, and can't help but wonder…what if? That's probably why I find myself asking, "So, are you considering the offer?"

Her eyes widen and bore into me from across the table. "You're kidding me, right? I'd rather walk across a football field of broken glass, barefooted, than work with that asshole. Plus, LA? Yuck!"

I snort a laugh and take a healthy bite of my food. It's a little easier to eat, knowing she still thinks Danny is a piece of work. And he is, especially after how he ended things with her at graduation. But I don't know, I guess I expected time to heal old wounds, or whatever. Honestly, knowing she wants no part in working with him makes me a little giddy.

But that's just stupid thinking, because it's not like there's anything there between *us*. I have no room for jealousy or any other weird emotion I may be feeling toward her or Danny. It's time to let go of this sudden crush and move on.

When our snacks are finished, the waitress returns to clear our food baskets and deliver a third round of drinks. It's been a while since I've had more than two beers, but it's so easy, so natural to talk to her that I find myself drinking a little more than normal. Though, three beers isn't exactly going to cause me any problems. I just want to keep an eye on Cricket. I want her to cut loose, if that's what she chooses.

I glance to the side and notice the empty dart board. I stand up and make my pitch. "Crick, I'm not really ready for this night to end. How about you go secure us the dart board while I use the restroom. Then, I'll come out here and pretend to let you kick my ass for a round or two before I really let you have it."

Her eyes brighten with mischief. "Let me have it, huh? You talk a big game for someone who hasn't experienced my abilities in a while. Maybe I've been practicing. We can play partners."

I shrug. "I'm not sure you're partner material."

She stands up and walks the few steps it takes to reach me. She's directly in front of me, the top of her head barely hitting my chin. She looks up with mischief and a bit of defiance in her emerald eyes. Cricket places a hand on my chest, and I wonder if she can feel my heart thundering. It's beating so loud, I'm certain everyone in the bar can hear it over the talking and music. If she can tell, she doesn't say anything. Instead she says, "I might be the best you've ever had."

My mind instantly makes her statement dirty. I've never actually wondered what it would be like to have sex with Cricket before today, but that doesn't stop my brain from conjuring up more dirty scenarios and playing them out on repeat. I swallow over the dryness in my throat and start toward the restroom. When her hand drops, I miss her touch immediately. It's only when I'm a few feet away that I stop and say, "Time to put your money where your mouth is, Crick."

Chapter Five

Cricket

Time to put your money where your mouth is, Crick.

I watch as he walks away, a shiver sweeping through my body at the deep, huskiness of his words. Sure, he didn't mean them sexually, but that doesn't stop my brain from going there. In fact, my mind is having a swell time picturing all the things Rueben would do to my willing body, if he had the chance.

Wait, no. I'm sure if he had the chance, Rueben would still keep us comfortably tucked in the friend-zone. Why wouldn't he? We've been safely locked there for more than a decade. But then I think about the subtle touches and lingering glances. He wasn't immune to them either, and I saw the desire swirl in his dark brown eyes when I touched his chest. Maybe he's thinking about me as more than a friend too. Or maybe he's just flirty and has no interest in me that way.

I groan aloud and put a dollar bill in the dart machine. This is stupid. It's been way too long since my last boyfriend, and that's the only reason I'm confusing friendship with sexual desire. I mean, it has been…a year and a half.

Holy shit!

I haven't had sex in a year and a half?

That's exactly what's wrong with me. It's the only logical solution for sending mixed signals and seeing things that aren't there. Lack of sex is clouding my brain and my judgment. I need to step back, keep my friendship with Rueben intact, and get through this weekend. Then, run straight home and find someone for a few rounds of bedroom Olympics.

I bet Rueben is fantastic in bed with those big strong hands and long, muscular legs…

I stop in my tracks.

You know what they say about big hands…

And big feet…

"Shut up," I tell my brain.

Just as I spin around to find the throw line, I run smack into a hard chest. The scent around me is familiar, but not welcome. It's definitely not Rueben's subtle, woodsy scent, but one I had long forgotten about. One that makes the hairs on the back of my neck stand up and my stomach drop to my shoes.

"Shut up? But I haven't even said anything yet," Danny responds, the familiar smirk spreading across his too-handsome face. God, I want to punch him.

"And yet, here you are," I retort with a bite, stepping out of the arms that seemed to wrap around me as we collided.

Danny does a scan from head to toe, lingering a little too long on my chest. I cross my arms and narrow my eyes, feeling nothing like I felt when Rueben did it earlier tonight. Instead, I want to stab his eyes out with a rusty butter knife and then throw darts at them.

"Good to see you, Cricket," he finally says when his eyes return to my face.

"I wish I could say the same to you," I mumble, stepping around him and finding the worn throw line on the marred hardwood floor.

"Come on, Cricket, it's been ten years. Surely you're not still pissed off, are you?" he asks, spinning around and following me.

I throw the first dart, ignoring his looming presence beside me. "Actually, yes, yes I am still mad." I throw the second dart. "You stole my car!" I state as I throw the third one with a little too much force and miss the board completely.

Danny retrieves my three darts before I can, bringing them back to where I stand. "I paid you for your half," he reminds me, cocking his head to the side as if it's no big deal.

"Six months after you left!" I thunder, feeling that familiar rage brewing inside me. Instead of punching him in the face—which is taking all the strength I have not to do—I focus straight ahead and throw the darts.

I can feel his eyes on me as I throw and tuning him out is proving to be harder than I'd like.

"You look good," he says as he retrieves the second round of darts.

"Fuck off."

Danny sighs and hands me the darts. He watches in silence as I throw the darts a third time. All of my throws are complete shit, probably because I can't even concentrate on the round board in front of me. It takes all my energy not to turn and "accidentally" toss a dart or two at his head. But then I think about prison and how horrible I'd look in those orange jumpsuits and decide he's not worth the energy or time. Plus, I'm not that great of a cook and I'd probably get stuck with kitchen detail.

"What do you want?" I ask, glancing over my shoulder and wondering where in the hell Rueben is.

"Saw you over here alone and thought I'd stop by and say hello."

"I'm not alone," I argue, then wishing I would have kept my mouth shut.

"No?" he asks, glancing around as if calling me on my bluff when he doesn't see anyone remotely close that could constitute as my date. A knowing grin spreads across his face—one that tells me he thinks I'm lying.

"No," I insist. "He's…in the restroom."

"Right," Danny snorts. "It's okay to be here alone, Cricket. I mean, I'm here alone too." He takes a step closer and those pesky hairs at the nape of my neck stand at attention again. "Maybe it's fate that we're both alone tonight."

"Or maybe it's because everyone who knows you knows what kind of an asshole you are and wants nothing to do with you."

He seems to straighten up at that. "And maybe it's because you're cranky and unforgiving and refuse to let the past go."

I practically growl at him. "Unforgiving? You're kidding me, right?"

"I've forgiven you for taking my job," he states, crossing his arms over his chest.

That makes me pause. "Excuse me? Taking your job?" What the hell is this guy talking about?

"You don't think I haven't noticed you're the bubbly new co-host of *Good Morning, San Francisco*?"

I roll my eyes. "That was four years ago, jerk. That position hadn't been yours in six years. In fact, you quit before you even started, remember?"

He doesn't seem to have an answer to that. It's almost like he's just trying to grate on my nerves, which pisses me off that I'm actually responding at all. It's like I'm letting him win. "All I'm saying is maybe if you were as bubbly in person as you are on-air, you'd have a date this weekend," he says with a shrug.

"I *do* have a date!"

"Really? Where?" he asks, a growing smile on his fucking face as he glances around once more.

Suddenly, I feel a presence behind me. It's familiar and, unlike Danny, a welcome one. Before I can even think about a consequence or a repercussion, I practically jump up and throw my arms around Rueben's neck, saying, "He's right here."

Then I kiss him.

Hard.

Rueben's arms wrap around me, drawing me against his body, and two things happen. My body ignites with desire, as if someone doused me with gasoline and lit a match, and the second is he deepens the kiss. His lips are firm, yet soft, as he plies my mouth open, his tongue delving inside and sliding against mine. It's intoxicating and invigorating, and frankly, out of this fucking world. I have no idea how long we kiss, all I know is I'd be okay with it never ending. His lips are masterful, and frankly, I've never been kissed like this before. Ever.

A throat clears behind me, a not-so-subtle reminder that we're not alone. Rueben pulls his lips from mine, our mixed breath both a gasp and a pant. My eyes struggle to focus as I gaze at him, maybe really seeing him for the first time. He glances over my shoulder and stiffens. That's when I recall exactly what drove me into my friend's arms, and more precisely, onto his lips. Rueben lets me slide down his chest until my feet hit the floor, though they're a little wobbly and struggle to hold my weight.

"Rueben?" Danny says, his voice full of question and disbelief.

I turn around to face my ex, sure that my own face will burst into flames at any second. The lie that I started continues easily, rolling off the tip of my tongue so effortlessly. "Oh, yeah, sorry. Forgot you were still here," I say casually. I can feel Rueben's presence directly behind me, but I ignore the pull that has me ready to turn back around and climb him like a tree.

Danny looks from me to his old best friend just over my shoulder. "So…you…and…him…"

"Yep! We're dating," I declare, hiding my cringe at springing this on Rueben and dragging him into the middle of my lie.

My ex continues to look between the two of us, as if watching a tennis volley, and suddenly, busts up laughing. "Oh, come on," clearly not buying the story.

Before I can even declare my lie the truth and nothing but the truth, I feel Rueben's hand slide against mine, our warm fingers entwine for the first time ever. He steps up, pressing his front to my back, and says, "It's true. We're dating."

The smile slowly falls from Danny's face as he seems to take in our words. "Seriously? You two?"

I nod frantically, unsure if I'll be able to get words past my Sahara-dry tongue.

"Wow," he says, running a hand through his hair. "I didn't see that one coming. How long have you two been...dating?"

"It's a recent development," I finally say, my lips still tingling from the Academy Award winning kiss.

"Yeah, sorry I didn't say anything earlier," Rueben starts, his hand still firmly latched on to mine. "I didn't want it to get awkward." His uneasy chuckle is ironic.

"No, I get it. I mean, it's not every day your friend starts dating your girl," Danny states.

My spine straightens. "I am *not* your girl. Haven't been in more than a decade."

He has the balls to roll his eyes. I want to punch them out of his head. "Semantics. Anyway, let's celebrate! I'll buy a round," Danny boasts, flagging down a server.

"No, that's not necessary. I'm sure you have things to do, others to bother," I argue, wishing he'd take the hint and leave us alone. Though, I can't speak for Rueben, I'm definitely not interested in spending the next half hour—or any amount of time, for that matter—catching up with Danny Ohara.

He flashes me the smile that used to melt my heart, and my panties. Now, I find it revolting and a bit nauseating. "I have no one else to bother but you. My plans for this evening was to find former classmates and catch up. I think I found exactly who I was supposed to run into." Then, he turns to the server and orders three draft beers in an old brand we used to drink when we were twenty-one and had absolutely no extra spending cash.

"So, tell me what you've both been up to?" Danny asks. "How do you make dating work if you're in Tennessee and she's in California?" he adds, glancing at his former roommate. If I'm not mistaken, there's a hint of mischief in his eyes. Maybe trying to catch us in our lie?

"Well, like we said, it's a fairly new development," Rueben replies, squeezing my hand. "We're still working out the logistics, taking it day by day." He shrugs his shoulders and reaches for his beer from earlier. I do the same, ignoring the fact that it's getting warm and starting to taste like ass, and practically chug what's left in the glass.

Our new skunky, cheap beer arrives, and Danny insists on a toast. "To old friends, reconnecting. And to you two lovebirds finding each other after all this time." He raises his glass, Rueben and I following suit, and we all clink our glasses together. The alcohol tastes vile sliding down my throat, but they don't seem to notice.

"How about I reset the board?" Danny asks, heading over to the dart board to insert a dollar.

Quickly turning to my pseudo-boyfriend, I whisper, "I'm so sorry about this. It just came out."

Rueben shrugs and leans against the closest pub stool. "It's fine."

Adamantly shaking my head, I reply, "No, it's not fine. I'm going to tell him the truth."

"No, don't do that."

I'm sure my eyes are wide with shock as I gape at him. With him leaning against the stool, we're closer to the same height, and I can't help but notice how close we're actually standing. "I'm the reason we're in this lie. I'll tell him I made it up." My heart hammers and drops into my gut. Danny's going to have a field day with the latest development. I'm sure he'll find it downright hilarious that I lied about having a boyfriend, but it's not Rueben's fault that I was too embarrassed to admit that I was here alone.

"Don't." He brings my hand up to his lips and runs them across my knuckles. A shiver races through my blood, even though it's warm in here.

"We can fake a breakup," I whisper, my throat hoarse and my breathing slightly labored.

He shrugs. "We'll figure it out."

"Ready?" Danny asks behind me. When I glance around, he's looking down to where Rueben is resting his left hand on my hip.

"Ready!" I holler, a bit too loudly and practically race over the board to retrieve my darts.

I end up playing Danny the first round, my mind not really on the game. Danny beats me easily, which never happened back when we were younger, and plays Rueben the second game. They chat easily, but to me, it still feels forced. I'm not sure if it's from their lack of communication over the last several years or the fact that Rueben and I are caught in faux dating hell. I mean, not that dating him would be hell—it would probably be very, very nice—but it's not real.

Those touches? The way his eyes danced as he gazed at me? Not. Real.

When they finish their game, I fake a yawn, because, apparently, I'm really good at faking things, and stretch my arms over my head. My shirt rises a bit, exposing my midsection, and there's no missing the way Rueben's eyes lock on that little sliver of skin. Inwardly, I grin and do a little happy jig as those dark brown orbs dilate even further. Since I'm already committed to my next fib, I say, "Well, I'm going to head back to the hotel. I'm beat." I go ahead and throw in another big fat fake yawn to complete my sell.

"I'll walk you," Rueben says, placing the darts back in the bin.

"No, you don't have to do that. Stay and catch up with Danny," I insist. Truthfully, I could use a little alone time in my hotel room. Maybe a bath in that small tub, a bottle of whatever liquor they've got stocked in the mini-fridge. A few moments alone to reflect on the mess I've made of our evening. Mostly, I could use a break from Rueben and the crazy excitement I feel inside at the prospect of actually being in a relationship with him.

"I'll walk you," he insists with more authority. "Danny, it was good to visit again."

"I'll head out too," Danny replies, finishing off his cheap beer and throwing a few bills for a tip in the center of the table. "You two walk?"

I nod, dreading the idea of walking back to the hotel, my ex in tow.

But that's what we end up doing, all three leaving the bar together, just like the good ol' days. Except this time, it's not Danny's hand I'm holding as we make our way through the streets of Carbondale. It's Rueben's. I'm not sure if it's to help sell our story or as a form of comfort, but I'll take the latter.

Danny chats about his job and life in Los Angeles. It turns out, he's been to a few fundraising events in San Francisco and even spent a long weekend there a few months back. Thankfully though, we've never crossed paths.

When we arrive at the hotel, another thought hits me. We make our way to the elevator, all three of us heading to the same floor. Would it be weird that Rueben and I are supposedly dating, yet staying in different hotel rooms? We did say it was early days, but Danny might find that odd and latch on to that piece of intel.

As we step into the car, the awkwardness trailing us as thick as fog, Rueben must sense my uneasiness. He puts his arm around my shoulder, snuggling me into his side. I admit, it's pretty fucking nice. Comfy, even. I've never been a big snuggler, but here I am, burrowing deeper into his embrace as if I can't get close enough.

When the car opens, we all exit. Rueben stops at his door, digging in his pocket for his keycard. I'm not sure what to do. Danny even hangs back, still blabbing about how great his life is and shares some story about being recognized at the airport. I take a step forward, prepared to head to my room and explain to Danny that we haven't been dating long enough to warrant a shared room, when Rueben pulls on my hand, stopping me. He opens the door and steps back, allowing me to enter first.

"Well, I'll leave you two for the night. I'm sure we'll see each other at the game. Hey, maybe we can meet in the restaurant for breakfast first. Say eight o'clock? I think we're supposed to be at the stadium by ten."

"Oh," I start, but stop, not really sure how to answer that. Do I want to have breakfast with my ex? Hell to the no. Do I want to have breakfast with my ex, while also having breakfast with my fake boyfriend who just so happens to be his former roommate and friend? Fuck that.

"That sounds great," Rueben replies, making my brain stutter to a halt.

What?

"Night, guys," Danny says, throwing a wave over his shoulder and heading toward his room.

I slip inside and am slapped upside the head with a familiar, sexy scent. The room smells like his cologne, and instantly, my heart starts to skip in my chest. I stand awkwardly in the little hall area by the bathroom door, unsure what to do. He waves me on and says, "You might as well stay for a little bit. You know he'll be watching this room. Wait until we think he's asleep and then you can sneak over to your room."

Good idea.

Moving through the room and stopping by the little desk, I say, "Smart thinking. But I have to ask, breakfast?"

He snorts. "You know he wouldn't let it go. If it wasn't this, then it would be drinks after the game or sitting together at the alumni dinner tomorrow. We have breakfast in the morning, and then he'll run into his former teammates at the game and talk about the good ol' days, forgetting all about us."

Seems simple enough. I've already endured an hour with the man, surely I could survive a quick breakfast in the morning, right?

"Okay, I get it. I don't like it, but I get it," I grumble.

Rueben grabs the remote and turns on the television. He finds a documentary on History Channel, which makes me happy. I love that channel. Not so much when I was younger, but the older I get, the more I appreciate learning about the events from our past, the things that made us who we are.

"I've been wanting to see this," I say, kicking off my shoes and crawling onto the top of the king-sized bed. My eyes remain glued to the screen.

"Make yourself comfy. I'm gonna use the bathroom," he says, disappearing into the small room off to the side, closing the door with a decisive click.

I take a quick moment to scan the room. His clothes are hanging in the closet, and I spy a black suit for tomorrow night's dinner. Truth be told, I'm a little anxious to see him in that bad boy. Back in school, he was a little lanky and lean, but now, with a little more muscle mass behind him, I'm quite certain he'll fill out that suit very nicely.

The rest of the room is well organized. I realize he hasn't been here long, but I can see he's already using the room. His laptop and a few other devices are sitting on the desk, an empty bottle of water tossed in the trash. There's a pair of jeans and a shirt folded up and set on the chair; probably the clothes he had on for the flight earlier today. Everything else is straightened and clean, just as I'd picture his living space at home.

I'm drawn back into the documentary about The White House. They're discussing the bunkers and the underground systems surrounding the most secured building in the world. Rueben joins me a few minutes later, but chooses to take the chair. He tosses the clothes onto the desk chair and kicks off his shoes, before throwing his long legs up on the ottoman and relaxing. If he's concerned about me making myself cozy on his bed, he doesn't say anything. We watch the show in comfortable silence, yet I'm definitely aware of his presence. Occasionally, I feel his eyes on me, but I try to ignore the pull that calls for me to look his way.

When the show ends and another one on the September 11th attacks begins, he gets up from his chair and goes to the mini-fridge. He pulls out two bottles of water and a package of peanut M&Ms. "Seriously? Gimme, gimme," I beg, reaching my hand out and taking the candy.

Rueben laughs as he hands over the cold chocolate and tosses a bottle of water onto the bed beside me. "I wasn't sure if you were still a fan," he says before taking his own drink of cold liquid.

"Not sure I'm still a fan? These are the greatest candies in the history of the world, my friend," I tell him, ripping open the bag and popping one into my mouth. "They're delicious," I say, slowly chewing and savoring the sweet and salty mix.

"I brought a few snacks for the plane ride but didn't eat them."

After popping a second piece into my mouth, I ask, "So you were saving them for the return flight home? And I'm eating them?" I don't even care that I'm talking with my mouth full.

He shrugs. "Eat anything you want. I can grab more at the airport. There's some Twizzlers in my bag somewhere too," he says, rooting around in his computer bag and coming back with a large zippered bag of licorice candy.

Rueben pulls a stick from the bag and throws it at me. "I should travel with you. You have the best snacks," I tell him casually, but notice that my heart kicks up a few extra beats at the prospect of traveling alongside him.

"So now the truth comes out! You're using me for my snacks," he teases, shoving half a Twizzlers in his mouth and smiling as he chews.

I reach for the one he threw at me. "You caught me. I'm only here for your snacks."

And because you're an amazing kisser and I wouldn't mind doing that again.

Shaking that thought off, I focus my attention back on the TV screen. Between the M&Ms and the licorice that is thrown my way, I find myself completely relaxed and enjoying the evening. My eyes start to get heavy as the show continues, breaking down the events that transpired on that September morning in 2001. Every once in a while, I hear Rueben adjust in his chair. I should probably offer to trade place so he can stretch out on his own bed. Of course, the bed is a king, so there's definitely enough room for us both.

I also realize the coast is probably clear in the hallway. It's been more than an hour since I joined Rueben in his hotel room, and if Danny's still awake, I'm sure he's not looking at the peephole, waiting for someone to walk by his room. I should definitely head to my room, take off my makeup, and snuggle up in bed in a nightshirt and all four pillows.

It's so nice and cozy here, though, too.

Maybe I'll head over in just a few more minutes…

Chapter Six

Rueben

I know the instant she falls asleep.

It's like I'm hyperaware of her and can sense the change in her breathing pattern. She's more relaxed now, almost angelic as her long brown hair hangs loosely in big waves around my pillow. Her mouth falls open just the slightest and every once in a while, a little snore slips past her lips. She's simply the most beautiful woman I've ever seen.

I sit in the chair for another hour, pretending to watch the program on TV, but really, I'm just watching her. The way she mumbles in her sleep and moves her mouth—a mouth that I've now tasted and can't stop thinking about. Cricket curls up on her side, facing me, and hugs the pillow. I'm sure it's clear for her to head back to her own hotel room, but honestly, I don't want her to go. Not only is she completely comfortable right where she is, but I like having her here. I *want* her here.

The whole scene tonight at Slim's was crazy. I knew the moment I walked out of the restroom and saw Danny talking to her that something was up. As I weaved my way through the growing crowd, a former classmate stopped me. We were in a computer class together and he wanted to know what I'd been up to these last ten years. I didn't want to be rude, so I stayed a chatted for a little bit, all while keeping an eye on Cricket and Danny.

I knew the moment he said something to upset her. Her body tensed and her spine straightened. He was smiling that cocky smirk and she took a step back, his hand reaching out to touch her arm. I was hollering a goodbye and a talk to you soon a split second later, making my way back to where I left my friend. Though I don't know the exact conversation, the first thing I heard when I was within earshot was her insistence that she *did* have a date. The next thing I knew, I was him and she was practically launching herself into my arms.

And kissing me.

Best. Fucking. Kiss. Ever.

My heart still pounds in my chest and my cock starts to harden when I think about it. And believe me, I've done a lot of thinking about it. I've been in a perpetual state of arousal since that moment, which is probably why it was so easy to go along with her little white lie. We're not in a relationship, but I'm willing to pretend we are just to get closer to her. Is it right? Probably not, but I can't seem to stop thinking about her in more than a friendly fashion, even if what she's asking of me is *because* of our friendship.

My own eyelids start to droop, and I'm torn. It's way past my usual bedtime, let alone throwing air travel in the mix. Cricket's day has been a mirror image of my own and she needs rest. Yet, all I want to do is stay up and watch her sleep like some crazy stalker.

I should wake her up, send her back to her room. I should crawl into bed and get my own rest.

Yet, I don't.

I sit here for a few more minutes and just take in her beauty.

Eventually, I move, pulling off my socks—because I hate sleeping in socks—and crawl onto my bed. It's a king-sized mattress; should be plenty of room for two friends to rest and maintain their distance. I've made a decision, one I'm not sure whether it's right or wrong. She's tired and I don't want to disturb her. So, I'll let her sleep.

Sticking to the edge of the bed, I roll to my side and continue to watch her. Cricket would probably be freaked out if she knew how much of a voyeur I've been, but that's a small price to pay. I don't want to miss a single moment, not one mumble or snore or eye flutter. After this weekend's over, I'll have those memories locked deep inside my brain to carry with me for the rest of my life. Memories of just her and the time I'll always wish "could have been more."

Because even though this is new and probably just a case of haven't-seen-you-in-forever-itis, I can't help but feel that this friendship could easily become something more.

It's a troubling thought, as I drift off to sleep, especially when those two people have lives several states apart.

A relationship isn't possible.

Not now.

Not ever.

***

I startle awake.

I'm lying on my side, my arm stretched forward and completely numb. The scent of fruit is strong and there's a tickle against my nose. Blinking rapidly, I focus on the beach scene painting on the wall and realize I'm in my hotel room. My bed.

And I'm not alone.

Brown hair is splayed across the pillow, my cheek, and my arm—you know, the numb one—and my mind instantly returns to last night. Watching the documentary, then watching her sleep. I was just going to lie down for a few minutes. I didn't even get beneath the covers. Neither of us did. We fell asleep side by side, on opposite ends of the king-sized bed, actually. Yet, here we are, entangled and cuddling, her ass pressed firmly against my very hard, very ready to play morning wood.

I know I should move. This is not how friends embrace first thing in the morning. Hard-ons don't usually factor into friendly sleepovers. Actually, that's an incredibly true statement. My last friendly sleepover was in eighth grade with Henry Forrester, and my usual teenage hormonal morning wood didn't even make an appearance that sunny morning.

But now? With Cricket snuggled into my side and her sweet ass pressed against my cock? Oh, it's very ready to play. More ready than the first-round draft in his first NFL appearance. Sure, there's a little bit of nerves there, but excitement and anxiousness reign supreme. And my dick is very excited.

It doesn't help that her subtle fragrance of fruit is penetrating my senses like the front infantry line crossing over into enemy territory. Sweet strawberries and pineapple slides into my nostrils and wrap around my brain, sending shockwaves of lust straight to my groin. I'm in a conundrum of hurt right now. I'm her friend and should keep my distance, yet I can't seem to get my brain on board with that plan.

I just…want her.

Cricket moves in my arms, wiggling that delectable ass against my cock and pressing her back farther into my chest. A little sigh slips from her lips as she relaxes once more. I wish I were facing her so I can see the contentment and serenity in her beautiful face while she sleeps. Last night I was treated to such a sight, but now, as morning light filters through the cracks of the curtains, I wish I could see her, committing it to memory too.

My time to lie here and just feel is coming to an end. I know it. Cricket shifts once more, her cheek pushed into the soft flesh of my inner upper arm. Her breathing is picking up a bit, not nearly as relaxed in sleep as it was a few moments ago. Now is the time to move, to dislodge my eager dick from where the crack of her ass is snug in those tight jeans, but I don't change quick enough. She shakes her ass once more against me, as if riding my cock, and I have to stifle my groan of pleasure. Well, of pleasure and frustration together, because even in my sex-fogged brain, I know this moment isn't going to end the way my dick wants.

A moan glides from her lips, sending shockwaves of desire through my blood, a moment before she stills and tenses. Cricket is awake, and can clearly feel how *awake* I am too.

"Rueben?" she whispers, her voice hoarse with sleep.

"Yeah," I reply, clearing my throat and pushing all thoughts of morning sex from my mind. This is my friend, not my girlfriend, even if that's the gig of the weekend.

She doesn't say anything for a few very long seconds, but doesn't move either. She's still pressed against me, our bodies way too close to keep those dirty thoughts at bay, at least on my part.

Grandma, grandma, grandma, grandma.

"What time is it?" she asks. Still. Not. Moving.

I look at the nightstand—the one that's directly in front of her face— and reply, "Six forty-five."

"Wow, I never sleep past four thirty, even on my day off," she says, almost absently.

Truth be told, I've never slept this soundly, this comfortably in all my life either. I've also never been a big snuggler. When a past girlfriend would stay over, I'd prefer to have my space. I'm a warm sleeper and the last thing I want is to wake all hot and sweaty, tangled in sheets and limbs. But with Cricket in my arms? I woke more rested and content than ever before.

Back to the problem at hand—or specifically, in my pants—I roll to my back and slide my arm out from under her head. Cricket sits up, adjusting her position on the bed and glances around the room. I, on the other hand, throw my legs over the bed and keep my back to her. I wish I could say not seeing her affects the hardness of my dick, but that would be a lie. It seems to remember exactly what it felt like to have her pressed against it and refuses to deflate.

"Um, sorry about not waking you. I meant to just lie down for a bit and let you sleep, but I must have dozed off," I tell her, striving for casual, yet hearing the sexual strain in my voice.

"It's okay. I mean, nothing happened," she replies, chuckling awkwardly.

"Yep, nothing happened. Just two friends sleeping in the same bed," I confirm, though my dick jumping in my pants is a reminder of how much he liked the whole sleeping in the same bed part.

Unfortunately for him, he's going to be unhappy with this morning's outcome. There will be no sex.

I feel his disappointment.

"Um, so I should probably go to my room and get ready," she says, the bed dipping when she stands up.

"Yeah, we have breakfast in just over an hour." The upcoming breakfast with Danny is like a cold glass of water thrown on my libido.

"Oh, shit. I forgot. What if he sees me going back into my room?" she asks, looking delightfully mussed in her post-sleep appearance.

Her question is a legit one. If he comes out of his room and sees her sneaking into hers, then he'll definitely know she lied about our relationship status, or at least about sharing a room. Then I'm afraid it'll be worse for her than before. He'll never let it go and will probably tell everyone who'll stand long enough to listen to him that his ex made up a boyfriend.

I can't let that happen.

"I'll sneak in," I find myself stating.

"What? How? Won't that be just as bad if he finds me?"

I shake my head. "No, I'll come up with some excuse, like maybe a work client meeting or something."

She seems to consider the options. "But then I'll have to shower and get ready here. We don't have a lot of time before breakfast."

I shrug my shoulders. "We'll make it work."

There's definite hesitation when she says, "I guess that would be all right."

"Great. Give me your keycard and I'll be right back."

She heads over to her little purse and pulls the plastic card from within. "I'll need all of my bathroom toiletries too. I had already unpacked everything."

"I'll grab it all," I tell her, our fingers grazing against each other's when I take the card. "It'll be okay, Crick."

She nods and lets go, severing our touch once more.

Needing a little air and a lot of distance, I quietly exit my room, the door making a distinctive noise when it shuts. Ignoring the fact that a beautiful, sexy woman is still in my room, I move quickly and softly through the empty hallway, to her door, and scan the card. The light flashes green and I'm inside a moment later. I sigh in relief at not getting busted by Danny and then groan as her familiar scent assaults me. Everywhere I look, I see Cricket. Her clothes, her reading device on the bedside table, that familiar bottle of lotion on the dresser.

Her suitcase is in the closet, so I make quick word at filling it. I grab everything from the dresser first, my heart skittering to a halt when I find her panties. I have no business lusting over anything in her drawers—the dresser kind, not the ones she's wearing—so I quickly toss them into the luggage, trying to forget the fact that they were blue and lacy.

Next, I remove everything from the top of the dresser and nightstand. Satisfied that I have everything from the main room, I make my way to her bathroom. The moment I walk in, I'm surrounded by Cricket. I grab the bag on the counter and fill it with her makeup and other items strewn across the bathroom counter. I unplug a flat iron thingy, as well as a blow dryer, and clear out the product left in the shower. I find a mesh bag on the floor and grab that too, which contains her dirty clothes.

Finally, I go back to the bed and toss everything in the suitcase. It's definitely full, and not even close to being the proper way to pack a bag, but time is of the essence here. My last stop before heading back to my room is the closet where the bag was kept. There, I find a gold sparkly dress that makes my cock twitch in my pants. There's also a pair of strappy black heels, and all I can think about his how fucking hot those will look on her feet later this evening. I throw them in the suitcase, grab the skirt and shirt set hanging beside the dress, and toss the garments over my arm.

With all of Cricket's possessions in hand, I slowly exit her room, grateful to find the hallway once more Danny-free. I don't need to knock on the door for admittance, as Cricket opens the door the moment she spies me in the peephole. She pulls open the door, grateful to see me with all her things.

Just as I start over the threshold, a door opens somewhere in the hallway, and Danny's familiar voice fills the silence. I'm not sure if he's talking to someone in his room or on the phone, but I don't hang around to find out. I dive inside, past Cricket's wide eyes, and hold my breath until the door shuts behind me.

Damn, that was close.

We both stand there, waiting to see if Danny knocks on the door, but it never comes. Panting a little, I say quietly, "I think I got everything."

"Okay," she whispers.

I take her bags and set them on the bed, ignoring the rumpled bedding and the divots in the pillows. Stepping aside, I let Cricket open the suitcase and start sorting her haphazardly tossed clothes. "Why don't I jump in the shower first while you unpack. Take all of the space you need. I think I only used the top dresser drawer, and there's plenty of closet space," I tell her, heading over and hanging up the gold dress and other outfit I took from her own closet.

"Thanks, Rueben," she says behind me. When I turn, she looks a little nervous and uncertain. "I'm really sorry I got you into this mess. If you want to tell Danny the truth, I'm okay with that. I don't want to force you to lie to your friend, even if that friend is a massive jerk."

I shrug. "Listen, Cricket. Things with Danny and me haven't been the same since graduation. I wasn't very happy with him when I found out what he did to you, and to be honest, we haven't spoken that much since, even after I drove his shit out to LA. It been years since I've seen him and don't exactly consider him my friend as I do someone I used to be friends with in school." It's the truth. Danny and I have been cordial since our time together in school but haven't kept in touch the way true best friends would. I guess you can say we grew apart since college. "My point is, I consider you more my friend than I do him, so if you need my help, I'm here for you. Even if it's pretending to be your boyfriend for a few days to fool a massive jerk."

She gives me a small smile, one that makes my heart gallop in my chest. "You're a good guy, Rueben Rigsby." Then she steps forward, into my personal space, and wraps her arms around my waist and hugs me.

I toss my arms over her shoulders and do the same, trying—unsuccessfully, mind you—to ignore the way she fits so perfectly against my body. "I'd do anything to help you, Cricket. I hope you always remember that."

That's the truth. Even though we lost touch after a while, both of us moving to different parts of the country, I will always consider her a friend. That's why I'm more than willing to serve as her pretend boyfriend if it makes her life a little easier, and at the end of the weekend, I'll head back to Tennessee and her back to California.

And our relationship—albeit fake—will be over.

"I do know that," she whispers, turning her head upward a little. When she does, her nose grazes against my neck and a shiver sweeps through my body.

Desperately in need of a little space, and a shower, I pull myself from her hug and retreat to the bathroom. "I'll only be a few minutes," I say, closing myself in the small room.

Exhaling deeply, I lean against the back of the door, realization setting in. These next two days are going to be the most trying of my life. The lines between friendship and more are starting to blur. That crush I've suddenly developed is big and alive, an ugly truth that I can't seem to ignore. I'm going to have to give the performance of a lifetime, and at the end of it all, pretend it never happened at all.

Shouldn't be a problem.

After a quick shower, one that uses more cold water than warm, I grab a towel and dry off. With the towel wrapped around my waist, I brush my teeth, run a comb through my hair, and place my glasses back on my face. Then, I turn to grab my clothes, only not finding any clothes. Probably because I didn't grab any from the dresser drawer before I closed myself off in the bathroom.

Sighing, I realize there's only one thing for me to do: walk out of here in my towel.

Chapter Seven

Cricket

I gather up my clothes as soon as I hear the shower shut off. It's weird to see my things intermixed with a man's, let alone Rueben's. I haven't lived with a male since my time with Danny in college, and even then, we weren't stuffed in four hundred square feet of joint space.

Rueben agreed to help me with Danny, but I still feel bad. It was my big mouth that got us into this mess, and I'm determined to get him out of it as soon as I can. Maybe we can stage a breakup tonight at the alumni dinner? Though, the thought of a breakup with Rueben—whether fake or real—doesn't sit well in my stomach.

I've kinda become attached to him.

When the sink turns off, I know my time to get ready is almost here. I make sure to have my travel cosmetic bag and other bathroom things, heading to the door as it opens.

And. Stop. Dead. In. My. Tracks.

Rueben is standing there in nothing but a white towel. My mouth goes dry and my tongue dangles from my lips. Truth, that last part doesn't happen, but it could, you know, just like those cartoons I used to watch when I was little.

"Sorry," he says, standing straight and looking both incredible and uncomfortable at the same time. "I forgot to take clothes in with me. I guess I'm not used to sharing a hotel room with anyone."

I'm already shaking my head. "No problem! I'm the one crashing your space. I'll just…go," I stutter, waving my full hands toward the bathroom and juggling my things like a clown at a birthday party.

Inside the room, which still smells like Rueben's soap, mind you, I drop all of my stuff on the vanity counter and start to sort it. Is it possible he didn't notice the way my eyes were riveted to his chest, not missing the way the V of his hips dropped low and disappeared behind that lucky terrycloth? God, I hope so. Yet, I'm pretty sure a blind man could have seen the way I was practically drooling all over myself.

I find my shampoo and conditioner, but the face scrub and body wash aren't here. I know I had them when I gathered my stuff for the shower. I guess I dropped them when I juggled my bath products and clothes. They're probably lying on the floor beside the bed. I'm sure it would be no big deal to use Rueben's body wash, but my face is sensitive enough that a change in product might not have a good outcome. I'll just slip out and grab my stuff.

I open the door and say, "Hey, Rueb, I think I dropped my—"

But the words stop on my tongue, my mind going completely blank. Rueben is standing there—naked—with his back to me, the towel that was once wrapped around his waist, now dropped on the floor at his feet. All I can do is stare at his ass. His incredibly firm and perfectly round ass. It's magnificent.

"Cricket?"

My eyes finally move up, taking in the muscled planes of his back and the way they tighten under my scrutiny. Words. Did he say something? I can't recall. I finally glance all the way up, my eyes locking on his. The chocolate brown is an even darker shade of molten black, and they stare back at me with question and astonishment.

"What?"

He's watching me over his shoulder, his bare ass still very much on display. "Did you forget something?"

I blink back. *Did I forget something?*

Yeah, my brain, apparently.

"Oh! Yes, I forgot my..." I glance around on the floor, spying my body wash and face scrub immediately. "Here it is!" I declare, picking up the misplaced bag. "Thanks for assing. I mean asking." My face burns with mortification. "I'll just..." I point over my shoulder as I backpedal to the bathroom.

Of course, my traitorous eyes drop down once more, drinking in one last, long look at that very fine derriere. Before I can slip into the bathroom, where I have a likely chance of accidental drowning in the toilet, my eyes flick up to his face, catching the hint of humor and the smile on his lips.

I practically slam the door shut and pray for the earth to open and swallow me. It never happens, however. What *does* happen, though, is a constant repeat of his naked butt right in front of me. I'll never get that image out of my mind, not that I want to. No, just the opposite actually. I'd take that picture with me through the rest of my life, happily pulling it out of my memory bank to ogle it over and over and over again.

Right now isn't the time, however. We're late for breakfast with my ex and a football game with half my graduating class. And I have to try to figure out how to not picture Rueben's ass every time I look him in the eye.

Should be easy.

Not.

***

"Sorry we're late," I state as we approach Danny's table. He's sitting there in deep conversation with a blonde woman. The moment they hear me speak, they both break apart, rather guiltily, actually, and turn to look at us.

Ellen Montgomery.

89

Well, this day just keeps getting better and better.

"Cricket, hi! It's so good to see you again," she coos, standing up to give me a hug.

I'm too shocked to return the gesture, but finally mumble a quick. "Hi."

"I'm glad you two could make it. I know what it's like being in a new relationship and never wanting to leave your hotel room," Danny says, wiggling his eyebrows suggestively to me and Rueben.

My fake boyfriend holds out my chair and waits for me to sit before taking his own seat. Always the gentleman. Danny never held out a chair or opened a door, unless it was to catch a glimpse down my shirt. I grab the menu, blatantly ignoring the awkwardness of this breakfast date after only the first five seconds. Unfortunately, I'm unable to ignore the way Danny reaches over and grabs Ellen's hand, bringing it to his mouth and placing a kiss on her knuckles.

There's a squeeze in my stomach, one that is both nauseating and revolting. Two things I've associated with Danny in the last decade. Rueben takes the seat beside me and squeezes my hand under the table. Comfort washes through me as we sit together, and our eyes connect. He gives me a friendly smile that makes my heart dance, and I can't help but feel grateful that the embarrassment from earlier this morning is gone.

We're back to friends.

Who cares if one friend has seen the other's naked ass?

We're both adults here. We can coexist and not fantasize about the other's nakedness, right?

Easier said than done, I'll admit, but I'm determined to do just that. I'm not about to ruin many years' worth of a friendship just because I can't handle a little ass. A very, *very* nice ass.

Shaking my head, I glance across the table and find Danny staring at me. I quickly look away, hating the feeling of him watching, dissecting me. The waitress arrives and fills up our coffee cups. I add a splash of cream and two sugar packets, stirring my drink and taking a long sip. Rueben sips his black, something I recall from college. He was the only guy I knew who actually drank black coffee. Danny prefers his not tasting at all like coffee. He's more of a fancy latte guy.

"So, are you both ready for the game?" Rueben asks our tablemates between sips of coffee.

"I am *so* ready! It's been so long since I've been to a football game. Of course, it won't be the same as seeing my Danny out on the field like I used to," Ellen replies. Again, Danny brings her hand to his mouth and nibbles a little on her fingers.

As sickening as it is to watch their gross display of affection, it's her comment that is more revolting. She makes it sound like he was hers way back when he used to play. I'm the one who was wearing his number. I was the one who joined him on the field to celebrate every victory and commiserate every loss. Ellen was the one in the stands, flirting with anyone she could, not even knowing who we were playing or what the final score was.

"It's going to be so great having you beside me," Danny coos, smiling blinding white teeth that have clearly been bleached to the max.

"So...you two are...together?" I ask, the bitterness of my coffee catching in my throat.

"We are!" Ellen declares, flashing her own too-white smile and giggling. Good to know her giggle still grates on my nerves, even ten years after I've heard it.

"Wow, congratulations. That must be a fairly new development," I reply. You know, considering she was trying to hook up with Rueben yesterday afternoon and Danny made no mention of Ellen last night at Slim's.

"We ran into each other last night in the hotel bar and got to reminiscing. The attraction is there, right? I mean, he's Danny freaking Ohara," Ellen boasts, waving her hand in front of the man at her side like she's Vanna White.

I can't help it, I roll my eyes. Really big like. So wide, I'm sure I catch a glimpse of my brain as my eyes are swirling around in my head. I try not to make a big showing of it, but I know Ellen saw. The glare is intense, and if I were a weaker woman, I would have definitely cowered under her stare, but I have years under my belt, covering Ellen's disapproval and less than sunny disposition.

Our waitress returns to take our orders, but I'm not sure I can eat much. Watching Danny and Ellen maul each other at the table is doing a number on my stomach. Even Rueben seems a little grossed out by the PDA our tablemates are putting on.

"So, Ellen, what have you been up to since graduation?" I ask, hoping that they'll stop licking each other long enough to have a conversation, even if I'd rather do anything other than talk to them.

"Oh!" she starts eagerly. "I moved to Chicago after graduation and worked for WKN as an intern. I did that for about six weeks and met Rodney. He was the CEO for the station. We got married about four months later in Aruba," she says with bright eyes.

"Wait, Rodney Jergeson? Wasn't he married?" I find myself asking, even though I already know the answer. I recall word hitting the streets, even all the way out in California. Rodney had been at WKN since he was in his early twenties, working his way up to CEO. He had married his high school sweetheart, and the world went nuts when his affair with a much younger woman came out. His wife left him and got half of everything, including their three houses and a boat.

"Oh, her," Ellen replies, waving her hand dismissively. "It was practically over before I met him."

Right.

"Anyway, I quit my intern position because everyone was accusing me of sleeping with the boss to get a better job," she goes on to say, but doesn't actually deny it. "But then Rodney started to get on me about spending money and the trips I was taking. I divorced him a year later."

I just stare at the other woman at the table. So, she quits her intern job to stay at home and spend his money, and then gets upset when he starts to push back about all of her spending?

"Anyway, I got half of his half in the divorce, considering his first gold-digging wife took so much of it." Ellen rolls her eyes dramatically for effect.

"So, are you working anywhere now?" I ask, almost afraid to ask. Ellen had big dreams of having her own syndicated talk show by the time she was thirty. Since I only recall seeing one Ellen on the TV, and it most definitely isn't Ellen Montgomery, I figure that dream didn't become reality.

"Nope," she replies, popping her P. "I don't need to," she adds with a shrug before chugging her mimosa.

We're saved from further elaboration when our food arrives. My ham and cheese omelet is still steaming, scalding the roof of my mouth with my first bite, but I don't care. I'm determined to get through this breakfast as fast as possible and away from Ellen and Danny. Rueben glances over, his eyebrows pulled together as he watches me shovel my food into my mouth. As if the lightbulb goes off, he grins and takes a big bite of his own food.

Throughout breakfast, I make occasional conversational noises, but for the most part, I drown him out. Danny is talking—again—about his career in LA. I hear things like ratings galore, charity ball, and Paris Hilton, but I tune the rest out. I don't really care that everything worked out exactly as it was supposed to. Yeah, I didn't miss that subtle dig either. Kudos to Danny for making something of himself, blah blah blah.

Is it wrong that I can't help but wonder who ironed his work shirts when he got to Los Angeles?

Probably some poor intern who wasn't even being paid to take care of the manchild.

When the check arrives, Danny reaches out and grabs the bill. I made no attempt to reach the slip of paper, nor do I offer to help with the tip. Instead, I let Mr. Perfect Moneybags take care of the forty-three dollar check, plus tip. Ellen seems very comfortable allowing him to pay.

Rueben makes a grab for his wallet, but I glare at him. "What?" he whispers, pulling a ten from the confines.

"He can pay. He owes me. And probably you too. Did he reimburse you at all for driving his crap all the way across the country ten years ago?" I whisper harshly.

The sober look on his face is my answer. The bastard didn't even pay for his friend's gas, nor probably his lodging during that time. What a cheap asshole.

Rueben still throws the ten on the table for the server and stands. He helps pull my chair out, his hand resting on my lower back as I stand beside him.

"Well, this was fun, but we really should be going," I say, even though fun isn't the word I'd use to describe breakfast.

"Aren't we going to the same place? We'll share a cab," Danny says as he heads toward the exit.

"Oh, no, that's okay. I'm sure you and Ellen want to enjoy the trip alone," I insist, but he's not having it.

"Nonsense. I'd love to catch up with you all more," he says, taking Ellen's hand and guiding her to the front entrance of our hotel.

"Seriously?" I ask, glancing up, as if asking my question to God himself.

Rueben snorts. "Well, it could be worse."

I glance up at the handsome man beside me. "Really?"

"Sure. He could have stuck you with the bill," he says with a smile before leading me outside to wait for our taxi.

Chapter Eight

Rueben

The stadium is packed by the time we arrive. Tailgaters are everywhere, wearing their maroon and white SIU Salukis fan gear and proudly screaming their excitement for today's big game. A welcome banner hangs from a portion of brick exterior on the new Saluki Stadium, right beside the school fight song. This is my first time visiting the new stadium, which opened the season after our senior year. It's a little surreal being back here, to the place I spent so many Saturdays for a handful of years. It's not, however, the first time I've been here with Cricket. Actually, we attended most football games together the second half of school. I wasn't a huge fan of the game, but I always came to support Danny.

The difference is today is actually the first time I've ever held her hand here.

"I can't believe I'm saying this, but I'm really excited to see the new stadium," Cricket says as we approach the entrance.

"Me too. I wasn't sure if I'd ever see it in person after graduation," I tell her, retrieving my ticket from my wallet. Cricket digs in her purse, pulling out her cell phone and bringing up her own ticket. When I purchased my ticket, I had the choice of an electronic ticket, but didn't pick that option. I'd rather pay the small processing fee and receive a physical paper ticket in the mail, I'm probably the only human alive that feels that way, but knowing what I know about computers and hackers, I'd rather not take the chance.

Our tickets are scanned and Cricket's bag is quickly searched. Moments later, we're finally inside the mostly metal interior of our alma mater's new football stadium. Of course, to everyone who lives here or attends school, it's not new. It's now ten years old. But to us, the students who left school two months before it opened, this is kind of a big deal for us.

"This place is pretty dope, right?"

I glance over my shoulder and find Danny still keeping up with us. I thought maybe we'd part ways, but that didn't happen. Instead, Danny insisted we share a taxi. Now, we're entering the stadium with them hot on our heels. "Uh, yeah, it's a nice upgrade," I reply, glancing up at the steel beams and the posters of past players.

"I need a pretzel with cheese. Lots of cheese," Cricket says, pulling on my arm. "We'll see you guys around," she adds, hollering over her shoulder to Danny and Ellen. "God, I thought we'd never get rid of them."

I snort a laugh. "I can't believe you're still hungry," I say as we enter the line for one of the food vendors.

"I'm not, but I needed a break from their kissy kissy faces."

"Kissy kissy faces?" I ask, unable to mask my smile.

"You know, the over-the-top googly eyes and almost awkwardly fake kissing? They can't keep their lips off each other," she says as the line slowly starts to move us forward.

"Isn't that how new love is supposed to be?" I find myself asking, pulling my wallet from my back pocket.

She shrugs. "I guess. It's just weird, right? Neither one of them said anything about the other yesterday, but now they're all over each other and throwing around closed-mouth kisses like they're kissing their grandma."

We step up to the counter and I order a pretzel with cheese and two bottles of water. "Umm, I hate to break it to you, but aren't *we* all over each other?"

Cricket stops and looks up at me, considering my words. Then she cocks her head slightly to the side and says, "Yeah, but it doesn't feel awkward and fake with us. Do you think they can tell?"

Now it's my turn to consider her words as I hand over twenty dollars, the pretzel and cheese and bottles of water almost eating up the entire bill. That kiss last night was pretty fucking amazing, and if I were watching it from the sidelines, I wouldn't think it was someone pretending to be in a relationship. I'd see a couple who was unable to keep their hands—and mouths—off each other. "No, I don't think they can tell. First off, they give each other these weird pecks on the lips," I say, grabbing both bottles of water from the counter and muttering a quick thank you to the workers. As we turn to head toward our seating area, I lean in and add, "Last night, we were all tongue."

Cricket gasps beside me, her face turning a beautiful shade of pink. She looks at me and smiles a knowing little grin. "True, we were." As we head to the area for alumni, she glances my way and adds, "So, what we're saying is our faking is way better than their faking, because I'm honestly not sure I believe they're dating."

"I would agree with that assessment. I'm not one hundred percent sure they're in a relationship either, but I am holding out on making my final vote on that topic."

"I can respect that," she says as we step out onto the concrete stairs and look down at the field. "I think we're over here," she points just off to the left, where a large section of seating is roped off for alumni.

As we approach, we find small groups of seats still open. Our tickets don't actually have seat numbers on them. The idea was to be able to mix and mingle with former classmates and teammates, catch up while watching the football game.

Cricket points to a few seats. "This okay?"

I nod, the noise around us pretty loud as I take in the ambiance. The team is on the field, warming up, and there's a buzz of excitement from the crowd. As I drop into a seat, I do see a few recognizable faces that grab my attention. A name jumps out at me for a tall, skinny guy with shaggy dark hair, while the others look familiar, yet I can't put a name to the face.

Off to the side, I see Danny. He's down along the railing, talking to someone from the coaching staff. Ellen is there, twirling her hair and occasionally glancing down at her nails. She's wearing a tight SIU Salukis shirt, one that may have come from the kid's department. Sure, I notice. I'm a guy. And not dead. But I'll take Cricket's brand of beauty over Ellen's in-your-face glamour any day.

Speaking of Cricket, she chose a fitted tee in maroon, but with a little more wiggle room in it. It forms nicely to her curves, but doesn't give it all away, if you know what I mean. She's wearing a pair of jean capris and cute white shoes. Even though we were under the gun this morning on time, she still straightened her hair and put on a little makeup. She looks stunning, making my dick twitch its approval in my pants, much like it did this morning when she stepped out of my bathroom ready to go.

We watch a few moments of pregame festivities until the man I recognized as Dylan Haskins heads our way. "Hey, Rueben Rigsby, right?" he says, extending his hand.

"Yeah, good to see you Dylan," I reply, placing my hand in his.

"I was hoping I'd run into you this weekend. How have you been?" he asks, taking the empty seat beside me.

"Good, yourself?"

"Can't complain," he says, glancing around, as if to monitor how closely the crowd is. "Listen, I have something I wanted to pitch to you. An idea the company I work for has. It might be right up your alley."

I consider his words for a moment as I take a drink of my water. "Like a job offer?"

Dylan shrugs. "Quite possibly. You available to talk? I know we have the alumni dinner tonight," he says, glancing over my shoulder to Cricket, "and I'm sure you have plans."

With Cricket. That's what he's insinuating, and in a way, he's right. Though we have nothing concrete, we're supposed to be dating, so it would be assumed we'd schedule things to do together with our downtime.

I'm not sure why I'm actually considering his offer to meet, other than I'm curious and want to hear him out. Am I looking for a new job? Nope. I'm happy where I am and get to work from home. I also make damn good money, so it's not like I'm looking for an increase in pay or more benefits. Yet, I'm curious as hell to hear what he's been up to and how it could factor into my future. "I can meet up," I find myself saying.

Dylan smiles. "Glad to hear it. I've been following the work you've been doing, and you'd be an asset. Here's my card," he says, pulling a small white rectangle from his shirt pocket and handing it to me. "My cell phone is on there. Give me a call when you have an hour or so free."

I take the card and palm it. "I will, thanks." Then, I stop and turn. "You've been following me?"

"Your work, man. Computer forensics is a small world. You've made a name for yourself."

He reaches out his hand, shakes mine, says a quick greeting to Cricket, and then leaves to go back to his group of friends. "That was strange," she muses, tearing off a piece of her pretzel and smothering it in cheese.

"It was," I confirm, reaching over and pulling off a small piece of her food and taking a bite. "Too salty," I mumble as I chew the dry, sodium-covered pretzel.

"It's supposed to be, dummy," she says, ripping off another section and covering it in cheese, coating her finger at the same time. "They're better with cheese." Then, as she shovels the food into her mouth, she licks and sucks the cheddar off her finger.

Lucky finger.

Clearing my throat, I tell her, "I was afraid to take any cheese. You're kinda hogging it."

"Am not!"

"No? You're licking your fingers like you haven't eaten in a week." With the knuckle on my finger, I push my glasses up on my nose, not even caring that they're slightly crooked.

Cricket glances down at her cheese to pretzel ratio, which is severely lopsided. "Fine, I guess to do like cheese. Everything's better with cheese," she states moments before she sets the pretzel down on the seat beside her and reaches for my face.

I don't move—I'm not sure I can— as she takes both hands and gently adjusts the frames on my face, carefully making sure they're straight. "There."

"Thank you." Why does my voice sound weird?

Her hands stay on the plastic, but her eyes are locked on mine. Something passes between us in that moment. Resolve, maybe? It's like we both completely give in to whatever it is that's holding us back. My lips tingle with anticipation. I'm going to kiss her, right here, right now, and it has nothing to do with who may be watching and everything to do with me flat-out *needing* to kiss her like I need air.

"These frames look amazing on you," she whispers, her voice deeper and with a touch of something raw and inviting.

My lips would look amazing on you.

Except the way her eyes widen, and her mouth falls open ever so slightly, I realize my mistake. I didn't think that statement in my head. I said it.

Out loud.

There's only one way out of my blunder at this point, and that's why I'm moving, her lips drawing closer and closer as the seconds tick by. Cricket licks her lips in anticipation, and as I take her jaw in my hand and thread my right hand into her hair, I give her ample time to say no, to tell me she doesn't want this kiss. She responds by tilting her head upward, her eyes locked on mine as she waits for the kiss.

Maybe she's giving me a chance to back out, to change my own mind, but that's not happening. No way in hell am I stopping the inevitable, and this kiss is unavoidable, like the waves crashing onto the shore. It just *is*.

Like the one we shared the night before at the pub, I feel like I'm punched in the stomach the moment our lips meet, but unlike the kiss from last night, this one is slower, tender, as if we're both savoring the feel of the other's lips against our own. She opens her mouth instantly, allowing my tongue to sweep inside and taste her. My left hand cradles her jaw protectively, while the fingers on my right hand tangle in those long, dark locks. The silkiness threads through them and my body responds in kind like an aphrodisiac. Who knew hair would be an undiscovered kink?

The kiss doesn't last nearly long enough, and I especially hate the way it ends. "Hey, you two. Enough of that in public. They'll call security on you."

Danny.

The reason we're in this pretend romance to begin with.

I slowly pull my lips from hers. There's a heartbeat's moment where I almost say 'fuck it' and kiss her again. Screw Danny. Screw the public. Screw the indecent exposure charge I'd be facing when I take the kiss a step or two further.

To be up front, I'm not sure how I feel about Danny in this moment either. I see exactly why she faked a relationship with the first guy to walk by. No, I wasn't exactly walking by, but you get my point. Even if he means absolutely nothing to her anymore, she didn't want to be made to feel unwanted.

Undesirable.

Fuck. That.

Cricket Hill is the most desirable woman I've ever known, and if we didn't live half a country apart, I'd make that fact well-known to her. Actually, fuck *that*. As her friend, it's now my solemn duty to show her just how wanted and desired she is. Even if it hurts to walk away from her at the end of our short time together, I'm going to give her that.

Prove to her that she's everything a man—a real man—could ever want, and more.

Cricket tenses under my hand, her eyes wide with disbelief. She looks to the left and finds her ex standing there. I can almost picture the smirk on his smug face, but I don't look over to confirm. My eyes are glued to the most gorgeous set of green ones I've ever seen. They're a little hazy and she blinks rapidly, as if to clear the desire and push it out of her mind. It doesn't work, though. I can still see it there, underlying and brewing a silent storm.

"Get a room, will ya?" Ellen says, dropping into the seat beside me.

Apparently, they're staying to watch the game with us.

Awesome.

A big part of my brain says to yes, get a room, but it's the other part that reminds me this isn't real. It's all fake, part of a scheme. A ploy to show Danny she's not still single and stuck in whatever rut he insinuated. Never mind the fact that she's successful and driven in her work. She's doing something amazing that she enjoys—or enjoys to an extent—and has really made a name for herself in San Francisco. She has nothing to be insecure about. She's amazing.

Just like that kiss.

And I want to do it again.

Chapter Nine

Cricket

My lips still tingle, even as halftime draws to a close. I've always enjoyed watching the marching band perform, yet I can't seem to concentrate on the action on the field. Instead, I keep reliving the action in the stands right before the start of the game, and instead of reminding myself that it shouldn't have happened, I wish it would repeat.

Now.

"So, Cricket, what made you move to co-host. I thought you were destined to be behind the camera forever," Danny says. I'm on the end of our foursome, while Ellen and then Danny sit to Rueben's right. When I glance over, I see Danny's arm casually thrown over the back of Ellen's seat, but other than that, they haven't touched the entire first half of the game. She has, however, bumped Rueben's leg or leaned hers against his at least half a dozen times. So much that he has actually started to angle toward me the further this game proceeds.

I tense in my seat and don't answer right away, which means Danny is left to fill the silence with his assumptions and preposterous insinuations.

"I mean, you're not bad and all, but I'm surprised they've kept you on camera as long as they have. They must have been super desperate," he adds, making Ellen giggle under her breath.

Just the slightest sound from her makes me want to punch puppies. Not that I would actually do that, mind you. I'm just saying… "Actually, yes, we were desperate, Danny. Our co-host left without warning, which I'm sure you already knew, considering she-was sharing a screen with you by six a.m. the next morning and a bed with you by six p.m. that night."

Danny laughs. Actually laughs. "Still care who's sharing my bed, Cricket?"

"Not in the least, Daniel. The only reason I even heard was because our entertainment reporter said pictures appeared on social media," I reply, glancing over at the man I used to love.

"What can I say? The camera loves me," he replies, giving me a wink and that cocky smirk.

Rueben takes my hand in his and brings it to his mouth, gently nibbling on the soft flesh. A warm shiver glides through my body, and I glance his way. His eyes are locked on the field, watching as the band finishes up their halftime routine to a stadium full of fans and alumni. But to me, it's as if we're the only two people here. His eyes might be trained forward, but I feel all of his attention directly on me.

As the third quarter begins, and Ellen's arm moves from the armrest to resting on Rueben's thigh, he quickly stands up and stretches his back. "I'm going to get something to drink. Anyone want anything?" he offers politely.

"Actually, I'll go with you," I state, happy to get up and away from our two tails for a little bit.

Danny asks for a bottle of water as I lead the way through our row of seats and reach back for Rueben's hand. I don't know why, exactly, but it's comforting. I like it when we touch. He doesn't seem to mind either, because he slips his hand in mind and walks beside me as we make our way to the nearest concession stand.

I try to gather my thoughts as I browse the menu items. The line is moving slower now, considering its lunchtime, and we silently wait for our turn to order. My mind keeps replaying what Danny said about being on camera. I knew this business was cut-throat, and that's a big reason why I didn't want it. I enjoyed the production room. I liked being behind the scenes and making the ship sail smoothly, even through rough, choppy waters.

"I don't really like being on camera," I state, unable to stop the word vomit from spewing out. "I know we've kinda already talked about my job, but the truth is… I hate it."

Suddenly, I find myself almost panting with panic. I've never actually spoken those words aloud, fearful that they'll be used against me and I'll suddenly find myself without a job in a city like San Francisco. But the truth is, San Francisco isn't home to me. Sure, it's a great city with great nightlife and things to see and do, but it's always felt like more of a landing strip than a home. For years, I associated that to my break up with Danny, and I was determined to prove that I could do it. Alone. But now? Now I crave the comfort and familiarity of roots, of home. Maybe it's being back here, to the place it all began. Or maybe it's Rueben's presence in my life. All I know is suddenly, I don't really have any interest in going back to my old life. I want something new, something exciting, something that gives me purpose and joy.

Rueben takes my hand and pulls me away from the food. "But what about—" I start, but he cuts me off with his lips. The kiss is firm and packs the punch of a thousand hammers to my soul. But it's also confusing. There's no one around to sell our fake romance to, so why is he kissing me? God, this kiss…is everything.

And that's when it hits me like a cold shower. He's doing it to calm me down. Not because he wants to kiss for the sake of really hot kisses, but because it's the only thing he can think of to keep the panic at bay and to take my mind off my life problems.

"Sorry," he stutters, blinking several times. "I didn't mean to kiss you like that. You looked a little freaked out, and I just…"

Called it.

Mortification sweeps in, branding my cheeks a dark shade of red. "No, it's okay!" I practically holler, wishing I had disappearing powers. Those would come in handy right about now. "I was getting a little worked up," I concede, glancing down at the floor.

His big, warm hands gently grip the sides of my face as he tilts my head upward. My eyes meet his. "You are an amazing woman, Cricket Hill, and if your job isn't making you happy, then I strongly feel you should consider other options. No, not the option you mentioned about switching stations and moving to LA, unless that's what you want. You need to look at yourself, deep inside, and do what makes you happy."

I can't help but smile a little, and I definitely don't miss the way his thumb gently strokes the apple of my cheek. "Like maybe become a professional poker player or competitive darts?"

Rueben snorts. "Anything but that," he teases. "But if that makes you happy, I'll be there, in the front row, and the first one to offer my condolences after you lose."

I can't stop the bubble of laughter. "Lose? I'm all winner, baby."

He just smiles this heart-stopping smile and says, "Yes, yes you are."

My arms move before I even consider the consequences. They wrap around his mid-section, the hard plains of his chest pressed firmly against my cheek. "Thank you for being my friend, Rueben." I pause for a few seconds as he wraps his arms around my shoulders. "I don't have too many friends in San Francisco."

I know he's looking down at me. I can practically feel his eyes on me and the sadness seeping from his pores. "You'll always have a friend in me, Crick. Always."

And I believe him. One thousand percent, without a doubt in my mind, I know I can count on Rueben Rigsby to have my back. The fact that we allowed our friendship to turn into a distant acquaintanceship is somewhat nauseating. Even in college, I knew he would be there if I ever needed him. I've missed that.

Tremendously.

"Thank you," I reply through raw emotion choking the very air I try to breathe.

After a few long seconds, we finally make our way back to the food line. It's a little longer than it was before my breakdown, but that's okay. We silently stand at the end and wait for our turn.

"I do have a few friends," I reassure him. "I'm good friends with Penny, my makeup artist, and I have a group of three girls that will hang out together at museums or dinner parties."

He smiles down at me. "I'm glad."

Clearing my throat, I continue. "I do consider them to be best friend material, even though I made it sound like I didn't. We've all shared a lot in the last six or eight years. They've been there for me when no one else was, and I hope they'd say the same for me."

He's watching me again, those chocolate eyes staring deep into my soul. "I get it. I'm happy you have them, Crick, truly. But I think what you really need is an awesome best friend."

"Really?" I ask, taking a step forward as the line advances.

"Yeah, I do. Someone who's just a call away anytime you need him. Maybe he wears glasses and is about six-two. Oh, and he's incredibly handsome."

I snort another laugh. "Handsome, huh?"

"*Incredibly* handsome, Cricket."

"My apologies." Again, we step forward. "Well, if you ever find that person, send him my way. He sounds great."

"You wound my pride, Hill."

"Your pride is fully intact, Ruby."

Rueben crosses his arms. "We can't be friends anymore. Not unless you vow to never use that nickname again."

I gasp. "What? I can't believe you'd force me to make such a promise," I respond, a performance worth of an Academy Award.

"Bullshit. Pinky swear, Cricket," he argues, extending his right pinky.

Sighing dramatically, "Fine, I won't call you Ruby ever again, Ruby."

His eyes widen. "You're already breaking the vow."

"I haven't even touched your pinky yet," I defend, raising my own pinky. Just before I wrap my pinky around his, I add, "Ruby, Ruby, Ruby." Then, and only then, do I entwine our fingers, sealing the deal.

"You're horrible. That was dirty."

"I'm a delight," I tell him.

Besides, he hasn't seen dirty yet.

As we order our lunch and step to the side to wait for it, he wraps his arm casually around my shoulder. "I'm glad you're my friend, Cricket."

I lean against his shoulder, relishing in the comfort he provides, as I reply, "I'm glad you're my friend, Rueben."

***

We arrive back at the hotel, exhausted, yet energized, still buzzing from the Salukis' big win and the sugary Swedish Fish.

After we ate our Chicago hotdogs, we decided to head over to a different section of Alumni and visit with fellow classmates a little. Mostly, we both just wanted away from Danny and Ellen. Rueben ran into Dylan again, and they quietly carried on a conversation. I bumped into a small group of ladies from my communications class, so I spent the rest of the game catching up with them. In fact, Jenna and Bridget invited me to have a drink with them before the alumni dinner this evening, which I accepted.

Rueben and I make our way into the elevator, hands touching ever so slightly as I press the button and wait for the car to move. "Today was fun," I say, watching the number creep up and stop on four.

When the elevator door opens, he waits for me to exit before he steps off the car. "It was fun," he confirms as I approach our door and wait for him to use the keycard to open it.

Stepping into the room, the cooler air conditioning hits my arms, prickly goosebumps peppering my exposed flesh. I set my wristlet down on the bed. "I was invited to go have a few pre-dinner drinks with Bridget and Jenna from comm class. We studied together on Wednesday nights through senior year. Do you remember them?"

Rueben tosses his keycard and wallet onto the dresser and turns to face me. "Yeah. Those were two of the women you were visiting with at the end of the game, right?"

"Yes, that's them. What do you think? Do you want to go have drinks before the alumni do-hicky?" I ask, plopping down on the bed and flopping on my back.

"That sounds good. I was invited to go meet with Dylan for a little bit. I could go meet him now and then come back and shower and go with you for drinks."

Rolling to my side, I face my friend. "That could work. I'll get showered and ready while you're gone."

Rueben lies back and stares up at the ceiling. "Sounds good. I'm not sure how long my meeting will take, but I don't think too long. He actually wants to do a conference call with his boss."

"On a Saturday afternoon?"

Rueben turns onto his side, resting his head on his palm. "The government doesn't sleep, Crick."

My eyes widen. "Dylan works for the government?"

"Apparently so. He didn't give me a lot of information to go on, but he swears it's legit. That's why he wants to do the conference call. He could probably tell I was a little skeptical at first."

"As you should be. But the government? That's pretty bad ass, Rueben."

"Yeah, I suppose. I'm pretty spoiled right now. I only have to go to Chicago once or twice a year, and working from home is pretty awesome. They pay good money, too. I'm not sure I'm looking for a change."

I shrug awkwardly, considering my head is resting in my palm. "Doesn't hurt to talk to him though, right? Maybe you won't like their offer, but maybe you will."

"That's what I was thinking." His brown eyes stare straight into me. "So, what are you going to do about your job? I hate to think of you as unhappy there, Crick. If that's not the job you want, then go find the one you do."

I sigh. "I know. I think I stay because it's comfortable, you know? When I first moved to San Francisco, that job was the only piece of the mess that was still mine. I had to break my lease on the first apartment because I knew I couldn't afford it solo. My dad had to drive me out there, help me find an even smaller studio that was within my measly budget. He bought me a car that was just old enough to not cost a fortune but wouldn't nickel and dime me yet. I worked at a late-night pizzeria to help offset the starting minimum wage I was being paid. But through all of that, I had the job, the station, and their support. It wasn't long before I was promoted from afternoon and evening assistant production work to the morning show, and from there, production director."

"You did what you had to do, clawed your way from the bottom, and made a name for yourself. I'm proud of you, Crick."

"Thanks. It wasn't easy, and believe me, there were plenty of times I almost packed up and came home."

"But you didn't."

"No, I didn't."

"Listen, I'm not telling you to quit your job. I'm just saying to think about it. Think about where you're at and where you see yourself in five years. Ten years. Don't stay if it's not what makes you happy. Life's too short to be anything but."

His words reverb in my brain. *Life's too short to be anything but happy.* Does my job make me truly happy? No. It hasn't in a long time. I've known that, but refused to really look at it. Now, the trick is going to be figuring out what that is and where I go from here. Do I quit my job and find something new? Go back to the production room, starting over again at the bottom? Or stay where I am because it's stable and the bills are paid?

My heart is leaning one way, but my brain is very black and white. Why would I leave if this job is everything I've ever wanted? Success, financial stability, and with great career opportunities for my future. But my heart, that pesky little organ, keeps yelling, "But why do something you don't truly love?"

Yeah, I have some major things to consider.

But not now.

Now, I need to get ready for the dinner party.

"Thanks, Rueben. You're the best," I tell him as I move into his side and give him a weird hug. It's more of an embrace, considering we're both on our sides. And that thought sparks memories of waking up in his arms this morning. You know, all snuggled into his hold, his very hard, very thick cock pressed firmly against my ass. Yeah, I won't be forgetting *that* anytime soon.

"It's my pleasure, Crick. And I'm serious. If you ever need to talk, I'm just a call away. I don't want to spend the next decade barely communicating like the last. You're stuck with me now, you hear me?" he says, the deep timbre of his voice vibrating against my palm.

"I hear you, bossy pants."

"Good. Now, why don't you go do what girls do when they're preparing for some big dinner thing, and I'll go meet Dylan. He's staying at the Marriott down the road, so I won't be too far away. I should be back by four thirty and we can head out for drinks by five."

"Sounds good," I reply, yet neither one of us move from our position on the bed. In fact, if I'm not mistaken, I'd say he's liking us being pressed against each other again, if you know what I mean. My lady parts are buzzing with dirty thoughts, my core starting to ache with need. Two things I'm still struggling to cope with in light of my friendship status with Rueben. Yet, here I am, ignoring the friend-zone and jumping straight into the wanna-jump-your-bones-zone.

His glasses are slightly askew, so I give them a little push. The side of my finger rubs against the coarse skin on his jaw, which is deliciously covered in today's stubble. What once was smooth this morning is already covered with a sexy five o'clock shadow. My hand lingers for just a few extra seconds before it drops completely.

"Thanks," he whispers, his voice deep and husky.

We finally separate, and he gathers up his stuff to leave.

"I'm going to stop by the front desk and get a second keycard. You keep this one with you," he says, setting the plastic card by my wristlet.

"Okay. Thank you, Rueben. For everything." I hope he knows I'm not just referring to our talk. It's so much more than that. His playing along when I ran my mouth about being in a relationship. His humor and ability to make me smile and laugh. And yes, his words of wisdom when I didn't even know how much I needed them.

He's a truly great friend.

I wish we were more.

Chapter Ten

Rueben

I walk down the block to the Marriott Hotel, sending Dylan a text on the way. Because of the nature of the meeting, he asked if we could meet in his room. I was a little hesitant at first, but after hearing a brief description of what Dylan does for the government, I admit I was intrigued. That's why I'm headed to a former classmate's hotel room instead of taking things with Cricket a step further.

And Lord knows I'm itching to take it further.

Cricket Hill is all I think about. Even when she's standing right beside me in a concession stand line or when we're seated beside each other at a football game, surrounded by hundreds of others I could be talking to or thinking about, it's only her. We're at this critical impasse, as far as our friendship goes. I'm still determined to show her how beautiful and desirable she is, but if I catch one iota of a hint that she's not interested, I'll back off. Until then, I'll continue to blur the line between friendship and, well, more than friendship.

My face still tingles where her fingers grazed my skin. She has this thing for my glasses, and who am I to deny her? If she wants to touch my face and adjust my glasses, I'm definitely not going to stop her. Every time her skin meets mine, I feel this sizzle of electricity. It's foreign and reckless, but it's a feeling I crave.

One I want to experience again and again.

Dylan texts to say he is in room 732, so I head for the bank of elevators and take it to the seventh floor. Within a few minutes, I'm standing in front of his door, and knocking, anxious to find out more about this meeting.

He opens the door with a smile and steps back for me to enter. His room is a small suite, complete with sleeping area, a little group seating area, and a big bathroom with Jacuzzi tub. "Thanks for coming by," he says, closing the door and waving toward the seating area.

"No problem. I admit, I'm very intrigued with what you have to say."

Dylan pulls out a device and sets it on the coffee table beside a laptop, and not a standard issue Dell or Mac. This baby looks custom built with a palm reader on the screen. "Before I call my boss, I thought I'd run down a few details pertaining to the position itself. Then, if you're still interested, I'll make the call. If not, then we move on, no harm, no foul. Sound good?"

I take a seat on the wingback chair, my palms a little damp with excitement and nervousness. I've only interviewed twice in my adulthood, and both of those were more of a formality. Those positions were basically mine before I even sat down for the discussion, and while I still feel that may be the case here as well, I know this meeting is government related, probably for an agency with three letters.

It only takes me a second to make my decision.

"I'm in."

***

The meeting took longer than anticipated. Much longer. In fact, at four thirty, I had to text Cricket and let her know I was still in the meeting. She replied and told me to take my time. We decided she'd go to meet her friends for drinks and then meet up with me at the dinner, which starts at six.

It's five minutes before six and I'm just getting to the event hall. My black necktie is already stifling me, but I do my best not to fidget with it. Instead, I push past the alumni gathered in the hallway and head toward the hall entrance. A table is stationed outside where we check in and are given a nametag. I stick mine on my lapel, smile at the two older ladies manning the entrance, and head inside.

Soft music fills the massive room as I step inside. The lighting is low and the room buzzing with laughter. Waiters walk around with glasses of champagne, while two long bars are stationed on each end of the hall. First up, grab a drink. Then, find Cricket.

I offer greetings to those who make eye contact without stopping to chat. When I'm in line at the bar, it's the first time I really take a deep breath. I'm not a fan of suit and tie affairs, especially when surrounded by hundreds of people. I should probably stick to beer, but that's not what I order when I finally make my way to the front of the line. "Seven and seven," I tell the pretty bartender in a fitted white dress shirt and long black skirt.

I pull a ten from my wallet as she makes my drink, and casually glance around the room to see if I can spot Cricket. I'm sure she's here already. Her plan was to meet up with her friends for a few drinks and then arrive in time for the six p.m. social hour, and even though socializing isn't exactly my cup of tea, Cricket is a natural in a crowd.

"Thanks," I say as I take my drink, throwing a few singles in the tip jar, before moving around the room.

I start in the back and work my way around the side of the room, slowly sipping my drink. The place is filling up quickly and finding Cricket is proving to be a difficult task. I make it all the way around the outer perimeter of the hall, resolved to moving to the inner part of the room, when I hear the sweetest sound. Her laugh.

My eyes scan the crowd until they fall on the most beautiful sight I've ever seen. Cricket Hill. She's wearing that sexy gold dress, which seems to look even more stunning hugging her curves than I could have ever imagined when I saw it on the hanger. The dress hits mid-thigh and is framed by lean, toned legs. She's wearing those strappy black heels, and now that I see them on her feet, all I can picture is how incredible they'd look wrapped around my waist. Her hair is down and her makeup is smoky. But the best part? Her lips are painted a deep red. The color of wine and bad decisions.

I feel it clear down to my toes when she slowly turns, her eyes meeting mine. Like a punch to the gut. And the heart. Her eyes light up as she smiles my way. Her legs chew up the space between us as she excuses herself and heads toward me. Cricket's eyes scan my suit, the appreciation evident in those intoxicating green eyes.

Even if I could talk, I'm not sure what I'd say. Words like beautiful, gorgeous, and stunning don't even seem like strong enough adjectives to describe the way she looks tonight. In that dress, those shoes, and that fucking smile that makes my heart gallop in my chest like a fucking racehorse.

"Fancy meeting you here," she says as she comes to a stop in front of me. Her eyes, so innocent and alluring, gaze up at me, so full of lust and need.

My eyes drink her in once more, my brain still unable to compute words, so I do the next best thing. The one thing that can convey my thoughts and my appreciation for how phenomenal she looks tonight. My lips press against hers, and she gives in to the kiss instantly. In fact, she steps forward, into my embrace, her hands pressing firmly against my chest. The hand not holding my drink wraps around her and rests on her lower back, while my lips devour hers. She tastes like champagne bubbles and mint.

"Well, hello to you too," she whispers against my lips as I nibble on the swollen flesh of her bottom lip.

"You look…wow." I glance down and take her in once more. She may not be mine forever, but she's mine for right now.

Cricket grins at me. "Thank you," she says, her eyes dropping to my shirt. Her hands skim my matte black tie before she straightens the knot at my neck, her fingertips dance across my smooth throat. "If I'm not mistaken, I'd say we planned this matchy matchy attire."

"Pretty crazy, right?" When I packed my tan shirt, it was because it was the only one that fit me right in the neck. But now, looking at Cricket's gold dress and black shoes, it's like it was fate.

"You look very handsome," she says, smoothing out my tie and resting her hands on my lapels.

"So, I don't look as uncomfortable as I feel?" I ask, taking another drink of alcohol.

"Not at all. You look great." Her eyes dance with excitement and happiness as she glances over her shoulder to the group she was talking to. "What do you say we snag me another glass of champagne, and then I'll go introduce you to my friends. They're dying to see you again."

"Well, let's not keep them waiting," I tell her as I take her hand in my free one and lead her toward the nearest waiter. I release her hand only long enough to snag a glass. The moment she takes it, I take her other hand and lead her back the way we came.

"Ladies, you remember Rueben Rigsby? Rueben, this is Jenna and Craig Dawson and Bridget and Phil Beckman."

"Great to see you again, Rueben. I remember you stopping by our study groups often," Bridget says, smiling warmly at my date.

"I do recall crashing your study sessions," I tell them, shaking their husbands' hands and theirs as well.

"It was a welcomed reprieve, believe us. Some of those books we covered were monotonous and boring," Jenna says.

We stand around and visit a little more as dinnertime approaches. When they announce that we can be seated at the tables, we find one that's still open, the six of us taking three quarters of the table, and making ourselves comfortable. Water is poured into the goblets on the table and the server takes our drink orders. I opt to stick with water for the duration of the meal and am surprised when Cricket does the same.

"So, did you both use your communications degrees for your careers?" I ask when the server moves to the next table.

"I did," Bridget says. "I went into radio. I host an afternoon program on a country station in central Illinois."

"And I'm not utilizing my degree at all, unless you consider arguing with toddlers all day as communicating," Jenna adds with a laugh.

"How many kids?" I ask. She holds up four wiggling fingers. "Four? Wow, that's great."

She laughs and looks at her husband. "It is great. I wouldn't change it for the world. We had our first two sort of back-to-back. We said we were done, but then were surprised with a third pregnancy."

"With twins," her husband adds with a proud smile.

"That's a lot of little ones," Crickets says.

"It is, yes. Most of the time we're outnumbered, outwitted, and outmaneuvered. I'm always tired and usually have something like food or spit up in my hair, but at the end of the day, I wouldn't change any of it," Jenna boasts, her loving eyes locked on her husband.

"She's the best mom in the world," he replies, kissing her hand tenderly.

Cricket glances over and catches my eye. It's the first time I really try to put myself into someone else's shoes. He has a loving wife, a brood of kids, probably mounting bills, and a mortgage that rivals the purchase of a small country. But he looks happy. Elated, actually.

And suddenly, I want that. No, not right this moment, but I allow myself to stop and think about it. A wife, some kids, and a house with a swing set in the backyard. Maybe even a horse or two in a pasture that we can take care of and ride. I haven't been riding in ages, but I grew up with a horse. We had Shadow until my dad passed. When my mom sold the house, she left Shadow behind for the new owners and their kids to love and ride. I've never really thought too much about that horse until now. It almost feels like another piece of me was lost when he passed away. The only difference is I can actually do something about one of them. I can't bring my dad back, or Shadow for that matter, but I can find a new horse, a new place to love, and maybe raise a family.

My daydreaming is interrupted by a familiar voice.

"Are these seats taken?" Danny is there, Ellen hanging off his arm like candy sprinkled in diamonds, and smiling down at our table.

"Oh, uh," Bridget starts, turning her panicked eyes to Cricket.

Cricket tenses beside me, and even though I don't have any issues with Danny—other than him being an occasional douche nozzle—my loyalty has changed. He's still my friend, but not the one I protect and want to take care of. That's Cricket, and if she's not comfortable with Danny and Ellen sitting with us, then I'll say so.

Before I can open my mouth to tell them those seats are reserved, she surprises me and speaks up. "No, Danny, they're not taken. You and Ellen are welcome to sit with us."

I glance her way, one eyebrow raised in question, but she just slips me a small smile and takes my hand under the table.

"Danny Ohara, good to see you again," Bridget says, taking a drink of her champagne.

"Ladies, lovely to see you again. I trust you've enjoyed the alumni celebration so far?" he asks, always charismatic, as he helps Ellen take a seat beside me.

Great.

"It's been a nice day," Jenna confirms, a hint of bitterness in her voice.

Apparently, the girls don't like Danny any more than Cricket does. I'm sure she told them all about their breakup and the way her life changed over the course of the next decade, which might be why they're both about a degree above frosty at this moment.

We're saved from more idle chitchat when our server arrives with a tray of salads. We all dig in, enjoying first the salad and soup, and then the main course of sirloin steak with roasted potatoes and green beans. Ellen, of course, chooses the vegetarian option, and I struggle to hold in my chuckle when Cricket rolls her eyes.

Throughout the meal, Danny monopolizes most of the conversation with stories of himself, and while that's not in the least surprising, what is, is the fact that Ellen seems completely bored out of her mind as he drones on and on about how amazing he is. He's definitely his own biggest fan, that's for sure, but I suppose that hasn't changed much. Danny was the exact same in college, whether in class or on the football field.

As our plates are collected and a chocolate mousse cake is passed out, the current school president of SIU takes the stage and welcomes the alumni. I try to listen to him talk, but to be honest, he could be selling trade military secrets to the entire audience and I wouldn't have a clue. I'm focused on the way Cricket's hand fits in mine. How she sips a fresh glass of champagne between bites of her chocolate cake. How she continually glances to the front of the room and looks as if she's truly listening to what the man is saying. When he finishes and turns the podium over to one of our classmates who became a young House Representative last year, Cricket continues to take in his words, a small smile playing on her lips.

Suddenly, she glances my way and our eyes lock. Hers dilate under the low lighting, her fork with a sliver of cake on it abandoned.

Cricket tightens her grip on my hand and her lips gently curl upward. I'm lost in a sea of green eyes and swirling emotions. Jesus, this woman is… amazing. She's breathtaking. She's everything.

The man with the microphone drones on and on about the state of Illinois and the success rate of college graduates, I focus all my attention to the woman to my left. I don't even care that I'm blatant in my staring. She's all I see.

A hand with eagle talons scores across my thigh. Considering Cricket is taking another sip of champagne with one hand and the other is tucked in mine, I'm willing to bet my left nut this hand belongs to the blonde viper to my right. I try to shift to my left, but the hand seems to cling to my leg like a monkey to a tree branch. I glance her way, but Ellen's attention is focused on the stage.

Reaching for my water, I chug most of the glass's contents, wishing it were something hard like scotch. Unfortunately, I'm left with ice water for the foreseeable future, since the servers and waiters aren't walking around during the speeches.

On stage, the speaker finishes up and introduces a woman I vaguely remember from school administration. Everyone claps as she takes the stage, and I'm relieved when Ellen does so too. I relax in my chair, anxious to get this part of the dinner over with. This was one of the worst parts of college, listening to the endless lectures and just trying to keep up, so if the professor called on you for an answer, you were at least following along.

When the room quiets down, the speaker starts talking about the alumni association, and how much of an impact it has on the school. At least this topic is a little more interesting, as opposed to politics like the last guy. Of course, the premise of her speech is about money and why we should be giving more of it to our alma mater, but I get it, it's part of her job. And to be honest, I could probably give a donation every now and again, especially when it goes to things like facility and education upgrades.

My mind is the furthest away from education though, when a hand cups my balls. I jump in my seat, my knee nailing the underside of the round table. Everything on the tabletop jumps, the clanking of glass and silverware heard throughout the entire hall. Cricket glances my way, her eyes wide in surprise, but what's more surprising, is that the hand on my balls hasn't moved an inch.

"Are you okay?" Cricket whispers as the attention returns to the front of the room.

"Fine, fine," I reply, my voice tight and breathy, and not in a positive way. "I'm going to use the restroom. Excuse me," I add, sliding my chair out quietly and forcing the fingers to let go of my boys.

Out of the corner of my eye, I watch Ellen. She doesn't even bat a mascara-caked eyelash or take her eyes off the speaker up front. She's cool as a cucumber as she sips her champagne, a coy smile playing on her lips. One that lets me know she knows I'm watching her.

I make quick work of exiting the hall and finding the closest men's restroom. Since the speeches have commenced, there's no one around except a couple slipping out of a closet, their clothes a little rumpled and their hair askew. Makes me wonder if they're here together or if happenstance brought them to that supply closet.

I use the restroom quickly, noting that no one else is inside. When I'm washing my hands, the door behind me opens. Glancing up as I'm lathering has my stomach dropping into my toes. Ellen stands there, her arms crossed, pressing her boobs up and practically out of her red dress. Reaching for the towel, I keep my eyes on her the entire time. Not because I'm attracted to her, but because I don't trust her.

"There a line for the ladies' restroom?" I ask, throwing the paper towel into the trash bin and turning to face her.

She smiles even wider as she slowly starts to walk my way. "No," she replies, coming to a stop directly in front of me. Her wide eyes are completely different than Cricket's. First off, the color is all wrong, but there's something else too. Where Cricket's are full of innocence and vulnerability, Ellen's are full of seduction and experience. "But the view is so much better in here than anywhere else," she adds, placing her hands on my lapel and sliding them upward.

I grab her hands and stop them before they can reach my neck. "Stop, Ellen."

"Stop what?" she asks, batting her eyelashes and giving me another coy smile.

"Stop playing games. I'm with Cricket," I tell her, taking a step back, my ass hitting the sink.

Ellen rolls her eyes. "Pssh, I don't mind sharing," she replies, throwing her arms around my neck.

I practically toss her off me, causing her to stumble in her too-high heels. "Well, I do mind," I state plainly, adjusting my cuff links and necktie. "I'm not interested, Ellen. Go back out to Danny."

Again, she rolls her eyes and steps up beside me at the sink, wiping any lipstick smudges off her skin. "Danny? And who do you think is keeping him company right now, Rueben?" she asks.

Jealousy races through me in a way it never has before. I don't want to think about Danny and Cricket together, not after everything we've shared in the last twenty-four hours. Yes, it's hard to believe it was only yesterday afternoon that we ran into each other at the airport, but so much has happened in that short amount of time, and I'm definitely not ready for that to end. Even more so, I'm not ready to lose her, especially to Danny Ohara.

"If you'll excuse me," I say, walking right by her and heading for the door. "My girlfriend is waiting for me."

She doesn't turn around, but our eyes lock in the mirror. "Don't be silly, Rueben. We both know she'll pick him. They always pick him," she says, vocalizing my greatest fear come to life and making my heart hammer in my chest.

It wouldn't be the first time a girl chose Danny over me. In college, before he was dating Cricket, there was this girl, Aimee, who lived in the same dorm building as us. She was a floor below us, but I often found us passing on the stairs or eating lunch in the common area at the same time. She was beautiful and driven—way out of my league—and had the sweetest smile. I saw her one night at some off-campus party Danny convinced me to go to, and I made the mistake of telling him I thought she was hot. I ended up heading home earlier than him, mostly because I wasn't into the shit that was passed around the later the night went on.

Next morning, I woke up and found her in my roommate's bed. He could have had anyone at that party, yet he took home the one girl there I told him I liked. When they woke, Danny played ignorant, like he had no clue how she got there, and I didn't call him out on his blatant lie. Should I have? Fuck, yes. In hindsight, I should have confronted him on taking her home, bringing her back to the small dorm we shared together, but I didn't. Technically, I had no claim to the girl. I was just a computer geek with a crush. So I let it go, but never told him of any of my crushes again.

Now, his girlfriend—or whatever it is Ellen is considered—is telling me he's out there, keeping my girl company, and insinuating they'll be back together in no time. My mind goes right back to that morning where I found him and Aimee in bed together. Jealousy is a bitter pill to swallow, and right now, I'm doing a terrible job of keeping it down.

Then I stop and picture Cricket. Sweet, beautiful Cricket. Someone who fell for his charms once before, but vowed she wouldn't be caught dead near the man again. In fact, she probably has a voodoo doll in his likeness, and late at night, she drinks a bottle of wine and sticks needles into his eye sockets and groin.

That thought makes me smile.

I realize in that moment, I trust her. With everything.

Including my heart.

I smile at the woman in the mirror. She returns the grin, thinking she has me under her spell. "You know what, Ellen, I believe you're wrong. Cricket doesn't want Danny any more than I want you." Her smile falls from her painted lips. "Have a good evening," I tell her as I turn and walk out the door.

My long legs eat up the carpet as I make my way back to the banquet hall.

Back to Cricket.

Chapter Eleven

Cricket

Where the hell is he?

I head for the bar, anxious to get away from our table. Away from Danny.

The moment Rueben excused himself to the restroom, I noticed Ellen's eyes follow him as he exited the room. When she turned and saw me staring, she only smiled that conniving, vindictive grin that let me know she was up to something. Before I could get up and follow him, she left, heading off to use the restroom.

Everything inside me wanted to follow her. I knew where she was going. But a bigger part of me realized I trust him. Even if our relationship is totally fake, Rueben would never do anything to hurt me, and that includes getting it on with Ellen in the supply closet. So that's why I stayed in my seat and listened to the chairperson of the alumni foundation speak on raising more money.

The moment she finished her speech, they started to clear the tables of dinner remnants and brought out a band for dancing. Danny took the opportunity to slide over two seats, occupying the one Rueben recently vacated. He instantly started talking about himself, about his contributions to the school, and blah blah blah, but my eyes kept wandering over to the door Rueben and Ellen went through not too long ago.

"You look beautiful tonight," he said, leaning in too closely for my liking.

"Thanks." My reply was short and sweet. He wasn't getting a compliment back.

"Listen, about us," he started, but I had already heard enough.

Standing up, my chair scooting loudly across the tile floor, I said, "There is no us. If you'll excuse me."

And then I headed for the bar.

Here I am, stepping up and ordering a glass of merlot to calm my frazzled nerves. I mean, who does he think he is? He left me, remember? More than ten years ago, the morning of our graduation and the day before we were to leave to start our new life together?

Fuck him.

"Fuck Danny Ohara," I mumble, as the bartender sets the glass of wine down in front of me and I hand over a twenty-dollar bill. When he slides back my change, I throw some in the tip jar. The moment my hand lets go of the bills, the hairs on the back of my neck stand on end, a familiar sensation I now associate with Rueben.

"Why are we saying fuck Danny Ohara?" he whispers, his warm breath tickling my ear as he presses his front to my back.

A familiar tingle courses through my veins as his hands snake around my body and rest on my stomach. He applies just enough pressure to hold me against him, my body feeling every ripple of his, the hardness between his legs. I gasp, the words to answer his question gone for good.

"Crick?" he whispers, his lips grazing over my sensitive earlobe.

"What?"

"What did he do?"

"It's not so much what he did say as what he was going to," I tell him. When he lightens his hold, I slowly spin around and gaze up at his dark eyes.

"What was he going to say?"

I shrug my right shoulder and glance around. The bar is starting to fill up, but no one seems to be paying us much attention. Shocking, considering we're practically blocking part of the bar.

"Truthfully, I didn't let him finish his statement. He started it with 'about us,' to which I politely reminded him that there was no *us*."

The corner of his lip turns up. His hand comes to rest on my lower back, and that familiar pressure is back as he holds me firmly against him. "And why is that?"

My brows pinch together in question. "Why is there no us?" I ask, a little dumbfounded by him asking. He nods once and waits for my reply. "Because I'm not interested in ever dating Danny Ohara again." I can practically feel him relax against me. "Plus, I'm sort of seeing someone," I add, giving him a knowing smile.

His little grin turns wolfish as he moves one hand and threads it in my hair at the nape of my neck. "Sort of seeing someone, huh?"

I'm not sure how it's possible, but he moves us even closer. I can barely think, let alone breathe. My mind is screaming to kiss him, my hands desperate to touch every inch of his body. I'm not sure if it's this man or the glasses of champagne I've had tonight, but a new boldness sweeps through my blood. "Yes, I'm seeing someone. He's pretty fucking great. Smart and funny." I move up to my tiptoes and lean in just a little to whisper, "Oh, and so fucking sexy."

He arches an eyebrow and grins down at me. "Sexy, huh?"

"Fucking sexy," I state, bringing my glass of wine up to my lips and taking a hearty drink. I'm afraid if I don't do something with my hands, they'll strip this man naked, crowd be damned.

We're locked in a stare down, both of us wanting something neither of us have vocalized yet. There's no question left in my mind when it comes to Rueben and whether or not he's attracted to me. I can feel *that* pressed against my stomach. There's also no longer any doubt that he's as lost to this attraction as I am. It's in the way his fingers linger on my skin, like he can't get enough. Or the way he holds my hand and rubs my knuckles with his thumb, almost absently. Or the way he looks at me, as if I'm the only woman in the room.

That's why I would never go back to Danny.

Because he's never made me feel this alive, this desirable, this wanted.

Maybe it was our age. Maybe a twenty-two-year-old doesn't really know enough about love. Or maybe it was *because* it was Danny and our story really didn't have a happily ever after ending. But this? With Rueben? *This* feels different. Better. The best. Exactly how all the fairy tales tell you it's supposed to feel. Maybe sometimes, you have to be shown the bad so you can appreciate the good when it comes along.

Rueben takes my hand and guides me back to our table. I notice Ellen is there, her and Danny's heads angled downward, as if having a private argument amongst themselves. We don't take our seats, however. My date takes the glass from my hand and sets it down, then with my hand still nestled in his own, guides me toward the dance floor.

There are several couples already swaying to the smooth melody of the slow song. My nerves kick up just a notch, and I'm not exactly sure why. I've never danced with Rueben, let alone this closely. Yet, it feels like the most natural, comfortable thing in the entire world. He pulls me into his arms, takes my left hand in his, and places his right hand on my lower back. He holds me close, our bodies aligned in perfect harmony. I can still feel his hard length nestled within the confines of his suit pants, and oh what I'd like to do with that cock right now. I'm grateful for the low lighting to help conceal my rapidly pinkening cheeks.

We sway in sync to the beat, and I realize Rueben has pretty good rhythm. I've danced at my fair share of charity events in San Francisco, and none of my dancing partners have been as smooth on the dance floor as Rueben Rigsby.

"Oh, I meant to ask," I start, glancing up. "How did your meeting go today?"

"Really well. They offered me the job."

"Rueben, that's great!" I exclaim, breaking our dancing formation to give him a hug. "I'm so excited for you. Can you talk about what you'll be doing?"

He glances around as we resume our dance. "A little of it, but some I won't be able to discuss. There's a huge NDA I had to sign just to even talk with the higher ups via video conference. It was a little surreal," he says.

"I'm sure. I bet you're going to be a computer spy working for the CIA, maybe in charge of communication between handler and agent," I whisper, my eyes dancing with excitement.

Rueben laughs. "Where did you come up with that?"

I shrug. "I like to read."

"Well, the job isn't anything like that."

"That you know of..."

He stops and glances down at me. "That I know of," he confirms, the corner of his lip turning upward, the poster boy for mischievous.

"So? Are you going to take it?" I ask, anxiously awaiting his decision.

"I asked them to give me a few days to consider their offer. I need to go talk to my grandpa tomorrow. He's always been my sounding board of sorts when it comes to these big decisions. I was planning to go visit them tomorrow anyway, so it'll be great to talk to him in person instead of on the phone."

Smiling, I reply, "That's right, you said you were going to visit them."

"Can you still go? You mentioned yesterday on the drive here you'd go with me, but I wasn't sure what your flight information was," he says, his eyes a little hopeful. Truthfully, I'm a little hopeful too. I'm not ready to end our weekend together yet.

"I fly out Monday night. I had planned to drive to Decatur tomorrow after the brunch and stay with my parents, but I'm going to need to hit up a car rental place first and pray they have a car available."

We stop moving. "I have an idea," Rueben starts. "What if, after the alumni brunch, we head out *together* and visit my grandparents. We can be on the road to Decatur by three or so and spend the evening with your family. I haven't seen them since graduation." He stops quickly, schooling his features as he adds, "Unless you'd rather just hit the road solo. I totally get that."

But I'm already shaking my head no, an idea already taking shape in my head. "No, I'd love for you to come with me. When is your flight?"

Rueben shrugs. "Tomorrow night, but it's changeable." He seems to swallow hard as he adds, "I'd rather spend the extra time with you."

My own throat seems to develop golf balls and it's hard to breathe over the emotions of his simple statement. Mostly, because I feel the same way. I'm much rather steal a few extra hours—a day even—with Rueben. My plan was to return to work on Tuesday, taking only one of my fourteen vacation days available. In fact, the last time I took a vacation or personal day was when I had the flu three years ago. Otherwise, I'm there, in the studio, ready to work.

But what if...

"What if we hung out a little longer?" I find myself whispering, searching for any sign of reservation in the depths of those brown eyes. When I don't see any, I keep talking, so much so fast I'm not sure he actually keeps up. "What if we visited my parents tomorrow night and left Monday afternoon. We could drive north to

Chicago and maybe stay there for a few days. I have hotel points I can use, and plenty of vacation time built up. We could stay up there through Thursday and then fly home on Friday."

I wait as he absorbs what I just said. He seems to be thinking about it, almost a little too hard, and I start to feel dread fill my gut. He doesn't want to hang out with me that long, does he. He's trying to come up with an excuse. Maybe he doesn't have any time off available and he needs to head back to Tennessee. I'm about to take back my suggestion when a smile spreads easily over his lips.

"I love that idea. I might have to do a little work, but I can work wherever, really. Can you move your flight from Monday to Friday?" he asks.

"I think so. I might have to pay a fee, but that's not a problem," I assure him.

Realizing we're just standing there in the middle of the dance floor, while couples around us sway to the music, Rueben starts to move us once more. "You know, I'll help with the hotels. You don't have to pay for it all. Actually, we could probably just share a room. It'll be cheaper that way," he says, glancing around at those surrounding us and not really making eye contact.

"We could do that. I mean, we already know we're capable of sharing a hotel room, right?" I reply with a weird chuckle. It sounds like I'm fake choking on air.

"Right."

"And we could get double beds. You know, if we need to."

Rueben's eyes finally lock on mine, and I feel the impact sweep through my body. Like a hurricane spiraling through my veins, my breasts start to tingle and my lady parts ache. "What if…we don't get double beds. What if we just share one. Together."

My throat is drier than the Sahara. Words seem to evade me, even though I want to scream my acceptance from the highest mountain. Nodding slightly, my brain and tongue finally communicate. "Together. I'd like that."

Relief washes over his features as his hand grips my lower back. He moves me even closer and everything around us just seems to disappear. This thing—whatever it is—brewing between us is its own force, its own entity, alive and breathing. It consumes me and washes through my blood. I can feel its power and am helpless to stop it.

Not that I want to.

I'm also helpless to stop the kiss. Rueben's lips are inching closer to my own. My tongue slips out, wetting them quickly as I close my eyes. I can feel his breath tickle my skin, causing goosebumps to pepper my skin. His lips are firm, yet tender, as he slides them across mine. When his lips finally settle on mine, he moves them expertly and lazily, as if savoring the taste and feel. Before I even have a chance to open my mouth, his mouth lowers, kissing down my jaw and across my chin.

This kiss…wow.

"I have another idea," he whispers, nibbling on my lower lip and making my body shiver.

"What's that?"

"What if we stay in Chicago through Wednesday and fly back to Tennessee. I'd love for you to see my place. You can stay there until Friday."

My heart is jackhammering in my chest as my brain screams, "YES! YES!" I let out a little gasp as he sucks my bottom lips between his teeth, my panties pretty much completely useless at this point. "I've never been to Tennessee before," I whisper in a voice that doesn't even sound like my own.

"Then it's my solemn duty, as your friend, to show you how gorgeous Gatlinburg is in the fall." He moves his hand slightly lower, his fingers dancing across the cheek of my ass.

"I think that sounds like a brilliant idea," I tell him, gripping onto the back of his jacket as if it were a life vest and I'm floating in endless miles of ocean.

"Yeah?" he asks, teasing the corner of my mouth with his tongue.

"Fuck yes," I gasp, practically grinding against the front of his pants where his erection presses hard into my stomach.

We continue to sway to the music, but I'll be honest, it could have switched to a fast song and I wouldn't have a clue. My brain isn't firing on all cylinders and the lust in my body is threatening to take over completely. In all my life, I've never felt this wanted, this appreciated.

This adored.

"I have another idea," he says, his mouth now dancing beside my ear.

"You're on a roll. Keep talking."

I can feel his lips turn into a smile as he tries to keep our dance PG. I'm pretty sure we already went way past that and are one nipple peek away from being straight out porn. "How would you like to get out of here?"

My heart skips a beat and pirouettes in my chest like a damned professional ballerina. I stop moving and pull back just slightly. Not enough to show the entire hall full of alumni what's going on down in his pants, but enough he can see my face when I reply, "I think *that's* the best idea you've ever had."

The smile that spreads across his face does things in my chest, and I already know, at the end of this week, I'm going to be crushed. I'm not going to want to go home, to leave him back in Tennessee while I fly home to California. I'm going to hurt and probably cry when this ends. I know it, yet I don't want to be anywhere than with him. Even if that means I'm left gutted and alone come next Friday night, I already know the line between friendship and more has already been crossed. It's in the rearview mirror, waving dramatically and begging me to come back. But I don't.

I can't.

I want more.

Even if there's an expiration date.

Chapter Twelve

Rueben

I'm ready to fly out of this room, dragging Cricket behind me as I go, but I don't. I can't. See, I have this little problem in my pants and if I move, everyone and their mother is going to know just how badly I want this woman.

That's why I keep dancing, even when the song changes to a slightly upbeat one, I keep us close, but put just a little more distance between us. If I don't, if I keep her body pressed against mine and the temptation of her lips so dangerously close, I'll never get this hard-on down enough to walk out of here.

And believe me, since the moment she uttered those words, it took Herculean strength not to throw her over my shoulder and run from the room. But I don't want to embarrass her any more than I already have, considering I've practically mauled her in the last five minutes in front of a room packed with people.

Definitely not my finest hour, and my mama raised a gentleman, which is why I keep her out on the dance floor just long enough to get my libido under control and keep my lips to myself. When the upbeat song finally ends, I take her hand and lead her off the dance floor. I can feel eyes on us, but I keep mine focused on our table and away from their judgmental glances.

When we finally reach our destination, my intention is to just grab her clutch purse and run, but I know that's not what will happen. She hasn't seen her friends in years, and I need to give her a chance to say goodnight.

I glance over at Bridget, who's wearing a cat that ate the canary grin as she sips her champagne. Her husband whispers something in her ear, making her smile widely and nod. I probably don't even want to know what he said, so I just give her a wink and reach for Cricket's purse.

"We're going to head out," Cricket says casually, her friends giggling.

"I bet," Jenna replies, standing up and giving Cricket a hug. It's the first time I realize Danny and Ellen aren't at the table.

I shake hands with the two husbands and give friendly hugs to Jenna and Bridget. We all make plans to sit together tomorrow morning at brunch before waving goodbye and heading toward the exit.

"I'm going to use the restroom quickly," she says, leaning up on her tiptoes and kissing my cheek.

I smile like the smug son of a bitch that I am as she walks to the nearest ladies' room. There are a handful of people milling around the hallway as the music inside starts to kick up a few notches. Any other night, I'd stay and find a few more classmates to catch up with, but tonight? No, tonight is all about Cricket and the things I want to do to her body.

Dirty, dirty things.

Over and over again.

"I didn't realize sparkles was your thing." I already know who's standing behind me before I even turn around. Danny's holding a glass with amber liquid, his eyes a little glassy, and the strong stench of alcohol seeping from his breath.

I glance down at the little sparkly clutch in my hand. "Oh this? Yeah, I've had it for years. Black goes with everything," I tease, smiling over at my old friend.

He doesn't smile back, however, as he sips his drink. "You two seemed awfully cozy out on the dance floor."

"Yeah?" I rock back on my heels, trying not to fidget too much under his scrutiny.

"Yeah. I have to say, I was a little ticked off when I found out you two were fucking. I mean, you're my best friend, right? And now you're fucking my girl."

I turn to fully face the man who'd been my good friend way back when, guilt spiraling through my entire body. "First off, she's not your girl anymore. She hasn't been your girl in more than ten years. You left her, remember? The text when you were how many states away already?"

Danny rolls his eyes. "Semantics. Besides, just because we weren't together then, doesn't mean we won't make our way back to each other now."

I stand up straight.

"Yeah, did she tell you she's interviewing with my station in LA? They want us to work together. I'm pretty sure she won't be able to turn away from the offer they've prepared, which will keep her in California. With me. And you're, where again? Kentucky?"

"Tennessee," I reply, my stomach dropping down to my shiny black dress shoes.

"So far away," he replies with a tsk.

My stomach churns as jealousy courses through my body. I've known all along Cricket wasn't mine to keep. She'll return to California after our time is over. Even dragging it out a few more days isn't going to quench this thirst I have for her. In fact, it'll probably make it that much worse. I'm going to send her home in six days, and quite possibly right back to her ex.

Reality has a dreadfully bitter taste.

Movement out of the corner of my eye has me turning to the ladies' room. Cricket walks out, that fucking amazing gold dress hugging her curves and sending my blood southbound to Boner

Town. Her eyes meet mine and light up like fireworks on the Fourth of July, and suddenly everything around me just...disappears. Danny and his insistent big mouth. The looming deadline on our time together. Ellen and her wandering hand. It's all gone, leaving just her and me.

Together.

I glance back at my friend and see his eyes so full of regret and longing as he stares at the approaching woman. "I can't predict the future, Danny. Whatever happens between Cricket and me could change tomorrow, the next day, or a year from now. I'm just enjoying the hell out of spending time with a stunning woman, who wants to spend time with me too. I'm sorry if that hurts you. It was never our intention."

"Sure it wasn't," he snorts, taking another sip of his liquor.

I guess, in a way, he's right. It was Cricket's intention when she told him we were dating. Maybe not to hurt him, exactly, but she wasn't being honest. There was nothing between us until she told him we were dating and jumped into my arms. From that second on, I was helpless to stop this freight train, even though we've both had ample opportunities to end the lie.

The truth is: I didn't want to end the lie. The prospect of Cricket being mine was more appealing than confessing our sins. Danny and I haven't actually spoken in nearly two years. It's been even longer since we've seen each other. When my dad died, I texted him to let him know. It took him two days to reply, and even then, it was a quick sorry. He hasn't initiated a conversation between us since he left. It's always been me to call or text or send an email. When he left Cricket, he, in essence, left me too.

He's been a shitty friend.

And I'm just now realizing it. In fact, there hasn't even really been a friendship since college, at least not one that I'd consider a friendship. There was sporadic communication, but that's it. That realization is both sobering and saddening.

I glance back to the approaching woman. Her eyes are skeptical as she comes to stand before us, a small grin on her dark lips. "Ready?" she asks, looking from Danny and myself.

Calmness takes over. I know I have a choice right now between Danny and Cricket, and it's an easy one. I choose her.

We were nothing more than friends back in the day, but now, I can see myself falling completely in love with her. Even if every second we're together leads us toward the end, I'll savor every single one of those seconds as if they were our last. There are no guarantees in this life, so I'm going to hang on to as many of those moments as I can to last me a lifetime.

"Ready," I tell her, taking her hand in my own.

"It was really good to see you, Danny," I tell him honestly, because at the end of the day, it was nice to catch up. Our lives took us in different directions. That's okay. We've moved on, our friendship not what it once was. I'll always wish the best for him, and hope he'd do the same for me.

Danny sways just a bit as he downs the rest of his booze.

I take a step closer and whisper, "You have to speak tomorrow at the brunch. Might want to lay off the alcohol a little."

He looks up and smirks. "That's right I do. I get to brag about how fucking successful I am, and how amazing my life is. I'm Danny fucking Ohara."

I'm pretty sure that's the alcohol talking, but then again, it's Danny and his immeasurable ego. "You are."

He slaps me on the back and watches a blonde with a very short black dress and caked-on makeup exit the restroom. "If you'll excuse me, I think that woman needs to be shown a good time in the supply closet."

142

And then he's gone, heading over to the woman and kissing her knuckles. Within a few seconds, he has her on the line and is making her laugh. She glances over his shoulder for a second before taking his offered hand and trailing off behind him. Off to the supply closet.

And that, my friends, is the real Danny Ohara.

"Well, I guess that answers the whole Ellen question, huh? Everything okay?" Cricket asks as we make our way to the front entrance of the hall.

I hand over my valet ticket and wrap my arm around her lower back. "Everything is perfect."

She smiles that heart-stopping smile. "It is."

I want to kiss her, but refrain. I know once I start, I won't be able to stop until those kisses turn to more and she's screaming my name in ecstasy, which I'm hoping happens no less than four times tonight. That's why I keep my lips to myself as we wait for my SUV to be pulled around. My hand, well, that's another story. I can't help it if it slowly creeps lower on her hip, my palm cupping the side of her ass.

We wait in silence for about five minutes before another couple comes out to the valet stand. They instantly start talking to us about the dinner, Cricket joining the conversation easily. I, on the other hand, am wound like a fucking clock. I smile politely, but don't engage in the speaking of the words. I can't. My brain is going a thousand miles a minute.

Taste her skin.

Hear her moan.

Slide inside her wet body.

Don't stop until she's coming.

And you can imagine what's going on in my pants, right? It's no secret I'm wildly attracted to this woman, and the thought of getting naked with her is messing with my brain. As in, it's not firing correctly. Like a gun that's misfiring, unable to even think about anything but sex. I haven't been this crazed since I was thirteen and found out what that thing in my pants was really for.

Realizing I'm going to embarrass myself if I don't get my raging hormones under control, I take several deep breaths and close my eyes. The September night is warm against my skin, the air carrying a hint of garlic and marinara from the restaurant across the street.

"Ready?" Cricket asks.

When I open my eyes, I see my rental in front of us, the driver holding the passenger door open. "Definitely," I reply.

I take her to the door and help her in, passing a ten to the valet attendant for his assistance. We're both silent as I make my way to our hotel. The vehicle is full of anticipation, desire, and maybe even nerves. The fog gets heavier the closer we get to our destination, the buzz of excitement practically audible. Fortunately, it's not that far of a drive, and we're pulling into our valet just a few minutes later.

I'm out, my key left in the ignition, as I hand the attendant my slip and another folded ten. Seconds later, I'm at her door, holding it open when she shimmies out of the passenger seat. Her dress is hiked up a little, giving me a good view of her thighs. They're tanned and toned and make my cock weep with joy.

"My eyes are up here," she says softly, her voice low and deep.

When I glance up and find those beautiful green eyes, they're filled with heat and mischief. My lips can't take it any longer. I kiss her. Hard and quick. Just enough of a tease to let her know how badly I want to be with her and how crazy her body in that dress is driving me. I take her hand and whisper, "Let's go."

Silently, we walk through the lobby and head for the elevators. There are a few other guests waiting to board, so we fall in line with them and shuffle in slowly when our car arrives. I move her close, her body shielding mine from anyone who may glance down and spot the baseball bat I'm smuggling in my pants. Of course, the vixen that she is, leans back just a little and wiggles her ass against my erection. I have to bite my tongue to keep the groan from slipping out.

We stop at each floor letting passengers out, until we're finally arriving on the fourth. Another man gets off before us and heads in the opposite direction. Thank God. She leads us off the elevator, her hand still nestled in mine. The moment the door closes and we're alone in the hallway, I spin her around and press her against the wall. "You're driving me crazy," I tell her, running my lips along the hallow of her throat.

"God," she groans. "Me too."

"Let's take this inside."

She nods but doesn't move. She's still pinned between my body and the wall, her eyes so full of trust and desire. "Inside. Now."

I already have my keycard out of my pants pocket when we reach 415. I slip it into door, impatiently waiting on that little light to flash green, and push the door open. The moment we're inside, she spins around and plasters herself against my chest. Our lips meet in a flurry of hunger and need. She's moving back, dragging me along until she stops moving altogether.

I open my eyes and find us in the bathroom, her ass pressed against the vanity. Cricket holds my gaze and reaches down, hiking up the hem of her dress and revealing a very skimpy thong underneath. The very one I had in my hand earlier when I moved her things from her room to mine.

With my hands under her arms, I lift and set her on the vanity top. Her legs instantly wrap around my waist, drawing me toward her body. Fuck, I can feel the heat from her pussy through that tiny scrap of material, through my suit pants and boxers. My mouth waters for one little taste, though I know one taste will never be enough. I want to dive into an ocean of Cricket and never come up for air.

"This dress…" I shake my head. "This dress is going to be the death of me," I say as I caress the soft skin of her shoulder and gently remove the strap of her dress. Before I reveal anything, I glance up and gauge her reaction. Her eyes are watching my movement, following as I lower the side of the dress and expose the top of her strapless bra.

My tongue burns with the need to taste her skin, so while the left hand lowers the other side of the dress, I caress the exposed swell of her breasts with my lips. The scent of her perfume wraps around me as her chest rises and falls with each breath she takes. When both straps of her dress reach her waist, I pull back just a bit to look at her beauty.

"You are without a doubt, the most stunning woman I've ever seen."

She blushes an even deeper shade of pink and gives me a grin. "You should see me without this dress on," she sasses, throwing a wink my way.

"Oh, sweetheart, I plan on it."

Reaching around, I unhook the clasp at her back and the bra falls away. Her breasts are perfect for my hands as I gather them in my palms and gently cup them. Her nipples are already hard as I roll them between my fingers. Cricket's head falls back and a gasp of pleasure spills from those luscious lips.

My mouth doesn't want my hands to have all the fun. Bending down, I suck one nipple into my mouth, running my tongue around the hard nub and drawing it farther into my mouth. She wiggles, pressing her chest out and resting her hands back on the counter. I pinch the other nipple between my fingers, drawing out another long moan. I cover it with my mouth and lavish it with the same attention I gave the first.

"You're wearing entirely too many clothes," she says, reaching for my tie.

I kiss between her breasts, running my tongue all the way down the valley between them. "If I take off my clothes, then this will be over before I'm ready. My clothes are the only thing keeping me from ravishing you right now."

Cricket pulls on the necktie. "What if I want you to ravish me? What if I don't want slow and nice."

My balls start to throb. "What do you want?"

Her fiery eyes gaze up at mine. Her lips are partly open. Her legs tighten around my waist, and her pelvis gyrates against me. "I want you to fuck me, Rueben. Not slow. Not easy. Not this first time."

"The first time?" I ask, the corner of my lip turning upward.

"The first time," she confirms. She runs her hands up the tie loosening it. "Something tells me you're a guy good for a few rounds."

I can't help but smile. "You're going to be worn out and sore by the time I'm through with you," I tell her, ripping off my necktie and tossing it on the floor. Her fingers are already working the buttons on my dress shirt, so I unclip my cuff links and toss them on the counter.

Nimble fingers practically claw at my belt, frantically trying to get it undone to lower my pants. I reach for my wallet, praying I still have that condom in there. It might have been almost a year since my last relationship, but not so long ago I have to worry about the rubber going bad. I'm pleased to find two condoms stuck in there. I guess the Gods of Random Sex With Your Friend were looking out for me this weekend.

"You know, I woke up this morning with *this* pressed against my ass," she says, reaching behind my zipper and cupping my cock. "I could feel how long and hard it was, and all I could think about was finding out exactly what it looked like." She takes my dick in her hands and squeezes. "And felt like." She strokes it. "And tastes like."

I can feel precum dripping from the end. There's no way I'm going to last, not with her hands on me. Ripping open the condom wrapper, Cricket pushes on my pants and boxers, sliding them down my hips. They gather at my knees, but I ignore them. Instead, I focus on the strip of material blocking the Promised Land. My fingers slide along the wet panties, gently moving them to the side and stroking her soft, bare flesh.

"You particularly fond of these?" I ask as I push a finger into her body. It's wet and warm and makes my blood hum with anticipation.

"The panties? No."

With my other hand I grab the thin material and give it a tug. It's not as easy as you'd think, but I manage to rip the lace off one hip and sliding the mangled material down the other leg. "They had to go."

She nods in agreement. "Definitely."

Cricket hikes her leg up on the vanity, and it's the first time I realize she's still wearing those heels. I grab the condom and slide it down my length. She reaches down and gently touches herself, her long finger sliding easily through the wet, swollen flesh. My brain practically explodes as I watch her move a single finger down her clit, disappearing altogether into the place my finger just was.

"Fuck," I groan, my eyes riveted on her movements.

"Yes, please," she replies, removing her finger and spreading her thighs even farther. She scoots until her ass is nearly hanging off the counter. I reach down and grab her ass, angling her pussy upward.

Her legs hitch high on my sides, the bite of her shoes dig into my flesh, but I ignore it. My cock is so fucking hard, it doesn't move very easily as I line it up with her body.

Gazing down at where we're about to join, I revel in the pure beauty of this moment. This incredible woman is giving me her body, giving me her pleasure. It's all I can do not to weep in joy. Instead, my eyes find hers and I gently push forward. Her body is tight, like a warm glove wrapping around my cock, and I make little thrusts as she adjusts. It doesn't take long before I'm fully seated inside her, my blood boiling with need, the tornado of desire forming in my stomach.

"Rueben?"

"Hmm?" I ask, my eyes still glued to where my cock is buried.

When she doesn't answer, I glance up and meet her eyes. "Not easy or slow, remember?" Then she reaches behind my neck and digs her nails into my skin. "Fuck. Me."

It's like that delicate thread between smart and rational just snaps. I pull back until I can see the head of my cock and then thrust forward burying myself clear to the root. Cricket gasps, but grinds against my pelvis. "Again," she groans, so I do. Again and again. Over and over again, I thrust hard and fast into her pussy.

Her hands hold on tight as she opens up her legs and rocks back. I position my hands on the counter at her hips and piston my hips forward. She's holding on to my shoulders, rocking in perfect rhythm and taking what she's after. My lips slam into hers, my tongue dipping into her mouth, mimicking my cock. She sucks on my tongue—hard—and groans as I drive into her pussy. "God, I'm so close," she groans, gripping tightly to my upper body.

"I want to hear you come, Crick," I demand, my own body gearing up for release.

"Fuck," she moans, her head rolling back. I take the opportunity to suck on the skin of her neck. It's soft and salty, a testament to the workout we're having. "God," she says, her body starting to clamp down on my cock.

The base of my spine starts to tingle and I know there's no stopping this freight train. The burn in my legs is ignored as I focus everything I have on her orgasm. My name is screamed, just how I imagined it would sound, as she comes on my dick, her body pulsing around me. My own release is triggered by the sound of my name, my balls pulling up hard and tight as I come in her body. Over and over again, I come more than ever before, waves of ecstasy rolling through my body like high tide.

Cricket starts to loosen her grip on me, but doesn't let go completely. I help hold her legs, since she doesn't seem to have much control over them and take her lips with my own. The kiss is softer, our frantic pants of exertion mingled together as we both try to calm our racing hearts. Her hands slide down my back and move to my ass. Cricket reaches down and squeezes before giggles slip from her lips.

"I'm not sure I like you laughing after that," I tell her, my lips trailing open mouthed kisses down her jaw.

"Do you know how long I've wanted to grab this ass? It's just as firm as I've imagined." She gives it a hard pat and a pinch to top it off.

"Maybe as long as I've wanted to grab yours?" I ask, sliding my hands up the outsides of her thighs and coming around to her backside. Since she's sitting, it isn't easy to work my hands in there, but I manage to lift her just enough to slide my hands between her ass and the hard vanity.

This has to be uncomfortable for her. Even though she hasn't said a word about it, I know her ass has to be sore. I mean, she's on a hotel bathroom counter, for fuck's sake. Not exactly the most comfortable seat out there, right?

I decide to rectify the problem and give her ass some relief by lifting her up. My cock is still buried inside of her, most likely because it's still half hard. Now that he's had a taste of Cricket Hill, I'm not sure he'll ever be soft again. He wants more, that's for sure. I walk out of the bathroom as carefully and slowly as I can, considering my pants are still around my knees. It takes a few long seconds to get to the bed, but that's okay. We fill the time by kissing, something else that makes my dick hard.

Carefully, I lower her onto the bed, my cock slipping from her body. Her dress is a wrinkled mess, all scrunched up around her waist. Her legs fall open and I can see how wet she is. I know I'm going to be ready for another round within moments, but that doesn't mean Cricket is.

She reaches down and unstraps her shoes, tossing them in the room. It's kinda sexy, watching her undress, as I finally remove my own shoes and socks. I push my pants the rest of the way down my legs and kick them off, leaving them on the floor. I quickly head back to the bathroom and grab my wallet, pulling the second condom from within. I remove the used one and throw it in the trash before returning to where I left Cricket.

I'm not sure what to expect. Her to be asleep maybe? Snuggled under the covers and ready to call it a night? What I don't expect is what I find. She's positioned in the middle of the bed, her legs wide open and her fingers teasing her swollen clit once more. All of my blood returns to my cock, and my half-hard cock is now fully engaged and ready to roll.

With the condom in hand, I head over to the foot of the bed and crawl on. My lips start at her knee and graze up her thigh, kissing along her pubis and her fingers. I go ahead and pull her finger into my mouth, sucking off the moisture and taste of her. Cricket's already breathing heavily, her legs widen even more and her hips starting to rock. I kiss up her stomach, lapping at her nipples. I move on, my mouth sucking on her neck and kissing her jaw until I finally get to her lips once more.

"Watching you play with yourself is the sexiest thing ever," I tell her, positioning my forearms beside her head and sliding my hands into her hair.

"You make me want to keep touching myself."

"Are you sure? We don't have to do this again," I tell her gently kissing that hallow point between her ear and her jaw.

She gasps just a bit and turns, offering the side of her head to me. "Are you kidding? Don't you remember what I said?" she asks as she hitches her leg up and over my hip.

"Something about the first time?" I ask as I push forward, my cock nestling right back inside her perfect body.

"Mmmm," she coos. "Yes, that was the first time. Now, we can move on to the second," she says as she rocks her hips, taking me all the way in once more.

I'm pretty sure I'll never get enough of her.

Not tonight.

Not ever.

Chapter Thirteen

Cricket

Warmth envelopes me. It's almost too hot, yet I find myself burrowing in even deeper, reaching for the heat and drawing in closer. A sleepy moan fills the silence, and I know it didn't come from me. I crack open my eyes and find Rueben in front of me, his arms wrapped around my back.

Adjusting my head to rest more comfortably on his forearm, I try to drift back to sleep, but that's not happening. My mind keeps replaying last night—and this morning. Three incredible times, and even then, I'm not sure I've had my fill yet. My body craves his, yearns for more. After the second time, we drifted off to sleep for a bit, but woke up in the early hours of Sunday for round three. Rueben was out of condoms, but after a quick glance in my purse, I found one lonely piece of protection that's been in there longer than I wanted to think about. But it was still good, so we made a point of utilizing it.

"What time is it?" he asks without opening his eyes.

I lift my head and glance over his shoulder at the alarm clock. "Six thirty. We have to be to brunch at ten."

"So we have plenty of time," he whispers, the faintest smile crossing his lips.

I move in closer and run my lips over his collarbone. "Time for what?" I ask, coyly. I'm pretty sure I know what he's talking about, and I'm fully engaged in this plan. He rolls over, pinning me between his body and the bed. My legs are free, so I go ahead and wrap them around his hips, aligning us up once more.

Rueben pulls back though, keeping his hard cock away from where I need him most. "Sorry, sweetheart, but we don't have any more protection," he answers when he sees the question in my eyes. Realization settles in. It's a startling and saddening feeling. I've never in my life been this sex-crazed, yet here I am, with Rueben, and begging for him to make me come a fourth time in under nine hours.

"But…" he says, kissing my neck and slowly working his way down my body. He stops to show attention to my nipples, his tongue licking and mouth sucking until they're hard and my core aches with desire. Pretty low blow, considering we're out of condoms. "But…there are *other* things," he adds as he continues his trek southbound. "Things that involve my mouth…and this." Rueben runs his tongue along my clit, making me shiver.

He presses my legs apart, positioning his broad shoulders between them. He starts slowly, licking and teasing my clit until I'm completely wet and practically panting with anticipation. Then, he slips two fingers deep inside me, stretching me and filling me. A moan of pleasure tears from my lips as my hips rock. He lowers his mouth back to my clit and sucks it hard. Stars burst behind my eyelids as the orgasm starts to build.

Rueben pumps his fingers in and out in a deliciously slow rhythm, his tongue continuing to lap at my swollen flesh. He rotates his hand, his fingers curl slightly upward as he slides them in once more. There's a slight stretch and burn, but that sensation is overwhelmed by the euphoria of him hitting that magical spot deep inside me. My legs start to quiver as I rock faster and faster, chasing that promised orgasm he dangles within reach.

He sucks my clit hard and massages my g-spot, sending me rocketing into outer space like a space shuttle. His name fills the silence as I ride the waves of my release, my body gripping his fingers like a vise. "That was definitely worth not having a condom," he says, carefully removing his fingers from my pussy.

"I happen to agree," I tell him, my body boneless and sated.

Rueben stays where he is, and after a few long seconds, I glance down. He's smiling, his chin resting on his hands as he watches me.

"What?" I ask, starting to get a little self-conscious at his open stare.

He shakes his head. "I just like seeing you, like this. Like anyway, actually. Here, in my bed, naked. That's probably my favorite way to see you, but also in general too. Does that make sense?" he asks.

I nod, because it absolutely does. Having him beside me, whether minimal contact or his entire body pressed against me, I've definitely liking it. A lot. "I feel the same," I confess.

He gives me a full-watt smile that melts my heart just a little more. This man is something. He's sweet and caring. Attentive and fierce. And the things he does with his body? Damn, he knows what he's doing in that department too. Rueben Rigsby is nothing like I expected, and everything I want.

But I can't keep him.

That depressing thought is like an ice cold bucket of water. I hate to think about our time ending, but it's a reality I must face.

But not today.

Today, we're spending the day together and going to see his grandparents. I can think about heading home later. Friday. That's five more nights with him, in a shared bed, in a shared space. Everything else that comes after those nights is just going to have to wait, because I'm not strong enough to deal with it now.

Pushing all thoughts of heading back to California out of my mind, a smile crosses my own lips. "What's so funny?" he asks.

"Nothing," I state, innocently. Sitting up, I push on his shoulders, causing him to roll to his back. I grab a pillow and shove it under his head, my eyes falling on my next task at hand. And holy hell, is that *task* quite large. Thick and long with the very slightest curve to the right. Much bigger than any other one I've had before, and my mouth waters in anticipation.

Rueben seems to realize what's about to happen. "You don't have to do that, you know," he says, always the gentleman.

"I do know that," I tell him as I reach down and grab his cock in my hand, sliding it slowly up and down the warm, hard flesh. "But this is something I've wanted to do for a while now."

He smirks and rests his hands behind his head. "A while now, huh?"

"Yeah, you know like twenty-four hours or so? Ever since I walked out of that bathroom yesterday morning and saw you standing there naked. Even though your back was to me, I was picturing you. This. I was imaging myself dropping to my knees in front of you and taking you all the way down my throat."

I didn't realize it was possible, but his cock actually hardens even more. His eyes burn hot and his breathing becomes a little harsher. "Fuck," he moans, closing his eyes and reveling in the sensation of my hand sliding up and down his length.

"Yep. With my mouth," I confirm, dipping down and licking the wetness from the tip of his cock. Adjusting myself above him, I lower my mouth over his cock, swirling my tongue around the head.

With my left hand holding him firmly, I start to move, taking him a little deeper into my mouth. He reaches down and grabbing my hair, holding it back and out of the way, as he watches me. I actually feel sexy and quite liberating, knowing he's watching me suck him, that I'm giving him so much pleasure.

His hands tighten on my hair as I start to move faster, my left hand starting to join the party and stroking his cock. I take him in as far as I can, until I can feel the base of his cock touching my lips. My name is like a plea as he watches me practically swallow him whole.

I gasp for air as I lick the head once more, beads of precum pouring from the tip.

Reaching down, I cup his balls with my right hand, lower my mouth again on his shaft, and stroke faster and faster with my left. I know he's close. His body is tight, his hips thrusting upward, his breathing erratic and harsh. I take him as far as I can once more, the head of his cock hitting the back of my throat. That's when he detonates.

His orgasm rips through his body as he shoots down my throat in hot bursts, his cock jumping and twitching in my hand. I slow my motions, gently letting his cock ease from my throat, as I lick the tip like a popsicle on a hot day.

"Fuck. That was…wow," he groans, his eyes closed and a hint of a smile on his full lips. He looks like a man happily sated, and a burst of pride spreads through my veins.

Crawling up his body, I lay on top of him. Rueben's arms wrap around my shoulders as he holds me close, breathing me in. "We're going to have to get more condoms today," I tell him, his strong heartbeat pounding against my cheek.

"Definitely. But it's good to know we've always got *that*, you know, when we run out."

I smile against his chest. "Yep, definitely good to know *that's* always on the table."

"Let's never take it off the table."

"Nope."

I close my eyes and catch a little more sleep until it's time for the final alumni event of the weekend.

***

The hotel hall is smaller than the one from last night, but quickly filling up with former students and faculty of SIU. The brunch is at our hotel, on the second floor, and features a big coffee and juice bar, as well as a buffet-style brunch.

When we sign in, I'm instructed to head to the front table, where I'll be sitting with today's speakers. I cradle my tablet firmly in my hands, the nerves of speaking in front of the group starting to take hold. Why did I agree to do this? I'm not the right person for the job, that's for sure. I might speak in front of thousands every morning, but that's different. I can't actually see the people watching me through their televisions. Rueben senses my uneasiness and wraps my hands with his, offering comfort in the simplest of touches.

"You got this, Crick. Your speech is remarkable," he says. This morning while we got ready, I had him read the words I wrote last week for this morning. I sat nervously as he combed through each sentence, ten long minutes of deafening silence. When he finished, he just smiled and said it was perfect.

"Thank you. Believe it or not, I hate speaking in front of large crowds," I whisper, glancing around the room at familiar and unfamiliar faces alike.

"You've got this. You're going to do great. Your message is solid. They're going to be eating out of the palm of your hand."

"Well, I don't know about that," I tell him, my eyes finding the front table. The dean of students is there, along with a few other faces I recognize, one being Danny, the other speaker for this morning.

"I do. Trust me, okay?"

I glance up at his chocolate brown eyes, framed with those dark plastic glasses I've come to love. He has so much faith in me, as a friend, sure, but hopefully as more too. "Okay," I reply, taking a deep breath. "I should head up front."

"I'm going to sit with Dylan, Bridget, Jenna, and a few others over there," he says, pointing to his left. "I'll be waiting for you after you're through." Then, he bends down and gives me a tender kiss on the mouth. "Kick ass, Crick."

"Thanks." I give him a smile and head toward the front of the room. As I approach, the three gentlemen stand up, eager to shake my hand and welcome me to the table. Danny stands too, pulling me into a hug and kissing me on the cheek. I catch a hint of expensive perfume on his skin and mentally roll my eyes.

"Good morning," he whispers, giving me one of those trademark killer grins. It does nothing to me however, and I step back, putting a little distance between us.

I take my seat between Mr. Donaldson from admissions and Danny, who quickly engages in another conversation with the table. Danny is very charismatic and easy to talk to. He's easy on the eyes too, I'll admit, but I feel absolutely nothing when I look at him. Not like I used to. I glance across the room and find Rueben watching me, a small smile on his lips. It feels good to know he's there, silently supporting me as I get ready to speak to the crowd.

Brunch is served, and we're invited to eat first. I take a little fruit and some ham, but nothing too big or heavy. My stomach is in knots, and I'm not sure there's room for food right now. My heart starts to pound and my hands shake. Seriously, why did I think this was a good idea? I can't give a speech about success in broadcasting. I'm the last person who should be up on that podium today.

As I approach the table, a warm hand gently grasps my arm, familiar and inviting. I turn to find Rueben there, holding a cup of coffee just the way I like it.

"I brought you this," he says, as if he could read my body language and sensed I was having a slight pre-speech freak out. His gaze is both calming and reassuring as he sets the coffee down in front of my place and squeezes my hip. "You got this, sweetheart," he whispers, kissing my forehead tenderly.

"I don't think we've met," Mr. Donaldson says as he joins us at the table.

"No sir, I don't believe we have officially, though I went to school here," Rueben says, shaking the extended hand in front of him.

"You did? I'm happy to hear that. And I take it you know our keynote speaker today," he says with a smile.

"I do. I'm Rueben Rigsby, and Cricket is my girlfriend," he says confidently, and it's the first time I really feel the words spread warmly through my blood. Before, they were a lie, a teeny tiny white lie, but now, they're a declaration, a truth.

"Well, it's nice to meet you, Rueben. We're very excited to hear what Cricket has to say today," he says, taking a quick moment to introduce Rueben to the others at the table.

When the pleasantries are done, Rueben heads back to his table to await his turn to get food. I take a seat and nibble at the food on my plate, my stomach a little better now that he came to wish me luck once more.

"So, Cricket, anymore thought to the offer in LA?" Danny asks, picking up a piece of bacon and shoving the entire thing in his mouth.

"Actually, yes," I answer and take a bite of pineapple.

"Well?"

"Well, what? You think I'm going to tell you whether or not I'm accepting the offer?"

"Well...yes!"

"Sorry, Danny, but that's not going to happen. I'll call George myself and tell him." George being the general manager who offered me the job.

I can feel his eyes on me, but I don't look his way. Instead, I focus on my food and trying to get it down my tight throat. I spy Rueben's table getting up and heading toward the food, his eyes on

160

me nearly the entire time. He looks concerned, as if he wishes he were up front with me, holding my hand, and reassuring me everything is going to be great. He offers me silent support so strong, I can feel it from across the room. There's also something else in his eyes that gives me pause.

Appreciation.

Respect.

Gratitude.

All things I've never really associated with past relationships.

But is this a real relationship?

Yes.

I feel *that* deep in my bones too. Even if there's an end looming in the background, I feel so much more with Rueben than I've felt in a long time. If ever. There was no way to stop it. It blindsided me like a linebacker rushing the quarterback. It caught me completely off guard and knocked me on my ass. Rueben knocked me on my ass.

But the crazy part of it all is that I like it.

I like Rueben, maybe even like him a lot.

I like the way he makes me feel.

It's all I think about as they collect our plates and the speeches begin. It's not Danny's words about being the best and rising to the top that have my attention, it's the man sitting at a table toward the back, absently pushing his glasses up on his nose. His eyes are on me, the slightest of smiles teasing his full lips. Lips that I've felt *everywhere* and am already wondering when I can feel them again.

"Thank you so much, Daniel Ohara. And now, I welcome Miss Cricket Hill to the podium."

There's a round of applause as I stand and glance to the front. My tablet is sitting on the table, but I don't reach for it. Suddenly, all of those words I spent hours, days even, pouring over don't seem right. They aren't the message I want to send today. So, I leave the device at my seat and walk confidently to the podium, even though my heart is racing and my palms are sweaty.

"Good morning," I say, adjusting the microphone to accommodate my height. I glance around the room, at the hundreds of eyes all focused on me. My old friends are smiling proudly, waiting for me to begin. Danny is off to my left, checking his phone before glancing back up at me expectantly. And then there's Rueben. He's sitting up tall in his seat, his hands in his lap as he waits for me to begin. He gives me a smile, one that calms my nerves and sends the message that he's here, for me and with me.

As my friend…and as my boyfriend.

Life's too short to be anything but happy.

Clearing my throat, I open my mouth and speak. "I'm honored to have been asked to speak to you all today, as an alumnus of Southern Illinois University."

Deep breath. "When I graduated college, I was afraid. Things in my life hadn't happened the way I had always envisioned them. Everything I had expected, had known, changed, and I was left reeling and trying to figure out what was next.

"My plan was California. I had an entry position at a small television station and was set to begin my career the next week. Over the course of the next few years, I put in the time and dedication, and moved up the ladder. I loved my job. Then, one day, it changed. I was…" My eyes close for a second as I try to slow my racing heart.

I look over at Danny, at his cocky smirk, the message he's sending is that his speech was better, his job is better. Then I look out at the crowd, to Rueben. He gives me the slightest nod, encouraging me to continue, to speak from the heart.

"Jobs change. Careers change. Life happens. Just like my life changed after college graduation. I was in a new city, a new state, and didn't know a soul. My family was supportive of my dream, and while they may have tried to convince me to find something closer, they never stopped believing in me. And while support of your family and friends is important, believing in yourself is key.

"A friend once said life's too short to be anything but happy. So that's the message I want to give you today. We go through life doing what we think we *should* do, instead of what we maybe *need* to. Do what makes you happy. Maybe it's going back to school or changing companies. Possibly it's a completely different career path altogether. Staying home with your children, so you don't miss any of those important milestones. Going for that promotion you may not think you'll get, but know you deserve. Or what if it's picking up your computer and writing that great American novel you've always wanted to write. Whatever your happiness is, do it. Follow your heart. Choose happiness... Because life's too short to be anything but happy.

"Thank you."

I take a deep breath and take a step back. Before my feet are firmly planted, the room erupts in a round of applause. Rueben stands, his hands clapping together and the biggest smile on his handsome face. I give him my own smile as a sense of relief and accomplishment wash over me.

I did it.

And my message was clear.

Now, do I follow my own words and change the course of my life or do I stick it out and keep my eyes open for my happiness?

Chapter Fourteen

Rueben

I knock on the door. *Family Feud* is blasting into the hallway, and I smile. At least I know my grandma's awake. She loves to watch "The Feud" while Grandpa takes his afternoon nap, which I always found odd, considering her need to blast the volume so she can hear it. How he can sleep through that noise has always baffled me.

The door opens and her aging face breaks out into a huge smile. "Ruby!" my grandma exclaims as she pulls me into a hug. Cricket snickers as I wrap my arms around Grandma and breathe in that familiar scent of Avon perfume and oatmeal.

"Hi, Grandma," I reply, her head hitting mid-chest as she squeezes me tightly.

"It's about time you came to see us. Your grandpa is napping, but will be so excited when he wakes up," she says, opening the door wide for us to enter. "Oh my, who is this pretty lady?"

"Grandma, this is my friend, Cricket. I don't know if you remember her from when I was in college. She came with me for a weekend visit one time," I say, entering their small one-bedroom apartment in the assisted living facility.

"Of course, I remember her! Cricket, you are even more beautiful than you were back then. What happened to the other boy? The pretty one who was always looking at himself in the mirror?"

My eyes meet Cricket's and we both smile. "Uh, Danny isn't here. They broke up after college," I tell her.

"Please, please, have a seat. I'll go turn the television down," she says as she shuffles into the living room area and grabs the remote. Grandpa is sleeping in the recliner, his feet extended out and his arms crossed over his chest. His glasses sit lopsided on his nose and his mouth is open wide enough to catch flies. I can't help but smile.

"There, that's better," Grandma says as she rejoins us in the kitchenette area. There's a small round kitchen table, just big enough for four chairs. "Now, what were we talking about? Oh, yes, that boy. Oh, honey, I'm so glad you're not with him. He was always a nice one, but a tad on the vain side. How my Ruby ended up with him as a roommate and a friend is beyond me," Grandma says, shaking her head.

"Come on, Grandma, he wasn't that bad."

"Hmpf," Grandma replies, waving her hand. "You definitely had done worse," she says to me, referring to my roommate situation from freshman year. Larry was a little...weird, and insisted on keeping his pet iguana in our room, despite the no-pets policy in the dorm. It may have been different if Spock (the iguana) was in an aquarium, but he rarely was. Larry kept him in his bed.

And sometimes, in *my* bed.

"Cricket and I just left our alumni reunion," I volunteer, intentionally being evasive. The last thing I need is for Grandma to be constantly asking about Cricket, long after she's returned home to California. It's going to be hard enough without her bringing it up every time we talk.

"Oh, that's right. Your mother mentioned it. I'm so glad you were able to take a little bit to visit," she says, reaching out and patting my hand.

"Of course. I wish I could stay longer, but we're only here for a few hours. But I promised Mom I was coming up with her at Thanksgiving again. I think Royce is coming too."

"That's perfect! We'll go out for dinner. This place cooks decent food, but not for Thanksgiving. I'll make reservations at the diner on Bowman Avenue."

"Sounds perfect, Grandma," I tell her happily. I'm truly glad I stopped by for a visit. I wish they'd move to Gatlinburg with us, but Grandma and Grandpa say this is their home and they're not ready to leave.

"So, tell me what you've been doing, Cricket," Grandma insists, turning and facing the woman beside me. They start discussing California, and Cricket tells her all about her job. She makes it sound exciting, but I know the truth. I know she's not happy being on-air, in front of the camera. I just hope she'll listen to her own words from her speech and find her happy.

The moment she didn't take the tablet up to the podium, I knew something had changed. After listening to Danny drone on for ten minutes about how awesome he is, it was refreshing to hear her speak about happiness, rather than herself. Her speech was much shorter in length but carried a message the other keynote speakers did not.

Passion.

Happiness.

And I was so damn proud of her for speaking the truth.

"Is that my grandson?" I turn and find Grandpa slowly getting up out of his recliner. I jump up and head over to offer help, but he waves me off. "I may be old, but I'm not that old," he teases, standing up and stretching his back. "'Bout time you stopped by for a visit."

"Sorry, Grandpa. I won't let it go that long between visits again."

"Good," he says, nodding. "Who's that pretty lady? She single?" he asks, nudging me with his elbow.

I snort a laugh and glance over my shoulder at Cricket. Yeah, she's definitely pretty, but single? How do I answer that? "It's...complicated." Seems like a canned answer, but it's all I've got right now.

Grandpa seems to notice the turmoil and indecision in my eyes. He studies them, acknowledges it, and then does what he always does. "I was just going to run down to the dining hall for some coffee. Care to join me?"

I smile and nod. Grandpa is offering an olive branch, taking me away so we can talk without Grandma's ears. It's not that I don't appreciate or want my grandma to know my troubles, but it has always been her husband that I talk to about the hard stuff. Especially after Dad died.

"We're going to run down and grab a cup of coffee," Grandpa says as he shuffles into the tiny kitchenette.

My eyes meet Cricket's. Hers dance with humor and ease as she sits with my grandma, eating vanilla wafer cookies and drinking tea. She knows of my plan to talk to my grandpa about the job situation, which is why she doesn't get worked up that I'm leaving her alone for a bit with my grandma.

"I'll be back in just a bit," I tell her, leaning down and catching a whiff of her fruity shampoo. I almost kiss her goodbye, but at the last minute, I stop myself. My grandparents are watching, taking in our interaction, with broad smiles on their faces.

I give her an awkward pat on the shoulder and step back, hating the flash of disappointment I see in her eyes. It's gone a split second later, but it was there. She wanted me to kiss her, expected it even, but I'm torn on what to do. We don't have to fake a relationship anymore. No one's here. We've decided to spend the week together, but does that mean we're including PDA in our relationship? What is our relationship?

Hell if I know.

Winking, I head to the door and wait for my grandpa as he kisses his wife goodbye. Then, we exit their apartment and head silently down the hall. As we make our way to the upstairs sitting room, we pass a woman wearing a bright red top and floral pants. Her hair is curled and her lips are stained a dark shade of burgundy. She gives us a friendly smile and greets Grandpa. He nods and offers a quiet hello, but neither stop to visit.

"That's Mrs. Donnelly. Her husband passed last year and now she's sleeping with ol' Elmer Fudd down the hall," Grandpa says quietly as we approach the sitting room.

I glance back just as the older woman knocks on a door. An elderly man opens it, grabs her hand, and pulls her gently into his apartment. Shaking my head, I turn back to the old man at my side. "Well, you know, everyone needs love," I tell him as we approach the coffee pot.

"That's true, boy. Very true. They think they're being all sneaky about it, but everyone knows. It's all our dinner table talked about this past week," he says, taking two mugs from the rack and pouring in the black coffee. "They usually keep this pretty fresh," he adds, his shaky hand offering me the first cup.

"Thanks," I tell him as I glance around and decide to take a seat at one of the small tables overlooking the courtyard in back.

Grandpa joins me after stirring in a scoop of sugar. "So, tell me what's up," he says as he takes the seat beside me, absently spinning the small stick in his cup.

Taking a deep breath, I spill. "I was offered a job yesterday. A good one."

"That's a good thing, though, right?" he asks, his eyes on me the whole time.

I nod my confirmation. "It is. I'm not sure what to do," I confess, knowing that I'm not just talking about the job offer. "I like my current position. I wasn't looking for something new," I tell him, taking a small sip of my coffee. "I was approached at our reunion by one of my former classmates and he asked for a meeting."

I go on to tell him about what I would be doing, without getting too much into it and revealing information I'm not allowed to. Grandpa listens intently, stirring his coffee between taking sips, and nods on occasion. He never interrupts, just lets me spill everything without reservation.

"So, you have two choices, Rueben. You stay were you are. You make decent money and have a lot of freedom to work wherever you want. There's a lot of security in staying put. Or you take this job with the government. You're working for a bunch of assholes who get off on hearing themselves speak. Not to mention, we're not the most financially stable country. Last I heard we were how many trillion in debt?"

"Yeah, then there's that," I concede.

Grandpa's silent for a minute, and I'm not really sure what to say. Do I want the job? Yeah, I think I do. But it's scary to step away from your security and stability, to take the chance on the unknown. That step into the dark and trusting the ledge to be where you need it. That the move you're making is a lateral one and not filled with regret.

"It would be a challenge, wouldn't it." It's not a question.

"Definitely."

"And you'd enjoy the hell out of putting those pieces together on that inter-web thingy, right?"

"Yeah."

Grandpa just gazes across the table, giving me a knowing smile. "Follow your heart."

I nod in reply, because I already know which way my heart is leaning. The nerves are undeniable, but it's something I have to do. It's something I *want* to do. A risk I need to take. "Follow my heart," I mimic, returning his grin.

He reaches over and pats my hand. We're both silent as we drink our coffee, glancing up occasionally to see the action on *Walker,*

Texas Ranger on the television. I'm thinking about the offer Dylan's boss made, which is definitely generous, but that's not the reason I'm about to accept it. I want the challenge, the thrill of doing a job that's going to be hard, yet rewarding.

And I can't wait to tell Cricket about my decision.

"So," Grandpa says, pushing his cup to the center of the table and leveling his gaze directly on me. "Tell me about this girl."

Chapter Fifteen

Cricket

"I really liked them," I tell Rueben as we make our way north from Marion to Decatur.

"They really liked you too," he says, glancing over and giving me a quick grin before returning his eyes to the road.

"Your grandma is a hoot."

He snorts.

Glancing out the window, I say, "I lost count of how many times she called you Ruby."

Rueben groans. "Of course you'd pick up on that."

"Kinda hard not to when she said it no less than fifteen times, Ruby," I tease, grinning from ear to ear.

He gasps and glances my way quickly before looking back at the interstate. "You promised!" he bellows in mock outrage.

Leaning closer, I drop my voice and whisper, "I guess you'll just have to punish me later."

I preen a little on the inside as he shifts his gaze to the road, his jaw tight. Rueben adjusts his pants, clearly having a little issue in the crotch area, which only makes me smile that much more.

The closer we get to Decatur, the more nervous I get. I haven't brought a guy home since Danny, and even though I sent my mom a text message to let her know I was bringing a friend, I didn't tell her who it was. Or the fact that my friend is a he. I'm not sure what they're going to say when we arrive.

"You okay?" he asks, following my directions to get to my parents' house.

"Yeah, fine. You?"

"I'm good," he replies, offering me a reassuring grin.

"So, my parents," I start, stammering a little bit on the words. "Erin and Alan, right?"

It makes me happy that he remembered my parents' names. I haven't mentioned it since we made our plan to spend the next several days together, and he hasn't asked. That means he recalls their names from more than a decade ago, and even then, they really only met twice. "Yeah, that's right. Anyway, they're expecting us," I tell him, adjusting myself in my seat to find a more comfortable position, but with the nerves I feel, there really isn't a position to help alleviate that.

"That's good," he says, focusing on the road.

"So... I may have mentioned I was bringing a friend, but I didn't say who."

He glances my way again. "Who did you tell them was coming?"

"I didn't go into details, which means they may be a little shocked when we arrive. I don't think it'll be a problem, but since I called you my friend, you're probably going to have to stay in my sister's old room."

He's quiet for a few seconds, considering my words. "Okay, that shouldn't be a problem. I'm sure I'll survive sleeping in another room for a night," he says, throwing me that sexy smirk of his as he pushes his glasses up on his nose.

"Right, I just didn't want to get into...*this* with them." Mostly because I don't know what *this* is. I mean, we're friends who are seeing each other for the next five days? That's not exactly a text message type of conversation with Mom, you know?

"I get it. I mean, we just spent time with my grandparents and didn't really define us," he says.

"Right," I confirm before telling him our turn is coming up. "But just so you know, your grandma did...ask me something."

He looks my way. "What did she ask?" his voice a little wary and full of concern.

"Well, she asked if I was playing hide the salami with her grandson," I tell him, somehow keeping a straight face.

He stops at the stop sign and turns to face me. His eyes are wide and his jaw practically unhinges in shock. "She asked that?"

"Well, technically, she asked if I was playing hide the salami with her Ruby, but I'm not supposed to call you that," I reply with a shrug.

"And what did you say?"

"Well, I couldn't lie to her!" I holler. "She could see my blush and told me it was all the confirmation she needed."

"Jesus," he mutters, closing his eyes and resting his head against the headrest.

"She told me she was happy," I tell him, recalling how her approval of us spending time together made me feel. She seemed genuinely happy Rueben was dating someone who made him smile. She said he never took his eyes off me, even in the short amount of time we were all together before he and his grandpa left the apartment.

Rueben's silent for several more seconds before a horn sounds behind us. He quickly pulls into the intersection, heading toward the house where I grew up. When we pull into the driveway and park, he unbuckles his belt and turns my way. "She really said salami?"

I can't help but laugh. "Oh, she definitely did."

"And what did you say?"

I blush again. "Ummm, well, I might have told her your salami was one of my favorite attributes," I say with a shrug.

His mouth falls open again. "Seriously?"

"Well, she caught me off guard, Rueben. What was I supposed to say?"

173

"Maybe you don't talk about my salami with my grandma, Cricket. How about that?"

I can't help but giggle a little at the embarrassment written all over his face and dripping from his words. The dark pink blush is super cute. "If it makes you feel better, she seemed very happy about my comment. She mentioned it runs in the family, and then she winked at me."

Rueben groans and brings his hand to his forehead. "I didn't need to know that. I don't need to know anything about my grandpa's...attributes."

"Well, you asked."

"No, no I did not."

The front door opens and my dad appears. Unclicking my own seat belt, I tap him on the forearm and reach for my door handle. "Time to go, Ruby. That's my dad," I say as I open my door and slip out, not giving Rueben time to respond to my use of his nickname.

"There's my girl," my dad says as he approaches, arms extended for a hug.

"Hi, Dad," I reply, the familiar scent of his aftershave and detergent wrapping around me in a warm hug.

"So glad you're here, even if it's just for one night," he says, kissing me on the forehead. It's then he glances over my shoulder and sees my friend standing there.

"Rueben, right?" Dad asks, looking down at me before returning his eyes behind me.

"Yes, sir. It's nice to see you again," Rueben replies, stepping forward and extending his hand.

"Good to see you too," he says, even though I can see the curiosity written on his face. "Let's get your bags inside, shall we?"

Rueben and my dad carry our two suitcases inside, casually chatting about the warm mid-September weather.

"Is that my Cricket?" my mom asks as she comes around the corner and joins us in the living room.

"Hi, Mom," I reply, my arms wrapping around her slim waist and holding on tight.

"You look amazing," she whispers. I can tell the moment she sees Rueben standing off to the side. "Oh, hello."

"Good afternoon, Mrs. Hill," Rueben says politely.

"Rueben?" Mom asks, glancing my way as she makes her way to Rueben. "When Cricket said she was bringing a friend with her, she didn't mention it was you! It's been so long," she adds, giving him a hug and broad smile.

"It has."

"Rueben and I ran into each other at the alumni reunion. We've been hanging out and catching up," I tell them casually, but I worry they'll be able to see right through my attempt to keep it nonchalant.

"That's nice, sweetie," she says, a knowing smile on her face.

"I'll take the bags upstairs," Dad says, pointing to the stairs.

"I can help, sir," Rueben states, reaching for his bag and following my dad upstairs.

"It's so good to have you home, even if it's just for a night," Mom says, squeezing my hand.

"It's good to be here," I reply, truly meaning it. I didn't realize how much I've missed them and this place until I'm back here after a prolonged absence. I usually come home once a year, around the holidays, but missed the last few years. Mom and Dad decided to take a small vacation for Christmas last year, making a short stop in San Francisco to see me. So, it's really been more than three years since I've been home.

Glancing around, I find the house exactly the same with the exception of updated pictures of my nieces. "These are new," I say, approaching the mantel.

"They are. Your sister had them taken last month at the park," Mom says, smiling fondly at the photos of her two granddaughters.

"Does Ash know what she's having this time?" I ask, referring to my sister's third pregnancy.

"Not yet, though we're all secretly hoping for a boy."

I gaze at my nieces' faces, their grins and their matching dresses. Even though there's a huge age gape between them, they still look adorable in their yellow and blue sundresses. Chloe is twelve and has long brown hair and green eyes like her mom's, while Courtlyn, at four, favors her father's lighter blond hair and freckled features. Truth be told, they don't resemble each other much, but that doesn't matter. They're sisters in every way that counts.

Chloe was the product of a short-lived relationship my sister had in college. She thought they'd get married and live happily ever after, which is partly why she quit school. But the ink had barely dried on the marriage certificate before he decided he wasn't ready for marriage and a kid. He left Ashley mere months after Chloe was born, sending her a check every month to help take care of her.

Ashley met Shawn a few years later at the supermarket. He helped her reach something on the top shelf and ended up chatting with Chloe while waiting in the checkout line. After that, they seemed to run into each other every Sunday morning when getting their groceries, and it wasn't long before Shawn was asking her out. There was only one stipulation, though: she had to bring Chloe with her.

They were married about six years ago when my sister got her dream wedding, and soon after, Shawn adopted Chloe. He makes her happy and doesn't care that Chloe's not his biological daughter, which makes him a winner in my book. Even after they had Courtlyn, he never treated my oldest niece as if she were any different. She is his daughter, and I appreciate him even more than ever.

"She's going to find out next month what she's having," Mom says.

"I can't wait to find out," I tell her, glancing at Dad and Rueben as they return from the upstairs. "I secretly hope it's a boy too." Turning to face the guys, I ask, "Did you get his things put in the guest room?"

I can already tell something's up by the look on Rueben's face. It's part humor, part surprise, which has me returning my gaze to my mom.

"Didn't we tell you?" she asks, an uncomfortable chuckle slipping from her lips.

"Tell me what?"

"We turned the guest room into a playroom for the girls," she says casually.

"Oh, uh, no, you didn't. So, where is Rueben going to sleep?" I ask, thinking about the layout of the house. My room consists of a full-sized bed, and while the thought of snuggling with him on that bed sounds like heaven, I'm not sure I really want to share my bed at my parents' house. Too many questions I'm not ready to answer.

"He'll have to sleep on the bottom bunk," Dad says, taking a drink of his sweet tea sitting beside the recliner.

"Bottom bunk?" I ask, glancing between my parents. When did they get bunk beds?

"Well, I assumed you'd want the top bunk since you're lighter. Not that Rueben won't fit up there, but it might be easier for you to climb up and down than him. The poor man will probably hit his head on the ceiling," Mom says.

"Wait, hold up. Bunk beds?"

Lacey Black

"Well, yeah. The girls wanted them for when they spend the night here, so we sold your old bed and bought them instead," she replies.

"So, Rueben and I have to sleep on twin bunk beds?"

Mom nods. "You might be able to fit on the couch, but Rueben's poor legs will hang over the end. It'll be more comfortable in the bunk, wouldn't it?" she asks Rueben.

"I'll be just fine, Mrs. Hill. Thank you for allowing me to stay with you tonight," he says politely, his brown eyes dancing with humor.

"Wait," I say, holding up my hands. "So my nieces, your granddaughters, decide they want bunk beds, so you just go buy them? Do you not recall me asking for them when we were little and you saying no because I could fall off and break my neck?" I ask, completely flabbergasted that my parents would say yes to the girls when they always said no to me and Ash.

"Well, yes, but they're much safer now," Mom insists.

"Safer how? They still have a ladder and a railing, right?"

"Oh, Cricket, don't be dramatic," Mom says, rolling her eyes. "We're meeting Shawn, Ashley, and the girls for dinner tonight at TGI Friday's in a half hour," Mom adds, essentially ending the bunk bed conversation.

"Fine," I grumble, crossing my arms in a slight pout. "I'm going to run up and change."

"Okay, be ready to leave in twenty," Dad says, following Mom to the kitchen.

When I enter my old bedroom, I find it decked out in pink princess everything. The bedding, the wall décor, and the curtains give the impression the room is fit for royalty, which I guess it is. Standing along one wall is a beautiful set of solid maple bunk beds with white twinkle lights hanging from the wall.

178

"Seriously?" I ask, noting how much time and effort went into changing this room from the tie-dyed mess I used to have to what it is now.

Rueben shuts the door behind him. "I'm actually kinda excited to sleep here," he says, picking up a small pink pillow shaped like a crown on the bottom bunk and tossing it aside.

"Really? Pink your thing?" I tease, stepping into his embrace and inhaling his familiar scent.

"Ehhh, not so much the pink as the roommate. Last time I was in a bunk bed was at horse camp. My parents sent me for one week when I was twelve. The kid I was bunking with had a small problem with wetting the bed. He, of course, was awarded the top bunk, even though I begged to switch."

"So, even you got to experience the awesomeness of bunk beds at one point in your life," I whine.

"Did you catch the part where he pissed the bed?"

I chuckle. "Yeah, I heard that. You don't have to worry about me peeing the bed tonight," I assure him, looking up and meeting his eyes.

"I had hoped. Plus, you're way hotter than Casper Short was," he tells me, his lips lingering just over mine for a few seconds.

"If you play your cards right, I might even forget to wear panties when I climb up that ladder," I tease him, my breath fanning across his lips and making my heart pump in my chest with anticipation.

"Definitely a bonus there. I might actually get to enjoy my hard-on instead of trying to hide it," he says, the softest graze of his lips across mine.

"Mmm, bedwetting and boys named Casper gave you woodies back in the day?"

"Baby, air gave me a woody back in the day. I was twelve. I was a walking hard-on," he tells me, making me smile against his lips.

"Speaking of," I whisper, reaching down and palming his thick erection through his jeans.

"Christ."

"I can definitely help with this guy," I tell him before I press my lips fully to his. He deepens the kiss immediately, sliding his tongue along mine and reaching down and grabbing my ass. He pulls me against him, my hand pinned between his body and mine, his cock pulsing with need.

"Shit," he grumbles, ripping his lips from mine and taking a step back. "We can't do this now. We have to leave in a few minutes, and I'd rather not sport a hard-on when I see your family again for the first time in a decade."

Stepping forward, I press one hand to his chest and the other goes right back to his hard length. "Then, we should take care of this before we go," I whisper just before I drop to my knees.

"Crick," he groans, his voice raw and full of desire. "We don't have time."

Reaching for his button, I flip it open and tug on the zipper. "We most certainly do have time, Rueben. Just watch," I tell him, pulling his pants down and freeing his impressive cock.

I waste no time at getting to work. Licking my lips, I hollow out my cheeks and smoothly take him into my mouth. He makes a choking sound that's a cross between a moan and a gasp, his hands fisting my hair at the nape of my neck. "Jesus, Crick," he whispers, trying to keep his voice down as his hips thrust forward.

"Mmmm," I groan, letting the vibration of my word course through his shaft.

His eyes are wide and dark as he watches me suck him deep into my mouth. I cup his balls, running my nails over the loose skin, and feel the pulse of his dick in my mouth. "Do that again," he groans, his eyes glued to my mouth.

I score my nails over his balls a second time and am rewarded as they draw in tight to his body. I can tell he's close, and knowing we don't have a lot of time to waste, I suck him hard and fast, one hand wrapping around the root of his shaft and twisting my wrist in time to my mouth. I keep the other hand on his balls, alternating between a gentle caress and the rake of my nails over the flesh.

"I'm going to come," he warns me, but it only fuels my own desire to finish him off.

Tightening my fist around his cock, I stroke him hard and fast, sucking him deep in my throat as he lets go, his cock twitching as jets of warm cum slide down my throat. He gasps a raspy breath and sags against the door behind him. I lick the tip of his cock, loving the shutter it evokes, as I let go of his cock and gaze up at him. Rueben reaches down and pulls me up, wrapping his arms around my waist and placing his lips against my swollen ones. "Thank you," he whispers, his lips sliding soft and tender across mine.

"You're welcome."

"We really do have to go," he tells me, not making a move to get ready.

"We do."

"And then I'm going to come back here and fuck you with my mouth until your face is buried beneath a pillow to cover your screams of ecstasy," he says casually and confidently, but it's his words that leave me wet and needy.

"I'm so wet right now," I tell him, kissing his jaw and backing away.

Rueben groans. "Christ, Crick, you're going to make me hard again. How am I supposed to get through dinner knowing you're ready for me?" he says, pulling up his pants and adjusting his already thickening cock.

I give him a sweet, innocent smile. "I'm sure you'll manage just fine. Let's just hope you're not sitting next to my dad during dinner."

His groan of frustration follows me into the bathroom.

Yeah, I know, Rueben. It's going to be a long night.

***

"Oh my god, Cricket! *That's* Rueben Rigsby? He's so…hot now!" Ashley whisper yells as she hugs me tight, her expanding belly pressing into my stomach.

"Shhh!"

"Seriously, sister. Those glasses and those muscles? If I wasn't happily married with a bun in the oven, I'd totally go all Lois Lane on his ass," she says, glancing over my shoulder and watching Rueben as he visits with my dad and Shawn.

"Lois Lane?"

"You know, the Superman thing? He looks one step away from ripping his shirt off and revealing a red and blue superhero costume underneath."

I roll my eyes, yet when I look his way, I can totally see it. He definitely has the whole Clark Kent thing going on with those plastic glasses and button-down shirt. My breath catches in my throat when he looks my way and gives me a wink and a smile before returning his gaze to my dad. "Jesus, I might have just orgasmed."

"What? Ashley!" I gasp and start to giggle.

"Sorry, sorry, but these pregnancy hormones are no joke. I can't stop wanting to bounce on my husband's dick like a pogo stick."

I groan, a disgusted look crossing my face. "Stop. Please," I beg.

"Fine, but you just wait. When you're finally pregnant, you'll understand what I'm talking about. One minute, you want to claw his eyes out with a toothpick because he's chewing too loud, and the next, you need him to bend you over the banister and make you scream. It's a horrible cycle, fueled by hormones and annoyance."

I giggle a little and pull her to our table. Mom is already seated, one granddaughter on each side of her, paying us all no attention. She's engrossed in grandma-time, and I'll be surprised if she even speaks to us the entire meal.

As I take my seat across from Ashley, I ask, "Oh, did you know our parents bought bunk beds?" I see Mom roll her eyes in my peripheral vision.

"Right? How much bullshit is that? How long did we ask to get bunk beds?" she asks, grabbing her menu and staring to look it over.

"Forever," I confirm, squinting at my mom in annoyance.

Rueben comes over and takes a seat beside me. "Hey, sorry, your dad was telling me and Shawn about his mole problem."

"His mole problem?"

He nods. "Apparently, your parents have moles in the backyard making a mess of their garden."

I look over at my dad, who seems to still be discussing his pesky backyard rodent problem with my brother-in-law. "Is this what we have to look forward to when we get older? Spoiling our grandchildren and complaining about animals tearing up the backyard?"

Rueben smirks. "Well, one day, when we have grandkids, I'm sure we'll understand why our parents did the things they did."

"I didn't mean…"

Shit.

"It's okay, Cricket. I have to admit, the thought of spoiling grandkids and bitching about moles doesn't sound so bad when you're in the picture too."

There's that familiar hammering of my heart as I take in his words. He offers me a small smile, full of reassurance and contentment before returning his eyes back to his menu. I, on the other hand, am unable to focus on any of the words in front of me. All I can think about is...grandkids. With Rueben.

That means we'd have to have kids first.

And that prospect actually sounds really, really...thrilling.

Dinner goes well. My family includes Rueben in conversation, asking him about his work and place in Tennessee. When I glance over at Ashley, I can see the questions on her face and written in her green eyes. She's wondering how we're going to make this work when I go to California and he goes back to Tennessee. The truth is, I don't know. I'm scared to ask, mostly because if the answer is nothing, if there's no way to make this work, I don't know what I'll do. I'll be heartbroken. I've come to really care about Rueben in these few short days we've spent together, and the thought of that just...ending, well it makes me terribly sad.

When the empty plates are collected and the check is delivered, the guys all fight for it. Ultimately, it's my mom that ends up with the tab and produces a card to cover the cost. "We can pitch in," I tell her, pulling my own debit card from my wallet.

"You will do no such thing. We rarely have the entire family at one table, and we're not arguing over something as trivial as the check," she says firmly before the server comes to collect the black folder.

"Thank you, Mr. and Mrs. Hill, for dinner," Rueben says as we all start to push back from the table.

"You're most welcome, Rueben. We hope you'll join us again one day soon," Mom says, glancing my way.

I ignore her stare and focus on pushing my chair in. I can feel her eyes on me and can only hope she can't read the war I wage with myself on my face. It's a horrible feeling, like floating between two worlds. The one I want and the one I have.

Rueben places his hand on my lower back and leads me out of the restaurant. When we step outside, my nieces come over and give me hugs, Chloe promising to call me and tell me how her first basketball game goes next week. Courtlyn throws her little arms around my neck and squeezes. I promise to FaceTime her soon so she can show me her newest baby doll. My eyes fill with tears as I give Ashley a hug. A sadness pulls down on me as I think about heading back home to California. I've never felt this homesick before, even after I moved. Sure, I was sad and missed my family, but it's nothing compared to the dread and regret plaguing me right now.

When she pulls back, there are tears in her eyes too. "I love you, little sister," she tells me.

"I love you too," I say, wiping at the wetness on my cheek.

"Mine is hormones. What is your excuse?" she asks with a laugh, dabbing at her own eyes. Eyes that are the spitting image of my own.

"I'll miss you," I tell her, pulling her in for one more hug.

"Come back soon," she whispers, giving me one final squeeze.

"I will. I promise."

Shawn shakes Rueben's hand and gives me a peck on the cheek before taking my sister in his arms and walking her and the kids to their minivan. Ashley gives me a teary wave as they pull out of the lot, a piece of my heart breaking a little more as she drives away.

"You ready?" Rueben asks, his warm hand resting on my back.

Unable to find words, I nod, trying to swallow the emotions I'm drowning in as my sister pulls out of sight. I slide into the back seat of Rueben's rental, Mom on the other side and Dad riding up front. Everyone chats easily as we make our way through the familiar streets of home, but I'm too lost in my own thoughts. I never thought it would be this hard to leave, especially not after I've been doing it for ten years.

But this time is different.

This time it's as if I'll be leaving a piece of myself behind when I go. A piece that I may not get back. Not while I'm in California. The war continues to rage in my mind, a mixture of restlessness and melancholy. A war that just may have started the moment I saw Rueben Rigsby in that airport.

Chapter Sixteen

Rueben

The moment her parents go to bed, there's a shift in the air. It's thick and heady with a buzz of anticipation coursing through it that I feel clear down to my toes. Cricket stares at me from across the table, practically glowing with desire and excitement. Without saying a word, I stand up and extend my hand to her. She slips her soft, delicate fingers between mine and stands, ready to follow me wherever I go.

Funny, I'd do the exact same.

That thought is both startling as it is thrilling.

We head up the stairs, Cricket flipping off the light as we go. When we reach her room, I carefully shut and lock the door, that hum of eagerness palpable in the room. "I'm going to go change into my pajamas," she says, grabbing a small bag and some clothes from her open bag and heading for the Jack and Jill bathroom between her room and her sister's former room.

When I'm alone, I glance around at the room that's the least sexy room I've ever been in. A bubble of guilt sweeps through me as I glance at the bunk beds used by her nieces. Oh, the things I want to do to her in those pink princess beds. Another wave of shame runs through my blood, as the door to the bathroom opens. Cricket is standing there, wearing my tan button-down from the dinner last night.

That shame is quickly replaced with a desire to explore her body and a hard-on that won't stop.

"Interesting choice in pajamas," I tell her, my eyes devouring her from head to toe.

Cricket shrugs. "I didn't bring enough things for a week, so I thought I'd borrow this," she says, her hand running along the seam of buttons to where it hits mid-thigh.

"It's yours," I say, need rushing through my veins and blood swooshing in my ears.

She takes a step toward me, and then another. "That's very generous of you," she whispers, her hands still moving, as if she can't stop touching the soft material of my shirt. She stands in front of me and reaches for the collar, bringing it to her nose. "It smells like you."

I reach for my shirt and give it a tug, her body pressing firmly against mine. My hands are anxious to explore, to feel her soft skin and her wet heat. "I can't wait to smell *you* on that shirt," I say just before my lips descend to hers.

My hands slide down the shirt, bunching it up around her hips and finding her ass bare. I grip that unbelievably perfect ass in my hands, wishing I could feel her body, her warmth against me longer. Longer than a week.

Forever.

I push that thought aside and focus on her pleasure. Helping her lie on the lower twin bed, I take my position between those magical thighs. She's already wet. I can see it, my mouth watering for a taste. Memories of her dropping to her knees before dinner flood my mind, that craving I felt to devour her pussy still very strong and alive.

"You have to be quiet, Crick," I tell her. "If you're loud, I stop."

When our eyes meet, I see her eagerness and willingness to comply. She's more than ready for the release I'm promising. Pushing up the tails of my dress shirt, I slowly lower my mouth to the apex of her legs, my eyes locked on hers the entire way. Her scent wraps around me, strangling my senses, as my tongue slides along her wet clit. I adjust myself on the small bed, ignoring the throbbing of my cock that begs for release too. I focus entirely on Cricket.

Hitching her leg up and over my shoulder, I suck on her sensitive flesh and feel her buck against my mouth. She bites her bottom lip, holding back the moan of pleasure I know is hovering near the surface, begging for release. I lick and suck, sliding my tongue into her pussy and savoring the sweet taste of her.

Placing my hands on her thighs, I spread her wide and devour her pussy. Cricket starts to shake, her thighs quivering under my hands, her inner muscles clenching around my tongue. She's so close, and while I'd love to prolong her release a little longer, the need to experience her orgasm is too great to ignore.

"I want to feel you come on my tongue, Crick. Come for me," I demand just before sliding my tongue back inside her hot, wet pussy, pushing it as far as it'll go and swirling it around.

She detonates like a bomb, biting her lip to keep her release from waking her parents and the neighborhood. I feel her pulse and quake in my hands and around my tongue, the sensations of her release washing over me like spring rain under the desert sun.

I run my lips over her thighs, trailing soft open-mouthed kisses over her tender flesh. Crawling up her body, I meet her lips with my own, relishing the taste of her release on our joined lips. Cricket wraps her legs around my waist, and just like that, I wish my jeans would evaporate into thin air. I sit up and hit my head on the bottom of the top bunk. "Shit," I mumble, trying to keep my voice down.

"You okay?" she asks between giggles, rubbing the spot on my head I just smarted.

"I'll be better when I get these pants off," I tell her, wiggling to get up and out of the bed to remove my jeans. The bed squeaks the entire way, the sound like a foghorn in the dead of night.

"This bed is noisy," she whispers, her grin like a beacon calling me home.

I lose my pants and boxers and grab my wallet for a condom. Thank God we stocked up with a quick stop at a convenience store earlier today. "Come down here," I whisper as I sit on the floor, reaching for her hand. When she stands up, I take a seat and help her straddle my lap.

Cricket reaches between our bodies and grabs my cock, stroking it a few times and making my eyes cross. Then, she lines it up with her pussy and slowly lowers herself onto it. My head falls back as pleasure shots up my spine and zaps through my veins. She's seated completely on my lap, my body begging her to move, yet my desire wanting her to stay just like this. To not move. To savor the feel of our bodies so intimately connected.

She doesn't get the message, though. Cricket rises up on her knees and falls back down, grinding her hips as she takes me all the way to the hilt. "Fuck, Crick," I groan-whisper, letting the sensations of pure indulgence sweep through me.

"Shhh, Rueben. If you're loud, I stop," she says, mimicking my earlier comment.

All I can do is hang on and enjoy the ride. I grip her hips as she controls the tempo, and really, my heart. It pounds in my chest as I watch hers rise and fall from both her breathing and her movements.

My mouth caresses her neck, her ear, her jaw, my hands kneed the globes of her ass. Her movements start to quicken, her body taking me right to the edge of sanity. I pay no attention to our surroundings, only the way our bodies align and our breathing syncs in a steady pant of silent pleas. My fingers dig into her hips as I pump up, racing toward that sweet bliss of release.

Then, I feel her tighten around me, her body gripping mine so hard it makes me almost blackout in pleasure. My spine tingles as I race to join in her in orgasmic paradise. I take her lips with mine, hard and bruising, as I thrust my hips up as she grinds down. I pulse, releasing everything I have into the confines of the condom tucked inside her tight heat.

When our bodies start to slow, I wrap my arms around her waist and pull her tightly against me. Our breathing is labored and mixed until eventually, we both sag against each other, her heart pounding against my chest. My lips find her forehead as I breathe in her scent and the sense of familiarity. She's familiar, even though I've only been with her hours. Days. Yet a lifetime of friendship that serves as our foundation.

As much as I hate to, I need to get rid of the condom and she's fading fast with exhaustion. First I help her stand, and then I help her get into the bottom bunk, pulling the pink comforter up to her chin. I slip into the bathroom and remove the condom, wrapping it in tissues to try to hide the evidence we're leaving behind in the trash can. Using a washcloth, I clean my body, then open my shaving kit and use my toothbrush.

When I'm done, I silently leave the bathroom and join Cricket back in the bedroom. Since I put her in the bottom bunk, I'm fully prepared to either climb that small ladder and maneuver my body into the space between the mattress and the ceiling or to just crash on the floor. That decision is not necessary when she opens up the comforter and slides over in invitation.

No other place I'd rather be.

I snuggle in behind her, our bodies pressed together in the small twin-sized bed, and just breathe her in. She's still wearing my shirt, and now there's a mix of her sweet scent tagging along with mine. It's the reason there's a smile on my lips as I close my eyes and hold her close, slowly drifting off to sleep.

***

"I want to see the Bean," she says as we walk down Michigan Avenue on Monday evening.

We left her parents' house in Decatur after lunch and drove north to the city. Cricket booked us a hotel downtown for two nights, just a stone's throw away from major Chicago attractions. I was able to extend my rental reservation, as well as switch up my flight home to Wednesday morning out of O'Hare. Now, after having pizza at Giordano's, we're slowly making our way, hand-in-hand, to Millennium Park.

"You got it," I tell her, slowly weeding through the crowd of people all making their way to and from one of Chicago's great landmarks.

"So, what's it like in Tennessee?" she asks as we carefully make our way around a mother and small child.

"Well, Pittman Center is a really small town. Like five hundred people, or so. I live on the mountain, which is pretty awesome. It's just slow enough and small enough for my liking, but is super close to all the touristy shit in Gatlinburg and surrounding areas."

"That sounds perfect," she says, a touch of longing laced in her voice. "I've never lived anywhere but in a city. I couldn't imagine being on a mountain, surrounded by trees."

"And a view. Don't forget about that, because the view is what sold me on my place. It's small," I tell her with a shrug, "but it suits me just fine."

She squeezes my hand. "I can't wait to see it," she says, a small smile on those kissable lips.

"What's San Francisco like?" I ask as we cross the street and into Millennium Park. There's a large crowd hanging out at the big stainless steel landmark taking selfies and group photos.

Cricket sighs. "It expensive," she says with a chuckle. "And believe it or not, it's actually small for a city. Everything is so close together. Did I tell you I sold my car after a few months?"

I glance down and shake my head.

"It was so expensive to pay for parking, and traffic is a nightmare. I could walk almost anywhere I needed. Plus, they have a lot of public transportation that made it easy to get anywhere I needed to go. It's super foggy a lot, especially during the summer. It's not hot and humid like I was used to in Illinois, and I remember my first summer there, I actually thought I'd missed that entire season. It was nothing like home.

"Real estate is crazy-expensive. It's like there's too many people and not enough places to put them. Rent keeps going up and up every year, which is really why I haven't moved. My place is rent-controlled, and every place I've looked at that might give me more space is three to four times higher a month."

"Sounds...interesting." Interesting? Not really, but it's her home, so what do you say? I think being on top of your neighbors sounds like a nightmare, personally, but I'm not about to tell her that.

She chuckles again, but it lacks humor. It sounds almost...sad. "Yeah." Then her eyes light up and she reaches for her phone. "Come on, let's go take a selfie!"

Cricket tugs on my hand and maneuvers us to an open spot in front of the Bean. She turns her camera to take the picture and stands in front of me. I wrap my arms around her shoulders and pull her into my chest, my chin hitting just above her ear. We both smile at the camera as she takes a few photos. I move, angling my head down and placing my lips just above her right eye. I close my eyes, savoring the feel of her body against mine, the way it seems to have been made just for me, and the taste of her soft skin.

I'm going to miss this when she's gone.

She slides her phone back in her bag and turns in my arms so she's facing me. There's so much I want to say. I want to tell her that these last few days have been the best of my life. That her throwing herself at me as my pretend girlfriend is something I'll never forget. That the thought of her getting on a plane Friday and flying away makes me want to throw up.

But I don't say any of those things.

Instead, I just hold her against my chest and let my mind venture into "what if." What if she stayed? What if I went to San Francisco? What if we really gave this whole relationship thing a shot? I want more than just a week, more than just phone calls and text messages.

I want her in my life.

And not as my friend.

When I glance down, I almost confess everything. I almost tell her she's quickly becoming my whole word, that she's everything I didn't even know I wanted.

But I don't say it.

I can't.

There's no way to make this work when we're so far apart. Our lives are leading us in two different directions, and that realization is startlingly sad.

So, instead of asking her to give us a real shot, I ask, "What do you want to see now?"

Her eyes flash a sorrow that I almost miss, but it was there. It's quickly replaced with something lighter and happier, a grin that makes my cock spring to life. "How about the inside of our hotel room?"

Chapter Seventeen

Cricket

"This is where you live?" I whisper, taking in the cabin nestled in the hills of the Smoky Mountains.

"This is home," he says, getting out of the passenger seat and back at where I stand.

When we landed at the airport, Rueben's brother, Royce, was there to pick us up. I had never met his older brother, since he was already in the military when we graduated college, but I had heard enough stories about him it felt natural and comfortable to be in his company. The brothers teased each other mercilessly, and I didn't miss the way Royce looked at his brother, the question and shock in his handsome face, as we stepped off the plane together.

"It's gorgeous," I say, in awe over the view.

"Wait until you see the deck," Royce says, collecting our bags from the back of his four-wheel drive SUV.

Rueben grabs my suitcase and wheels it toward the front door. I join him, taking in everything around me, from the pair of white wooden rocking chairs on the porch to the flower boxes hanging from the railing, as he unlocks the door and pushes it open for me to enter first.

When I step inside, air catches in my throat. It's...beautiful. And not in a feminine, pretty way, but in a rustic, gorgeous way. The living room is straight ahead with a comfortable brown couch and recliner. There's a fireplace with stunning stonework around it adorning one wall, and a sliding glass door off to the side.

"Come on, I'll give you a tour," he says, dropping the bags at the front door.

"I'm going to head out. I'll text ya later," Royce says, clearly trying to give us privacy, yet wanting his brother to know there will be a conversation about my presence here.

"It was nice to meet you, Royce," I holler over my shoulder, my eyes sweeping from floor to ceiling.

"Nice to meet you too, Cricket." And then he's gone.

"Rueben," I whisper, taking in the spiral staircase that leads upstairs.

I can hear the smile in his voice as he says, "Come on, Crick. Let's start up here."

Taking my hand in his, he leads me to the staircase. "I bet this made moving in a little complicated," I say, my hand running along the smooth wooden handrailing.

"There's actually another set of stairs in the back of the house that doesn't spiral. We used those to move me in," he says.

When we reach the landing, there's a huge floor-to-ceiling window directly in front of us that looks out over the mountains. This view is breathtaking. I could see myself waking up every morning and standing right here in this very spot, enjoying the spectacular display of nature while enjoying a cup of coffee.

Rueben opens the first door on the left to reveal his office. It's a good-sized room, running the entire width of the house. The ceiling is sloped toward the center of the house, but it doesn't feel small or cramped. There is great lighting from two skylights and a large window overlooking the spectacular view.

The second door on the left side of the hallway is a small laundry room, which is clean and organized. He leads me to the only door on the right side, and I already have an idea of what's beyond that doorway. Rueben pushes open the door, revealing his bedroom. The bed is a king-sized bed with dark headboard and footboard and hues of blue bedding. There's a five-drawer dresser along one wall and a comfortable chair and table in front of the window.

"I like to watch the sunrise and drink coffee there," he tells me, nodding to the tan chair.

"I bet," I reply, loving the open, airiness of the room. Of course, the skylights and floor-to-ceiling window only enhance the view, giving it a feel that you're floating amongst the clouds.

"There's a bathroom through there," he says, pointing to one of two doorways. "The other is a closet."

After glancing in and taking in the complete room one last time, my eyes finally return to his. Even though I'm a little worn down from so much travel, there's a buzz of anticipation, of exhilaration in the room. It's thick and heavy, weighing on my chest and my heart. My legs start moving before I even process it, his arms wrapping around my shoulders and pulling me against his chest when I approach.

We stand there for a few minutes, just drinking each other in, as if us standing there together is the most normal and natural thing ever. It sure feels like it is. I hear Rueben exhale, his warm breath blowing my hair. "Want to see the rest of the house?" he asks without making a movement.

"Yeah," I reply, sighing against his chest. "Show me this magical deck."

"My pleasure."

***

"How's your barbecue?" Rueben asks from across the table.

"Orgasmic," I tell him, shoveling the last few bites of my mac and cheese into my mouth. I have no clue where I'm putting it. I was full five minutes ago, yet here I am, stuffing even more food into my face. I'm going to have to spend a lot of time on a treadmill when I get home.

Another wave of misery sweeps through my blood as the hours slowly tick by, the minutes steadily press on without so much as a care. Every time I look at a clock, I get more and more depressed with each passing second.

Last night, he took me out to eat at Blake Shelton's restaurant in downtown Gatlinburg, and then we took an aerial tram up the mountain. The views were breathtaking; almost as gorgeous as the ones Rueben has from his back deck. Afterward, we came back to his place and took advantage of the hot tub until we were both relaxed, tired, and ready for bed.

But we didn't sleep.

Not at first. We had our fill of each other, first with me pressed against his bedroom wall and a second time bent over the bed. Then, and only then, did we finally pass out from exhaustion, our own bodies to the point of collapsing, despite the desire we may have felt swirling around for each other.

Today, he took me on a tour of the town. We did a few touristy things, including buying matching T-shirts and coffee mugs. We visited the Titanic Museum and rode go-karts at an outdoor racetrack. We ate taffy and pretzels with cheese as we walked amongst the people, our hands linked whenever we could.

Now, we're at this hole in the wall barbecue joint with the best BBQ brisket sandwich I've ever had and trying to ignore the fact tonight is our final night together. "I come here a lot," he confesses, wiping his hands on his napkin. "I've never had bad food."

"I can see why. If I lived here, I wouldn't cook at all. The food is to die for," I confess, patting my belly with one hand and shoving my cardboard tray away with the other. "So full."

Rueben chuckles and reaches for my hand. He's been doing that all day, as if he can't stop touching me. "Ready to head back?" he asks, tossing a few bills on the table for the tip.

"You may have to roll me up the mountain," I groan.

He throws me a smirk and a wink. "You still look pretty fucking fantastic from here." To prove his point, he takes a slow perusal, his eyes scanning me from head to toe, each second feeling like a caress.

We head out together, and when we reach Rueben's vehicle, he asks, "So what do you want to do tonight? More sightseeing? Maybe head to Dollywood for some rides?"

I stop at the passenger door and turn to face him. Shaking my head, I wrap my arms around his shoulders and slide my hands along his neck. My heart hammers in my chest and emotion clogs my throat at the words he hasn't said. What do I want to do...*on my last night here.*

"I don't want to do any of those things," I whisper, sliding my hand up into his hair.

Rueben pulls me flush against his body, his hard erection pressed between us. "What do you want to do?"

"Be alone. With you," I confess, stepping up on my tiptoes and grazing my lips along his.

I can feel his smile. "I was hoping you'd say that. Come on."

Rueben lets go before the kiss can turn into something indecent and opens the passenger door. He drives quickly along the now-familiar streets, heading to his home in the mountains, my hand still in his on the console. Everything about this trip has been so unexpected. From running into him at the airport to sharing a living space for the past week. My eyes burn with unshed tears at the prospect of this all being gone tomorrow.

When we pull into his driveway, Rueben hops out and comes around to my door. I'm getting used to this little touch of chivalry, something I wasn't accustomed to in past relationships. He leads me into the house, stops and locks the door. He turns and frames my face with his big hands, the softest of touches that make my body ignite.

"Go put on your swimsuit," he tells me.

"Umm, I don't have a swimsuit, Ruby," I tease him. He already knows full-well that I wore only a T-shirt last night in the hot tub.

"Oh, that's right. That's okay. You look better in my T-shirt anyway," he tells me, running his finger along my bottom lip. "Go get ready and I'll turn on the jets."

Upstairs, I find another one of his shirts in his dresser. Bringing the material up to my nose, I inhale the scent of laundry detergent and Rueben's unique smell. It's like the scent of his skin carrying the shirts to the dresser absorbed into the material. It smells amazing, just like him.

Just one more thing I'm going to miss come tomorrow.

I slip into the bathroom, pull my hair up high on my head, and freshen up my lady bits, donning only Rueben's blue tee when I return downstairs. Outside, the air holds the slightest chill as the sun drops behind the trees and darkness starts to fall. Rueben is there, wearing only his boxers and holding two glasses of wine. I take the offered drink and bring the glass to my lips. The liquid is cold and sweet, a favorite amongst white wines. I glance down, his erection very much present as he looks at me over his own glass, taking in his large shirt hanging on my smaller frame.

"Interesting swim trunks," I comment, sipping my drink.

"I figured since you were going all casual, I'd do the same," he says. Last night he threw on his trunks before hopping in the hot tub. I have to admit, I like this view much better.

He takes my hand and helps me slide into the heated, jetted water. A moan of pure pleasure rumbles from my throat as I lean back in the seat, my body instantly relaxing in bliss. I take another sip of my wine to help cool my throat, but the moment I see Rueben take off his glasses and get in the tub, all thoughts of keeping myself cool fly right out the window.

His hand wraps around my ankle as he gently pulls me in his direction. He takes my glass and sets it on the table beside his as I straddle his waist, my arms wrapping around his neck. The shirt I'm wearing is floating on the water, and frankly, getting in the way. So, I reach my arms up in invitation, one that Rueben quickly jumps at.

It's difficult to take off a soaking wet shirt, but we manage, drenching my hair and face in the process. It doesn't matter, though. Nothing matters. Only him. Us. My lips are eager as I start the kiss, my naked body wrapped around his like a spider monkey. I grind against his hard cock, wishing he hadn't worn those boxers into the tub.

His hands are everywhere. My neck, my back, my breasts, and even my throbbing pussy. I'm on sensory overload right now, but I wouldn't change it for anything, because tomorrow, these memories will be all I have left.

"I've never had hot tub sex," I tell him, my hand sliding between our wet bodies and stroking his erection through his boxers.

He makes a choking sound, his head falling back in ecstasy. "Me either," he confesses, lifting his head back up and locking his eyes on mine. There are a million emotions I see, but only one I latch on to: longing.

It's the look I'm going to miss the most.

Our lips meet again, slow and leisurely, as we explore each other's mouths, tasting and savoring this one perfect kiss. The tighter I hold his cock, the more urgent his lips become. He takes what he wants, devouring and controlling me with the simplest of actions. I'm not sure how long we sit there, my body wrapped around his, as we kiss. It feels like a lifetime, yet not long enough all the same.

Gasping for sweet oxygen, my eyes are glued to his as I slowly stroke his cock from root to tip, memorizing the way his jaw tightens and his gaze burns hot like lava. He pulls me against his chest and stands up, taking a seat on the edge of the hot tub. I start to tug at his wet boxers, sliding them down to his ass and freeing his cock.

Rueben reaches to the chair beside the hot tub and grabs his pants. While he fishes out a condom, I take a few moments to trail kisses down his neck, tasting the spiciness of his cologne and reveling in the burn of his stubble against my lips. When he sits back up, he rocks back on his ass and tugs his boxers down his legs. I take the opportunity to get the condom and rip it open.

Slowly, I caress the soft, velvety skin over his rock-hard shaft. A throaty moan rips from his mouth as I position the protection over the head and gently slide it down, taking my time and enjoying the feel. When I reach the root and glance up, I find his eyes on me, as if he's doing the same thing I am.

Remembering every moment.

Rueben holds me by my hips as I guide myself to his cock and lower myself down. There's the familiar stretch as I accommodate his size, my body tingling in all the right places, my blood rushing through my veins. With one hand, he cradles the back of my neck almost protectively, his thumb gently stroking circles on the nape of my neck. Every hair on my body stands on end, a sizzle of desire zaps me. My body has never felt so alive.

Our eyes meet once more as I lift my hips and slide back down, swirling my hips and grinding against his pelvis. My hands grip his shoulders, but the need to touch him everywhere is too great. I caress his arms, chest, back, and neck. I memorize his face with my fingers, outlining every line, every dimple, every blemish.

My nipples scrape against his chest, sending shockwaves of lust through my extremities. I start to feel that familiar tightening deep inside me, but I fight it off. I don't want this to end. I want to stay right here, in this moment, for as long as possible. Unfortunately, with each thrust of his hips upward, the end draws near. My body craves release. The one Rueben is promising.

When I gaze into his eyes, he starts to blur. Words rush from my brain to my tongue but refuse to come out. Words like forever and home. Words that can bring the ultimate peace or rip me in two. I don't even realize the first tear falls until I feel his thumb catch it on my cheek. He strokes so lightly, so gently that it makes my heart ache. He continues to caress my cheek, catching every tear and wiping them away.

The end draws near, my release racing for the surface and ready to break free. I cling to his shoulders and hold on tightly as I explode, crying out into the dark of night. Rueben takes my lips with his, breathing new life into me as he finds his own release. My world starts to fade, but he refuses to let go. He holds on tight, swiping his lips across mine and whispering, "My Cricket."

This time, he's unable to catch the tears before they fall. They come too quickly. Wrapping my arms around his neck, I draw him into me and breathe him in. I don't ever want to forget this moment. The way the moon hangs high in the night sky. The coolness of the air as it kisses our overheated bodies. The scent of sex mixed with woodsy soap and fresh cotton fabric softener. The way we fit so perfectly together, it's as if he were made just for me.

The way my heart cries out to stay right here.

With my head on his shoulder, he lifts me up and adjusts me in his arms. I could walk—and probably should walk—but it feels too right.

Rueben turns off the jets and grabs his wallet and glasses before heading back into the house. I hear him engage the lock and turn off the light. He ascends the stairs and heads up to his room, holding me tightly against him as he goes. We make a quick pitstop to the bathroom and grab a fresh towel, drying our bodies as best we can, considering he's still holding me.

When we reach his bed, he tugs on the comforter before setting me down. "Be right back," he whispers, running a hand over my wet hair and kissing my forehead.

I hear the water turn on the bathroom, and while I know I should get up and get ready for bed, I just can't find the energy. So, I lie still, the moonlight filtering through the windows and listen to the now familiar sound of Rueben getting ready for bed.

Tomorrow night, there will be nothing but silence.

When he returns, he doesn't set his alarm. He crawls into bed, his arms reaching for me and pulling me close. It's warm nestled in his arms and pressed against his chest, but that's okay. There's nowhere else I'd rather be. Even as my skin starts to boil, I just lie there and feel.

I start to wonder if he's fallen sleep. His breathing seems to even out, his warm breath fanning across my forehead. When I make the slightest movement to adjust my arm, he tightens and reaches for me, as if he's afraid I'm going to disappear.

The night wears on, but neither of us sleep. We don't speak either, we just hold each other tight and try not to let ourselves think about tomorrow. At least, that's what I'm doing. I'm trying not to freak out by being overly emotional or too blasé. It's a fine line between being too eager to stay and too eager to go. I hate it, actually. Life shouldn't be this complicated.

Sometime in the night, my eyes finally draw closed. As much as I'd like to stay awake, my body is physically and emotionally too exhausted to comply. At least I have Rueben. His arms around me and his steady heartbeat against my cheek.

"I'm falling for you." It's those whispered words I hear as I drift off to sleep.

Chapter Eighteen

Rueben

I slept like absolute shit.

The only thing that made it better was having Cricket in my arms. Everything—the ticking clock and the looming finish to our week together—hung like an anvil, heavy and despondent, but being with her, having her naked skin pressed against me, seemed to make it all a little more bearable.

When the sun starts to peek over the horizon, I exhale slowly. The last thing I want is to get up and moving, but that's just what I need to do. Not to rush what little time I have left with her, but because I need to start pulling away before it's too late. Before I say or do something I shouldn't do—like ask her to stay. Her life is in California, and mine is here.

Gingerly, I roll out of bed, careful not to wake her. Sunlight reflects off her long, brown hair, and something tells me I'm never going to look at morning light the same way. I open my dresser and find a pair of lounge pants. After slipping them on, I slide my glasses onto my face and really drink my fill of the beauty in my bed. Her hair is splayed against my pillow, her mouth slightly agape in relaxation. The blankets dip low, revealing a nice view of cleavage. She's like a wet dream come to life.

Instead of doing what I'd rather do—which is crawl back into bed with Cricket—I slip out of the bedroom and head downstairs. The sun has risen and the birds are chirping. Opening up the deck door and front window, I let the warm breeze blow through the house and get to work in the kitchen, flipping on the coffee pot. I'm not a huge cook, but I manage. I chop up some mushrooms and peppers and throw them in a small pan. Next, I dice some sliced ham and cheese and add them to the mix, finally adding half dozen eggs to the concoction.

I flip the omelet over and plop four slices of toast in the toaster. The minute they start to pop up, I slather them in butter and toss them on a plate. I remove the omelet from the pan and cut it in half, placing a half on each plate. Adding the buttered toast and two cups of coffee, I take my tray (cookie sheet) up the stairs and to my room.

When I enter, I'm surrounded by her scent. Cricket is a goddess, all wrapped up in my blankets, and like the goddess she is, draws me to her. Carefully, I set the tray on the nightstand and crawl onto the bed. She stirs as I reach my hand over and swipe the thick strand of brown hair off her cheek. Then, I follow the trail of my fingers with my lips. "Good morning, sunshine," I whisper.

Those emerald eyes slowly open and a small smile spreads across her lips. "Morning," she says as she stretches beneath the blankets, the material falling below her breasts as she moves her arms over her head.

I ignore the desire swirling through my body and thickening in my pants. Now isn't the time to have Cricket. We're down to mere hours left together, and the last thing I want is for her to think I'm only after sex. What I want from her is so much more than a physical release. I just have to figure out a way to tell her.

"That smells delicious," she mumbles, sitting up and grabbing for the sheet to keep her covered.

"Well, I'm hoping it tastes as good as it smells," I confess, grabbing the tray and setting it on the bed between us.

Sheet forgotten, she reaches for the coffee and takes a sip. I hand her a fork and watch as she dives into the omelet, devouring half of it in no time, as if she hasn't eaten in days. "Oh my God, this is so good," she says, her mouth full of food. Smiling, I grab my own fork and take a hearty bite of eggs.

"I accepted the job," I tell her between bites.

Her entire face lights up with excitement. "You did? That's so wonderful."

Shrugging, I reply, "Well, the money's hard to pass up, but I get to work from home too. I'm not sure about working for the government, but if it doesn't work out, it shouldn't be too hard to find something in my field again."

Cricket smiles, her damn face lighting up and making my heart trip over itself in my chest. "I'm proud of you."

We chat through breakfast, but we stay away from anything heavy. Mostly the warm weather, the amount of time it took me to update and renovate this aging cabin, and how many times I've seen bears. We avoid all of the things that really matter, like how would we make this work long distance and what if we can't find time to schedule another visit. Those are the things I don't have answers for. Not yet. So I keep them to myself.

After breakfast, we snuggle in bed, watching the clouds roll in and the sky turn a darker shade of gray. Just like my mood, I can feel the storm looming in the near future, and also like my mood, I can't do a damn thing to stop it.

My eyes keep watching the clock, and the closer it gets to the witching hour, the more tense we both get. When I know it's time to start moving or risk her missing her flight—which wouldn't be that bad—I take her by the hand and lead her to the bathroom. I crank up the water, getting it as hot as I can without burning our skin, and help her inside.

This shower is like nothing I've ever experienced before. There are no words and even no sex. We spend thirty minutes touching each other, as if it could be the last time. I memorize every curve of her body, caressing every square inch. I pretend not to notice the extra wetness on her face, allowing the shower water to wash away those tears. But I know they're there. I'll remember them for the rest of my life.

After our shower, I wrap us both in a thick towel, and we start the painful process of getting ready for the day. The atmosphere is somber, the air thick with pain and regret. Not regret of what has happened, but regret that our lives are in two different places. Sure, easy fix, you'd say, but there's so much more to it. My new job. Her job. Mortgage and rent payments. Plus, there's the fact that this relationship is so new, we haven't even really had a proper "dating" period. We skipped right over it and jumped headfirst into practically living together and meeting each other's families.

Not to mention that it all started with a lie.

A tiny little fib.

I know we've done this all backwards, and it's going to take time to straighten out. The problem is we just don't have any time left.

As we head to the airport, our fingers entwined, I just don't know what to do or say. The one thing I know as certain as my name is: I don't want her to go.

Chapter Nineteen

Cricket

As far as days go, this one's pretty fucking shitty.

It's not the company, not in the least. It's not the gloomy, rainy sky that really just seems par for the course. It's not even the fact that I'm heading home with more questions than answers. It's the fact I'm leaving Rueben behind. My friend. My lover. The one I've grown so incredibly close to in the last week that the prospect of not waking up beside him tomorrow weighs heavily on my heart. The one who makes me smile and be a better me.

The one I'm falling in love with.

I tell myself a thousand times over I won't cry as we approach the McGhee Tyson Airport. I won't let myself get lost in the sadness of the moment, but will rejoice in our time spent together. It's better to have loved and lost than to never have loved at all, right? Bullshit. This sucks.

He doesn't pull up to departures, which I'm grateful for. Instead, he heads for the parking garage and finds a spot near the entrance. With heavy legs, I start to exit the SUV, only to find Rueben there, offering me a hand. When I take it, I ignore the tremble in my fingers. If Rueben sees it, he doesn't say.

At the back of the vehicle, he pulls my big suitcase out, locks the doors, and pulls it toward the entrance. He wraps his arms around my shoulders and pulls me close as we walk side-by-side through the dark, wet parking garage and into the bright yellow airport lights.

He hovers at my side as I check in, taking my bag over to the counter to help me check my bag. I have my carry-on and purse with me, and the moment his hands are free of my big bag, he takes my smaller one and throws it over his shoulder.

Then, we head to security.

My throat is so tight, I'm not even sure how I'm breathing. Emotions clog my airway and those pesky tears cloud my eyes once more. When we reach the point of no return, I turn in his arm, his body wrapping around me in comfort. My body shakes as the tears come hard and fast. He doesn't care though, just lets me cry into his T-shirt and rubs soothing circles on my back.

"This week was the best I've ever had," he whispers, his own voice thick and raspy.

"Me too," I tell him, pulling back just enough to glance up. His eyes are shiny, and he doesn't seem the least bothered by it. His tears don't fall like mine, though.

"I…" he starts, clearing his throat. "Cricket, I… I don't want this to end."

My heart starts to beat a little harder than before, which considering it was pounding so loud I swear everyone in the airport could hear is really saying something. "I don't want it to end either."

He gives me a smile of relief. "Okay. So, we have a lot to think about, right? I mean, the logistics of this aren't going to be easy."

No, it's going to be downright hard.

"With me starting my new job, I just don't know when I can get away for a visit yet. And you, I know it's not easy for you to get time off."

Realization weighs heavily on my chest. He's right. There are so many things working against us in this moment I'm not sure if we can actually make a long-distance relationship work.

I nod.

"I'll call you or text every chance I get, okay?"

211

Again, I nod my head, unable to find the words to ease the discomfort settling into my chest.

Rueben pulls me back against his chest and squeezes tight. "I promise we'll figure this out, Crick."

"We will," I find myself saying, though in my head, I just don't see it happening.

Before I pull back, I inhale against his shirt one last time. I want to remember the exact way he smelled as I'm traveling to the other side of the country, away from the man I'm falling in love with.

When I pull back, he swipes at my tears, his eyes so full of longing and regret. "I'm going to miss you," he says, giving me a small smile.

"I'll miss you too."

He places his lips on mine and just holds them there, savoring the last and drawing out our connection just a little longer. When he finally pulls back, it feels like my heart is being ripped from my body. Rueben lets go of me and takes a step back, removing my small bag and handing it to me. Our fingers touch as I take the bag, that familiar sizzle of electricity still ever present.

"Bye, Ruby," I tell him, trying with everything I have to put on a brave face and give him a grin.

"I'll make you pay for that," he says, but the words hold no bite. Instead, they hold regret. Probably because we both know it may be a long time before he can make good on his idle threat.

If ever.

"I'll hold you to it," I still reply, goodheartedly, even though it feels anything but good.

My heart feels bad.

Horrible.

I give him a little wave, paste on my best "I got this" smile, and turn toward the security gate.

"Hey, Crick?" he says, making me stop and turn back around. "I'll see ya soon."

The flood of tears rushes my eyes, but I refuse to let them fall. Not yet. When I fall apart—and heaven knows it's coming—it's not going to happen at the airport. Not with Rueben standing right in front of me in sexy worn jeans and a tight T-shirt. Not with those intoxicating chocolate eyes staring at me, witnessing my breakdown.

So that's why I lie.

That's why I say, "See you soon."

Even though I know I won't.

With a quick wave, I turn back to security and get in line. I don't glance behind me again. Not because I don't want to see him standing there, watching me go, but because I don't want to risk him *not* being there anymore.

I keep my eyes forward.

On heading home.

Even though my heart will be left behind in Tennessee.

***

Saturday morning is rainy and shitty. Shitty and horrible and...yeah.

Shitty shitty shitty.

Worse? My texts from Rueben last night were... different. Cordial, yes, but there was an underlying sadness in our normal pleasant conversations. I was exhausted by the time I reached home, after four hours of flying and then public transportation to get me back to my San Francisco neighborhood.

Even worse yet? My cell phone is ringing for a second time this morning with a number I had hoped I'd never see again.

Danny.

I'm about to let this one go to voice mail, but realization hits me. He won't let this go. He'll keep calling and calling until I either change my number or answer the phone. So, I do the one thing I don't want to do yet need to do to move on.

"Hello?"

"Hey, Cricket, it's Danny."

"Yeah, I know."

There's silence for a second before he replies, "So, you still have my number programmed into your phone?"

I exhale. "Yes, I left it in my phone, but changed your name to Asshole. I wanted to make sure I always knew if you were calling."

He chuckles. "Ouch, Crick."

The way he says my name causes pain to shoot through my chest. Danny has never called me Crick. It was always Rueben's nickname for me.

"What do you want, Danny?" I ask, annoyed that he's ruining my Saturday of sulking and whining.

"I take it you haven't checked your email?" he asks.

"No."

"Well, after we talked at the brunch, I got the vibe that you weren't interested in the co-host position in LA. So, I came back and talked to my producers. They've gone to the bosses, who have made you a new offer."

"A new offer?" I ask, trying to keep up, but I wasn't exactly paying attention to him in the beginning, so now I'm left trying to figure out what he's talking about.

"A beautiful offer, Cricket. One that gets you to LA and on my television set by Monday morning."

"What?" I gasp. *Is he high?*

"True story, love. They're prepared to buy you out of your rental contract and put you up in one of our station-owned condos temporarily. They'll pay for your entire moving costs, as well as offer a sign-on bonus to be here Monday morning."

"Hold on," I tell him as I grab my laptop. I boot it up and retrieve my email. There's one from Thursday, addressed to me from the man who offered me the job weeks ago. I pull it up and start to read.

Wow.

That's their offer?

No wonder everyone jumps ship from our small station to climb the ladder at the larger stations. Not only is the salary about seventy-percent greater than the one I have now—and I've always thought it to be a great wage—the bonus is enough to get me out of the shoebox I'm living in and into a decent-sized apartment with neighbors who don't sell questionable products out their back door.

"Are you there?"

"Yeah," I whisper, scanning the email once more.

"So, as you can see, it's a logical move up for you, Cricket. You can drive here today, get settled in your new place, and be ready to start Monday morning," he says, as if it were the most reasonable explanation ever.

My heart starts to gallop and I'm having a hard time thinking, let alone sucking sweet oxygen into my lungs. I get up and start to pace, taking my small bag from the counter and emptying the contents. Danny continues to talk about the station, as well as how successful he is, but my mind is reeling.

I glance down and look at the object in my hand. It's the coffee mug I bought at that little souvenir stand in Gatlinburg. The match to the one Rueben has. Tears well in my eyes for like the four thousandth time since I've returned to California. The familiar ache is there, front and center, and holding the mug in my hand is just another reminder of what's back in Gatlinburg.

I catch pieces of his pitch, and he doesn't seem to realize the conversation is completely one-sided. He wants me to move to Los Angeles and work with him.

"No," I interrupt, with a little too much force.

"No?" he sputters

"You heard me, Danny. No. I don't want to move to LA. I don't want to be your co-host. I don't want to switch jobs. I don't even know if I want *my* job."

He's quiet for a few seconds before he asks the burning question, "What is it you want, Cricket?"

Funny he should ask that, because it's the one answer I can give easily. The one thing I know as certain as my own name. "Rueben."

Danny sighs, and at first, doesn't say anything. "Talk to me, Cricket," he finally whispers as another wave of warm tears fall from my eyes.

"I think I love him."

Danny chuckles. "You *think* you love him?" I don't reply. "Listen, Cricket, things that happened back then, I know I messed them up. I was just…young and stupid. I knew we weren't going to last long term, and I was too chickenshit to just say it. Instead, I led you on and mapped out the move with you. I fucked that all up."

"You got that right," I mumble, snuffling and reaching for a tissue.

"But it's not because I didn't love you. I did. We just wanted different things in life. I think you could see it too," he says.

Sighing, I know he's right. Deep down, I knew Danny wasn't the right one for me, but I was angry at him for blindsiding me with the graduation day breakup. "I think you're right."

"Oh, I know I'm right. I'm always right, baby. I'm Danny Ohara," he replies, and I swear I hear him pound his chest through the phone line.

I snort. "Please. I couldn't give two shits about Danny Ohara."

"Maybe that's true, and I'd totally deserve it. But do you know what, Cricket Hill? I still give two shits about you. That's why I'm going to ask you this: Why are you in California?"

"What?" I ask, standing up and starting to pace.

"Why are you in California? That wasn't your dream. It was mine, and you know it. I know you got that job at the station, which was right up your alley. I heard you were awesome and promoted up to a production director within a few years. Then what happened?"

"You screwed one of our morning show hosts and she left to join you."

"And then you were put in her place, right?" He doesn't wait for me to reply. "So why did you stay? Why keep doing it if it wasn't what you wanted? Security?"

"Yeah, part of it," I confess. "I do enjoy my job. It just isn't...what I love."

"And what do you love?"

Rueben.

"I don't know," I say instead.

"Let's not do that, Cricket. We're way past lying. Be honest. What do you love?"

I sit back down on the couch and close my eyes. "I love the thrill of taking something raw and making it complete. Of working on a project and putting my own spin on it. I love mountain views and bear warnings. But most of all, I love the way it feels to wake up in his arms and fall asleep against his chest."

I realize I'm crying again, which I hate, because I've never been this big of a cry baby before.

"Then let me ask you this again. Why are you in California? Why are you there when he's in Tennessee?"

Exhaling, the emotion of the past twenty-four—hell, forty-eight—hours starts to weigh me down. "Because I'm stupid."

"Because you're scared. What happened to the girl who called me up, chewed my ass up one side and down the other, and then loaded up a rental and drove to California the next day? Was she scared?"

"She was terrified," I tell him honestly.

"She was brave, even if a little afraid on the inside." Now it's Danny's turn to exhale. "I gotta tell ya, Cricket, when I saw you and Rueben together at Slim's two things crossed my mind. How dare my old friend date my girl," he says, and I'm already opening my mouth to argue. "And," he starts, disrupting my almost-interruption, "do you know what the second thing I thought was?"

"No."

"I thought if anyone was perfect for you, it was Rueben. He's probably the best guy I've ever known, honestly. He was a good friend in school, and that's one thing I've always regretted about leaving. I never really kept in touch with him.

"Cricket, I don't know what's going on with you two, but I do want to tell you this: if Rueben makes you happy, then go for it. Whatever the hang-up is you two have, figure it out. Because I truly believe he's the best guy for the best girl I've ever known."

I close my eyes and absorb his words. They're kind and reassuring, two things I'd never associate with Danny Ohara anymore. But he's shown a little piece of his decency today, and for that, I am grateful.

"Be happy, Cricket. That's all anyone can ask for in this life."

I'm still quiet for a few seconds, recalling those last few minutes with Rueben in the airport. It doesn't seem possible to feel the way I do for him after only a week, but here I am, falling in love with my friend.

"So, what do you say about the offer? You know you can just stay with me if you choose to come to LA, right? My bed is nice and warm, Cricket, and doesn't squeak like the one we had back at Carbondale." I can practically hear him wagging his eyebrows.

I snort, a mix of disgust and laughter. "Gross. Not happening, Daniel."

He laughs in return. "I kinda already figured that, Cricket. I was just kidding. Well, unless you're really interested in another ride."

I laugh hard. "Thanks for the offer, but I think I'll pass."

"Suit yourself. I guess I'll go ahead and tell my boss to keep looking for a new co-host," he says with a smile.

"Yeah, that's probably for the best. You know, if you'd stop sleeping with them, they wouldn't get pissed off when you break it off with them and quit."

"But what fun is that?" he asks, a relaxed and familiar chuckle fills the phone line. "I guess I'll let you go. Oh, and Cricket? If you ever need anything, call, okay?"

"Okay," I reply. Honestly, I don't know if I ever will, but it's nice to know he would be there if I needed him.

"Oh, and tell Rueben I said he's a lucky man." The sincerity is evident in his voice.

"Bye, Danny."

"Bye, Cricket. Take care and be happy."

"You too."

Long after we've hung up, I sit there with my phone in my hand, trying to figure out my next move. I need a plan. I know where I am, and I know where I want to be. I just have to figure out how to get them both, without losing myself or the man I'm falling for.

Shouldn't be too hard, right?

Chapter Twenty

Rueben

One week later

"You okay?" Royce asks between sips from his beer bottle from across the deck.

"I'm fine," I repeat for what feels like the millionth time. Between my mom and brother, and the easy lie I keep telling myself on a regular basis, I've said those exact two words more times than I can count.

"You're not fine. You're a grumpy bastard."

I finish off my third beer of the night and toss the bottle into the recycle bin. "I have a lot on my mind." That's putting it mildly. In the week since Cricket left, I've been a miserable fuck. I know it. Apparently, my brother knows it. That's probably why he refused to listen to my declined invitation for tonight and just showed up with food and beer.

"Would any of it be about a beautiful brunette with pretty green eyes?"

My cheek ticks and my jaw tightens as my brother talks about Cricket. She's been back in California for seven days. Seven days of hell on earth, missing her like crazy and wishing she would have stayed. But I also know it wasn't the right time. She has commitments and obligations back west, which is why I didn't just ask her to drop everything and stay.

Even though I wanted her to.

"Mind your own business," I mumble, grabbing a fourth beer from the cooler.

"Your grumpy mood is my business." He doesn't continue, just looks out over the Smoky Mountains landscape. "Why didn't you ask her to stay?"

I take a long drink of my bottle to give myself time. Time to formulate an answer to the burning question of the week. "It's not the right time. She has a life out there, shit to do. She couldn't just drop everything and stay here with me," I tell him.

"Why the hell not?" he asks, his facial features showing he's genuinely confused.

"Because," I start, frustration sweeping through me like a furnace, hot and fierce. "You just don't understand," I end up saying, even though it's a weak retort at best.

Royce leans forward, resting his elbows on his knees. His eyes lock with mine and I can tell he's not going to let this go. "Explain it to me."

Sighing, I take another drink of my beer and end up setting it aside. "There's all this crap stacked up against us right now. I start a new job in another week, and my free time and leisure travel isn't going to be what it was, at least not for a while. She's a morning show host on television, Royce. She can't just take off whenever she wants to come to Tennessee."

"How do you know? You made it sound like she doesn't even like her job."

And here's where it gets tricky. "She doesn't. Not really. But... I guess I just wanted her to want to make the decision on her own, ya know? I don't want to be a major influence on this life-changing choice, and then she come to regret it down the road." And that right there is the main reason I didn't ask her to stay. I'm terrified she'll hate it here, hate the life she gave up everything for, and regret her decision. Regret me.

"How is she going to make that decision if she doesn't have all the facts? You want her to come here, right? So ask her. Lay your cards out and see where they fall. She's hot, Rueben, but something tells me she's not a mind reader."

I look over at my brother, my heartbeat thumping a heavy melody in my chest. "She is hot," I finally say with a cocky grin.

"Dude, I'm still trying to figure out what she sees in you. I mean, you're not even the hot Rigsby brother," he teases.

I snort my disbelief and shake my head. My smile falls from my face as I get back to more serious matters. "There's so much to decide. Where will she work? Will she want to live with me? If not, where is she going to stay during peak tourist season?" I start firing off, and while I know how I'd answer all of those questions—she'd be with me—I don't know that we're exactly ready for that. That's why I add, "It's been like…a week."

Royce shrugs. "What does a calendar have to do with it? You think just because you were with her a week that it means you can't love her yet?" I feel his eyes burning into me, reading my mind and my soul. "You do love her, right?"

The answer is immediate. "Yes."

He just smiles back across the deck. "Hearts don't lie, little brother."

"That's pretty deep for a man who's never been in love before," I tell him and watch in fascination as something passes through his eyes. Regret, maybe? Longing? Yeah, there's something there, but it's pushed aside quickly and replaced with a grin. "No time for love, little brother."

I just grin at my older brother. "You're going to fall hard."

"Whatever," he mumbles, looking down at his beer. Finally, he sits up straight and gives me a pointed look. "Wanna know what I think you should do?"

"Yeah."

"I think if you love her and want to give it a go, you should tell her. You guys can make it work long distance for a while, until you get to know each other better and maybe figure out where it's going. I think you need to tell her how you feel, even if you're afraid. Who cares that it's only been a week? You're miserable right now, right? So fucking do something about it."

Do something about it.

I let his words soak in. Is a long-distance relationship going to be easy? Fuck no. Anything has to be better than these uncomfortable phone and text conversations we've been having for the last week. Every time we call, there's awkward silence. It's like we both have things to say, but don't want to say them. At least, that's how it is for me. Neither of us wants to discuss the hard stuff, so we stick to the basics. Work, weather, and television.

Fuck that.

It's time to take what I want.

It's time I get Cricket.

Reaching for my phone, I pull up my internet app.

"What are you doing?" Royce asks, resuming his beer drinking.

"Checking on flights to San Francisco," I tell him, clicking on the first available flight that pops up. *Yikes.* Last minute flights aren't cheap.

"Don't go tonight," my brother says, my fingers hovering over the purchase button.

"What?"

He shrugs. "First off, we've been drinking. It's probably not a good idea for me to drive, nor you to travel. Plus, I hate to be the one to say it, but you kinda look like shit. When was the last time you shaved?" His eyes are teasing, but I can tell he means them.

Running a hand over my face, I stop and try to recall when the last time I actually shaved was. When Cricket was here? Even then, it was probably closer to our time at the reunion. "You're probably right," I tell him, hating to say those words to my brother. I know he'll latch on to them and remind me that I said them as often as possible. "I should do this without beer in my system, but I don't know about the shaving part. She seemed to really like my stubble," I retort, wiggling my eyebrows suggestively.

Royce laughs. "TMI, little brother. Find a flight out tomorrow sometime. I'm crashing here tonight, so I can take you whenever you need."

Not the first time he's crashed on my couch after having a few beers on this very deck. "Fine, but it's your turn to make breakfast in the morning," I tell him as I resume my search for a flight to California.

"Deal."

When I find one that doesn't leave too early, I pay for my ticket and set down my phone. A weight has been lifted off my chest as I picture reuniting with Cricket tomorrow afternoon. I'll have to get her exact address, but that shouldn't be too hard with a little computer forensics work. I'm not sure what her reaction is going to be when she opens the door to find me standing there, but my brother's right. I have to tell her how I feel and let her make the next move.

I just pray it's a move in my favor.

Chapter Twenty-One

Cricket

"To Cricket," Penny says, raising her glass high in the air.

"To Cricket," a chorus of well-wishings echoes above the music as we all clink our glasses together.

"I can't believe you quit," my friend Kristie says, taking another sip of her margarita. "I mean, I thought you'd be the Good Morning girl forever."

Me too.

Truth be told, I probably would have stuck it out for a while yet, maybe even until I retired. The problem with that is it wouldn't be me living my best life or truly being happy. Funny, it took me talking to the one man I despise more than anyone to really make me see it, and act.

"I think she's going to do great at her new job," Rachelle adds as she licks the sugar off her own margarita glass.

Diving into the chips and salsa on our table, I say, "I'm really excited. It's something I'd never thought I'd do, but still utilizes my communications degree."

"Plus, all the hot guys you get to work with," Penny adds just before shoveling her own chips and salsa in her mouth.

"Hot guys? Ummm, there's only one guy in the office."

"And he's hot!" she replies, earning double nods from Rachelle and Kristie.

"Whatever," I chuckle, sipping my peach mango margarita.

When our entrees are delivered, I switch from the chips and salsa to my taco salad and listen to the girls talk about their week. Rachelle works at a hotel and always has some juicy gossip to share, while Kristie is a bookkeeper for a law firm. She's pretty straight laced during the week, so when she goes out and cuts loose, it's usually pretty entertaining.

"So? Tell me about the guy," she says between bites of her chicken fajita.

"Who says there's a guy?" I ask, thankful for the low lighting in our favorite Mexican joint so they can't see the blush on my face.

All three of them roll their eyes. "There's always a guy," Rachelle chimes in. "No one just ups and moves halfway across the country for anything but a guy."

"Not true. I moved out to San Francisco without a guy," I argue.

"Semantics. You had a guy until he left without you and broke your heart. You may not have come out here with a guy, but he was definitely the reason you were here."

"Yeah, it was like one final fuck-you to that jerk with an average sized penis," Penny adds.

I snort, because I know they're right. It was my way of saying *screw you, Danny. I could do it on my own without you.* "Fine, you got me there. But that doesn't mean I'm leaving now because of one. I have my new job," I counter.

Kristie gasps. "Watch out, ladies. Her pants are on fire!"

Rolling my eyes, I reply, "Oh, stop, they are not."

"You're a total liar. It's written all over your face." Rachelle leans in and smiles. "What's his name."

Clearing the taco shell from my throat, I take a quick drink of alcohol. They all stare at me eagerly, waiting for me to drop them the smallest of crumbs. "Rueben."

"I knew it!" Kristie bellows.

"Totally called it," Rachelle adds.

"Tell us about him," Penny says.

In unison, they all lean forward, their eyes wide as I tell them all about my reunion and how Rueben and I crossed paths. I leave out the good stuff—you know, glossing over anything that has to do with naked bedroom aerobics—and focus on our short time together. By the time I'm done with my story, they all have those googly heart-shaped eyes and are practically picking out bridesmaid dresses.

"That's so sweet!" Kristie exclaims, clapping her hands a little too dramatically.

"Does he know you're coming?" Penny asks, finishing up her dinner.

I shake my head. "No, he doesn't. We talked this morning, but I left out pretty much anything of any importance."

"Where are you staying when you get there?" Rachelle asks.

"Well, honestly, I'm kinda hoping with him, at least for a few days until I can get a place of my own. If it doesn't go well, then I guess I'll stay at a hotel for a few nights."

Penny gives me an odd look across the booth. "Why would it not go well?"

I shrug. "I don't know, lots of reasons, maybe? First off, I don't know how he really feels about me. We've never really discussed it other than a vague declaration at the airport. Plus, even though we've known each other for like twelve years, we only reconnected two weeks ago. A lot can happen or change in that short amount of time."

Kristie's already nodding her head. "He'd be stupid not to want to be with you."

"True!" Rachelle adds, raising her glass once more. "To men not being stupid!" she hollers, drawing the attention of a few surrounding tables and booths.

"And to them being better than average on the penis length scale!" Kristie throws out there. I'm pretty sure I hear a mom nearby gasp as she holds her hands over her young son's ears.

"Todd has a below than average penis," Penny says, her eyes dropping to the table in sadness.

I, on the other hand, have had enough booze to find her comment funny. Apparently, once I start laughing, I can't stop either. "I'm sorry," I reply, holding my hands up in surrender.

She shrugs. "Don't be sorry. It's not your fault he's all talk and no girth."

Kristie giggles uncontrollably. "So why do you keep sleeping with him?" she asks.

Penny looks her dead in the eye and says, "Because his tongue gets the job done."

We all burst into laughter, and another weight lifts off my chest. I'm going to miss these girls. We've hung out for a handful of years now, and whenever I look back on my time here, it'll be with them in mind. Texts and the occasional phones calls won't be the same, but we'll make it work. That's what friends do.

"So, Penny, tell me about this tongue," Kristie whispers, leaning in to hear all about it.

She dives into sex-fused stories about my former co-host before I can stop her, so I just sit back and enjoy what's left of my time here. Unlike a week ago, when I was leaving Tennessee, this time I smile. Sure, I'm sad to leave my friends, the girls I've grown close to during my time in California, but I'm moving on to something bigger.

Something better.

Something real.

***

"Delta flight 8742 to Las Vegas, now boarding at gate 18."

I grab the suitcase I'd barely unpacked just over a week ago, and head toward my gate. I throw my empty paper coffee cup in the trash, wishing I'd bought a second one before takeoff. Not that I need the extra caffeine, but because there's something about hot coffee that's so soothing on my frazzled nerves.

I'm nervous as hell for this flight, but that doesn't stop me from taking it. I'm mere hours away from seeing Rueben. I'm not sure how he's going to react when I show up on his doorstep, but I'm hoping elated and happy are a big part of it.

I guess we'll find out, right?

Chapter Twenty-Two

Rueben

"American Flight 2411, nonstop to San Francisco is now boarding at gate 22."

I shoot my brother a quick text to let him know I'm boarding and stow my phone in my carry-on. I decided against bringing my laptop, even though a few hours of time on the airplane would do wonders for tidying up last minute details before my last day of work. Instead, I'll use the time to catch up on a book I've been wanting to read, or at least, that's what I tell myself. I already know my time inflight will be occupied the same way it's been since I ran into Cricket again.

My mind will be on her.

Hell, I can't even dream without her having the starring role. She's everywhere, including my house. I see her in my room when I look at my bed and in the kitchen every time I use the Gatlinburg souvenir mug we each bought. I can't even look at the hot tub without picturing our last time together. The way our bodies aligned perfectly and the soft gasps of pleasure that slipped from her lips.

Adjusting myself discretely, I pull out my printed boarding pass and jump in line. I watch as the businessmen and women enter first, followed by families and priority boarding. We slowly move along, my mind trying to figure out the right words to say. What do you say to a woman you're about to surprise with a visit and a possible love declaration?

I'm hoping I get that figured out before I land.

"Thank you, sir, enjoy your flight," the polite woman says as she hands me back my scanned pass.

With a quick nod, I head down the jetway and board the plane. Every step brings me closer to Cricket.

Chapter Twenty-Three

Cricket

My hands are already shaking as I follow the GPS on my phone to Rueben's place. It's mid-afternoon, the sun is shining high in the sky, and I'll take that as a sign of happy, bright things to come. I have to. Otherwise, I'll be even more nervous and probably wreck my rental car off the side of the mountain and die in a fiery crash before I can even confess that I'm falling in love with him.

Speaking of rental car, it's a little freaky to be driving up a mountain in a Ford Focus. I probably should have taken the advice of the voice in my head to get the bigger SUV. But when you're spending a big chunk of your savings on moving expenses, you have to cut corners wherever you can, and for me, that cut came in the way of Focus versus Toyota Highlander.

When I pull into the driveway, my heart starts to skip around in my chest like a kindergartener on her first day of school. Excitement and apprehension mix together, making it almost difficult to breathe. "It's now or never, Cricket," I whisper aloud, unbuckling my belt. I take a few deep, cleansing breaths and glance at my reflection in the rearview mirror. Today's appearance is much better than that first time we ran into each other at the airport. My hair is up, yet stylish, and doesn't reflect a big football helmet. I'm wearing comfortable leggings, which he seemed to appreciate every time I wore them before, and a cut cold-shoulder top. I even threw on a little makeup; a look that doesn't scream late-night booty call.

I take one last deep breath and slide out of the driver's seat. When I do, I can't help but giggle at the thought of Rueben trying to get his big, long body in or out of this tiny car. Squaring my shoulders,

I shut the driver's door and keep my eye on the prize...or the front door. It's open, that beautiful mountain air moving through the downstairs as it did so often when I was here with him.

A quick glance at the driveway reveals his SUV, along with one I know to be his brother's. I'm not really enthused about doing this with an audience, but it is what it is, right? No turning back now. I'm sure he heard my car pull in anyway.

As I take my first step up the stairs, I catch movement out of the corner of my eye. Royce walks around the corner of the house, his eyes wide and his mouth hanging out. Almost in disbelief. Yeah, he's definitely surprised to see me. I just hope his brother's shock is of the happy kind. "Shit," he mumbles.

Okay, not really the response I was going for.

"Hey, Royce," I say, my voice a little shaky. "Sorry to just drop in on you guys, but I was sort of hoping to see Rueben. Is he in the house?" I step off the stairs and head toward the older Rigsby brother. He's standing with his hands on his hips, watching me approach.

"Uhh, no," he says, running his hand over the back of his neck the way his brother does.

Dejection sweeps through my blood as I take in how uncomfortable Royce looks. It's like he doesn't know what to say to me. "Oh. Okay. Ummm, do you know where he is?"

Finally, he smiles. No, he doesn't smile. He laughs. He bursts into a fit of hard, belly-shaking laughter, which causes him to double over and put his hands on his knees, confusing me that much more. He doesn't say anything for a few long seconds, which turns into a minute. When his brown eyes finally meet mine, his dances with humor.

"Funny story, Cricket..."

Chapter Twenty-Four

Rueben

I raise my hand and knock on her door. There's music coming from the apartment, some slow melancholy bit by an artist I don't know. My heart starts to pound a heavy beat, much like it did the moment I landed in San Francisco. It took me longer to get here, mostly because I struggled to figure out their public transportation system. I'm not used to cable cars and figuring out stop schedules, so after taking one wrong car, I finally was able to get myself close enough to Cricket's apartment and just hoofed it on foot.

Now, I'm here.

Ready to claim the woman I've fallen in love with.

When the door opens, I'm struck stupid and speechless. The woman in front of me is staring at me, expectantly, waiting on me to speak. "Uhh, hi?" I say, my words coming out a question.

The woman is pretty with her long dark hair pulled up in one of those messy buns and a tight T-shirt and black yoga pants. The problem is she's not Cricket. She gives me a smile. "Can I help you?"

I glance behind her, as if waiting for Cricket to magically appear, or at the very least for the camera crew to jump out and scream "gotcha!" I find the small apartment filled with boxes, some opened and discarded, while others stacked up along the back wall, waiting to be unpacked. A man walks around the corner and gives me an inquisitive look. "Can we help you?" he asks as he approaches the door and throws his arm over the woman's shoulder.

"Sorry, I must have the wrong apartment," I mumble, glancing down the hall and checking the number on the door.

"Who are you looking for?" the lady asks.

"Cricket Hill?"

Why did that come out a question?

"Oh, she doesn't live here anymore," she replies.

Wait, what?

She gives me a grin. "We just moved in today. We're subleasing."

I'm not sure how long I stand there, but it's long enough to make them uncomfortable. Finally, the man says, "So..." leaving it hanging open for me to finish.

Clearing my throat, I ask, "Do you know where she went?"

They both shake their heads. "Sorry, no. The moving van was here this morning when we arrived to get the keys. She was gone about an hour later."

My heart drops to my shoes. I can't believe she's...gone. I mean, we talk all the time and she never once mentioned moving. Maybe that's a sign that our relationship isn't what I thought it as, wasn't going to the place I had hoped. It's not sadness I feel take root in my chest, it's utter despair.

"Oh, okay. Well, thank you," I tell them, taking a step back and then another. The couple watches me go, finally shutting the door when I reach the stairs to head back down to the ground.

Outside, the air is thick and almost gloomy, which is par for the course, considering my sudden mood. I don't know what I expected, but it wasn't that. It wasn't her being gone completely, without so much as a goodbye or kiss my ass.

My phone rings in my pocket, and a part of me wants to let it go to voice mail. When I see Royce's ugly mug on the video chat, I almost do just that. I don't even want to talk to him right now, let alone have him on video chat. The asshole will be able to read my features from a thousand paces, and that's not something I want to get into right now. Right now, I just want to figure out how to get back to the airport. I didn't book a return flight yet, in hopes that I'd be able to stay a few days with Cricket. But now? Now I can't wait to get the fuck out of the city and home to Tennessee.

When the call hangs up, a text message arrives.

Royce: *Answer the fucking phone, dickhead. I have something for you to see.*

I'm pretty sure I don't want to see whatever it is he wants to show me, and the moment the second video call starts ringing, I almost hit decline. But I know the jerk won't let up and will probably keep calling and calling until I finally give in.

That's why I swipe my finger over the screen and paste on my best 'I'm fine' grin.

"Hey," I reply, taking a seat on the front steps of Cricket's building. *Or her former building.*

Royce smiles so big, all I can see are teeth. "Hey, little brother. How's it going?" he singsongs like a fucking lunatic.

"Fine."

"Fine? Really? Have you been to Cricket's place yet?"

I open my mouth, but nothing comes out. I could totally lie and tell him I haven't made it here yet, or I could tell him the truth, that she's not here anymore. Both options suck, if you ask me. I don't make it a habit of lying to my brother, and I'm not really in the mood to listen to his "it'll be okay, there are plenty of fish in the sea" speeches right now.

"Uhhh…" I reply, glancing around as if by some miracle, Cricket will appear.

"Listen, so the reason I was calling was to tell you a visitor just showed up." He's still smiling. I want to punch him in the face.

"Okay," I reply with a shrug. What's he getting at?

"Damn, what a hot little number she is too," Royce says, making the hairs on the back of my neck stand up. "And since you're not here, I might as well keep her entertained, right? I mean, isn't that what a good big brother does?"

"Stop torturing him!" I hear, just as a hand appears on the screen and hits Royce in the arm. That's when I stop breathing all together.

The phone is jostled around until the most beautiful sight fills my screen. Way better looking than my brother. "Hey," Cricket says, a gorgeous smile on her face.

"Hi," I reply, sitting up straight and grinning myself. "What are you doing there?"

Cricket shrugs. "I was in the neighborhood…"

"Yeah? You just happened to be in Pittman Center?" I ask. *Why am I smiling so big?*

"Actually, yes. I just moved here."

My blood swooshes in my ears. Did I just hear her right? "Really?"

Cricket nods. "Yep. I start a new job in Gatlinburg in a week."

"A new job, huh? Doing what?"

"I'd rather tell you about it in person, but you seem to be…not here."

I glance back at the front of her former building. "Yeah, I decided to take a little trip."

"I see that. So…how long are you staying in San Francisco?"

I stand up, collect my bag, and start walking down the sidewalk in the direction I originally came. "I'm not."

"No?"

"Nope, I'm headed home. As quickly as I can get there."

Now she's smiling again. "Good to hear."

Reaching the end of the block, I glance around at the street signs, wishing I'd have paid better attention the first time. "Go left for three blocks and take the next trolley," she starts, giving me step by step directions to get to the airport quicker.

"I'll text you when I have my flight booked," I tell her, elation rushing through me like a tidal wave.

"I'll pick you up at the airport," she says.

"I'll keep her company until you get home!" my asshole brother hollers from the background.

"You'll keep your filthy hands off her!" I yell back all in good fun. I know my brother wouldn't actually mess with Cricket, but still, his comment causes an automatic reaction.

Cricket shakes her head at our banter. "I'll see you soon?" she asks, nibbling on her bottom lip.

"You can bet your sweet ass you will," I confirm as the cable car pulls up. "I have something I want to say to you."

She grins again. "I have something to say to you too."

"See you soon, Cricket," I tell her, and as much as I want to add a declaration of love, I hold back. That's not something I want to do over the phone, even if we're on a video call. When I finally tell her how I feel, it'll be with her standing right in front of me, when I'm able to kiss her and hold her close.

"Bye, Rueben."

After we hang up, I smile the entire way back to the airport. I don't care how much this impromptu trip has cost me. It'll all be worth it to tell her how I feel.

Chapter Twenty-Five

Cricket

I yawn, but I'm not tired. Not really. I'm nervous and excited, all at the same time. His plane just landed, and I've started to pace in anticipation.

The airport is practically deserted as the clock strikes just after one in the morning. Unfortunately, Rueben wasn't able to get an immediate flight out of San Francisco, and the first one available wasn't a direct flight. They took him on a trip to Denver first, before finally sending him back to me in Tennessee.

Royce helped me get settled in Rueben's room, and even though I don't have confirmation that I'm staying with him, the older brother insisted, swearing Rueben would be okay with it. He even made me dinner, even though I wasn't really hungry. Nerves reigned supreme while I waited for Rueben's flight details and then for the hour I could go pick him up. Royce offered to go with me, considering the flight wasn't landing until one a.m., but I insisted he go home and sleep. Royce ended up staying until it was time to go back to the airport, and honestly, I'm grateful. It was nice to have someone to talk to to help pass the time, especially since he filled me in on all his younger brother's most embarrassing moments growing up.

Now, Rueben's flight number shows landed, and I'm waiting for him just outside of the security checkpoint. A few people head my way, pulling small carry-on suitcases and travel bags. My heart starts to pound as I scan each face, looking for the one that makes my heart skip a beat and brings a sense of home.

I hear the pounding of feet echo through the mostly empty corridor, and when I glance up, I see a man running my way. Not just any man. Rueben. He's carrying a duffel bag and making his way through the security checkpoint exit, darting around two businessmen in suits and offering a quick "excuse me."

My smile is instantaneous as he skids to a stop in front of me, drops his bag, and holds out his arms. I launch myself into them, plastering my lips to his. He's home.

I'm home.

Right here in his arms.

"Fuck, I missed you, Crick."

"I missed you too," I reply, my lips still pressed to his, tasting and savoring the softness of those full lips.

The kiss is almost indecent, my body wrapped around his, as he runs his hand through my hair. He pulls back and looks into my eyes. "I can't believe you're here."

Shrugging, I reply, "Nowhere else I want to be."

He sets me down in front of him, his hands framing my face. "I'm falling in love with you. I'm pretty sure I started to fall the moment I ran into you in St. Louis, but I knew it for fact the second you left. I know we have a lot to figure out, but I want to try, Cricket. Fuck, I want to try more than anything."

I smile up at him, his words washing over me like a spring rain. "I've fallen completely in love with you," I confess, my heart feeling freer and lighter than ever before. "That's why I came. I wanted to tell you in person and see if we could figure out the next step. Together."

He exhales and smiles all at the same time, as if he's relieved by my response. As if he thought there was a chance I'd turn him away. "I'm so fucking glad you're here," he says, pulling me into his arms. "Being in that lie was the best thing that ever happened to me."

"Me too. But I don't want it to be a lie anymore."

Rueben shakes his head. "It's not. No more pretending. You're mine for as long as you'll have me."

We're quiet for several minutes, just breathing each other in and reveling in the feel of our bodies pressed together.

"You went to San Francisco," I point out, my cheek pressed against his chest as I breathe him in.

"I did. Imagine the shock I received when a woman answered your apartment door who wasn't you," he says, resting his chin on my forehead and inhaling the scent of my shampoo.

"I'm sorry. I wanted to surprise you."

"That you did, Cricket. That you did." He pulls back and wraps his arms around my shoulders, my arms instantly going to his waist. "So what now?"

"Now we head back to your place. I'm sure you're beat from so much flying."

He gives me a little smirk. "I'm not *that* tired."

Laughing, I turn in his embrace. Rueben picks up his bag, keeping his arm around my shoulder, and guides us toward the exit. "You know what? I'm suddenly not really that tired either," I state, that familiar tingle between my legs visiting as I think about getting him back to his place. Alone.

"Let's head home then, shall we? I want to hear all about this new job on the ride."

Epilogue

Rueben

1 year later

Damn, I'm proud of her.

Cricket is at the top of the mountain, getting ready to zipline down. It's part of her new series on taking risks in their new tourist web-series, sponsored by the Chamber of Commerce.

When she moved to Tennessee a year ago, it was to start her new position within the Chamber. She was helping with PR for their new tourist division with a focus on highlighting all things Gatlinburg and the surrounding communities of Pigeon Forge and Sevierville. It's a joint effort from the three communities, with Cricket spearheading the project.

She's been in front of the camera many times, but that's not where her expertise lies. Once they shoot her videos, she's the one to produce, edit, and prepare the final video for publication. *That's* where the magic happens. *That's* where Cricket shows her professionalism and love for her job. The final product, every single video she's created, is outstanding, and I'm not just saying that because I'm prejudice.

Though, I am a little.

She's really fucking amazing.

But now she's at the top of the mountain, a video camera strapped to her helmet, and getting ready to zoom down the mountain. She's terrified, I already know. That's why she's put off making this particular video, even though ziplining is one of the biggest draws to the Smoky Mountains. But Royce wasn't letting her out of it this time.

He's up there with her, determined to ease her discomfort and help her through this particular assignment.

I'm on the ground, waiting for her arrival, and I'm probably just as nervous as she is.

It's just for different reasons.

"She's almost ready," Royce says into the walkie talkie he provided me. It's how he communicates with his team stationed at the different ledges on the mountain. Her trip isn't just a single shot down the mountain at a high rate of speed. She's zigzagging over the terrain, stopping at little ledges amongst the landscape.

I just pray she keeps her eyes open. It's the only way my plan will work today. Royce assured me she will, even though I'm not so sure he's right. I know my girlfriend and she's terrified of heights like this. The prospect of freefalling to the ground will have her throat closed in terror and her body shaking like a scared puppy. The only reason she agreed to do this is because Royce is going with her. He'll be riding on the line beside her, making sure nothing happens to my girl after they complete their interview at the top.

Of course, she thinks it's all part of the set-up. Only, it's not the video set-up she's thinking. It's for my set-up.

"Passengers are strapped in and ready to go. Everyone ready?" Royce asks, his voice calm and sure.

One by one, each platform responds with a go.

"Rueben?" he whispers, as if not to draw attention to me.

"Yeah, uh, ready. Definitely ready." My heart is trying to crawl out of my chest.

Royce's chuckles filter through the small handheld device in my hands. "Cricket, are you ready?" he asks loudly.

"I guess. Let's get this over with," she mumbles, her voice wobbly with worries.

"You'll be just fine, darlin', I promise. It'll be the best ride of your life," my brother says right before he gives the countdown.

Three.

Two.

One.

***

Cricket

Worst. Idea. Ever.

I don't want to do this, I almost yell as Royce counts down from three. The moment he hits one, my eyes squeeze shut, and I hold my breath.

I feel the fall. The wind is whipping through what little hair isn't contained in the helmet. It smacks me in the face. It chokes the scream that's ripping from my lungs. I know I should open my eyes, but don't want to witness the ground approaching, getting ready to send me to my death.

"This is unreal!" Royce hollers. I want to punch him. Hard. "Cricket! Do you see this?"

"No, I'm good," I tell him, squeezing my eyes so tight the tears seep through the corners. I don't even care I'm recording this fall, my screams of terror, and my less than graceful reaction to ziplining. All I care about now is surviving this stunt and getting both feet safely on the ground.

There's a jolt and I stop hard, two hands wrapping around my arms. "You okay, Cricket?" Royce asks. I admit, it does give me the slightest sliver of comfort knowing he's making this trip with me.

Out of respect for him and his profession, I crack open my eyes. "Am I alive?"

Royce chuckles, moving his harness from one line to the next. "You're very much alive, darlin'." When he's securely locked in place, he turns to face me. I glance up at the man beside me, moving my security cord from one line to the next, a reminder that this trip is only a fourth of the way done.

Royce looks me square in the eye. "How about this? Close your eyes for a second as we make the initial fall, but then I want you to open them up. Can you do that?"

I shake my head.

"Yes, you can do this, Cricket. Open your eyes. You're not has high up as you think you are," he says, glancing down.

I make the mistake of doing the same and I swear the landing platform moves under my wobbly legs.

"I promise it'll be worth it," he whispers, stepping over and squeezing my arm.

"I don't know," I whisper, my throat thick with emotion.

"Crick?" I hear through the walkie talkie at Royce's shoulder. He takes it off and hands it to me.

"Rueben?" I ask, wondering why he's on the radio.

"Hey, baby. I just watched your first leg, and I have to tell you, you did good."

I can't help it, I laugh, though it lacks any actual humor. "Good? Did you hear me screaming?"

He laughs too. "Yeah, I heard. The entire city heard, baby. But you can do this. I know you can. Just listen to Royce and relax. Enjoy the fall, Crick."

I swallow over the very large, very hard lump in my throat. "Listen to Royce? Aren't you the one who's usually telling me to *not* listen to him?"

That makes both men laugh. "True, I have been saying that. But this time, promise me you'll listen to him. Just this once."

Exhaling, I look over into Rueben's brother's eyes. They're full of respect and trust, and I realize I need to do the same. "Okay. I'll do it."

"Good girl. Now get that sexy ass down this mountain so I can kiss you," he says into the walkie talkie, making me giggle.

Royce takes the device and reattaches it to his shoulder. "You heard the man. Let's get down this mountain. You ready?"

I swallow back the reply I want to give and say, "Yes. I'm ready."

"Good. Let's do this!" Royce hollers, getting everyone into position for the next leg of our descent.

Three.

Two.

One.

I close my eyes as we plunge off the platform and start another crazy fall. I want to open my mouth, to scream my protests, but I don't. Instead, I recall the promise I just made to Rueben. To listen to Royce and enjoy the ride.

Slowly, I crack open one eyelid, the swoosh of air hitting my eyeball. When I see I'm still tethered to the line, I crack open the second.

"Open your eyes, Cricket."

I put all my trust in Royce and open them completely. We're zipping along the trees, zagging down the mountain at a much higher rate of speed than I'm used to, but it's...not that bad. The next platform is in sight, but that's not what draws my eyes. I'm focused on the wooden sign positioned all by itself on the side of the mountain.

It reads... Will.

"Will? What does that mean?" I ask Royce, who's sitting beside me, a wide grin on his face as he relaxes into the harness, his arms and legs spread out. "Oh my god! A will? Is that what this means? I didn't get a will! Royce, why didn't I get a will before I did this?" I holler, just as my feet hit the next platform and my body jolts to a stop. "I don't have a will, Royce!"

He's smiling wide as he moves his next carabiner. "It's fine, Cricket, I swear. That wasn't a notice to update your will."

"Really? Are you sure? It was like this big white sign telling me I'm fucked for not doing a will before I die." Who cares about the cameras? I can edit out that part.

"Ready for the next trip? This is the third one," he says, ignoring another one of my freak-outs and making sure we're all secure for the next trip.

When they nod that I'm set, I grumble, "Fine. Let's get this over with."

Royce smiles that boyish grin that's exactly like his little brother's. "Just remember, Cricket. Keep those eyes open!"

And then they start to countdown and we're off again. This time, I force my eyes open a little quicker on the fall, and find myself actually taking in the breathtaking scene around me. Another spot of white on the landscape catches me eye. This one says "You."

You? What the hell does that mean?

My feet hit the third platform and those hands reach out and grab me, steadying me, before moving the carabiners and getting us ready for the fourth and final leg of our trip down the mountain.

"You still with me?" Royce asks, checking his connection and getting ready.

"I'm with you. I'm not sure what that sign meant though. Did you see it? It said you. What does that mean? Is that God calling? He's here for me, isn't he?"

Royce lets a full belly laugh fly, doubling over like he did that day I showed up at Rueben's house a year ago. "Oh, Cricket, you're something else. I can see why my brother loves you so much."

Standing back up, he adds, "Well, let's go. He's waiting down on the ground."

And just like that, we're ready to make the final journey down.

"Cricket?" Royce says, pulling my attention to where he hangs beside me.

"Yeah?"

"Promise me you'll sit back and enjoy the ride, okay? Keep those eyes open. It'll be worth it." There's something in the way he says it, but I find myself nodding in understanding.

The countdown begins one final time and then we let go. I don't close my eyes this time, choosing to enjoy the entire freefall as best as I can. Right away, I see another white sign approaching. It's the same size as the others, the letters printed in big black block script.

"Marry," I whisper.

What the hell is going on?

Before I even have a chance to try to piece it together, a fourth sign appears. Me.

Marry me?

Something catches in my throat and I gasp. It's not at the scenery or the fact that I'm ziplining, even after swearing to God and all things holy that I'd never do it. The signs.

Oh my God! The signs!

Will.

You.

Marry.

Me?

Holy shit, someone is proposing! But who? I barely have time to considering the options when my feet touch down on the fourth and final platform, mere feet off the ground. When I glance at Royce, he's grinning like a loon, which makes me smile as well.

"Did you see those signs? I think someone is proposing," I tell him as they remove my safety harness and get me out of the contraption I had to wear for this expedition through hell. But I have to admit, despite the screaming and the fear and the pleas to save me, I did actually enjoy myself.

Don't tell Royce.

"Really?" he asks, glancing down to the ground where his brother stands. "What did the signs say?"

"Will you marry me?"

"That's odd. Who could be proposing?" he asks after making sure he's free from his zipline harness.

"I'm not sure. Maybe it's someone coming down the mountain?" I follow him down the stairs that lead to the ground.

Oh, sweet, safe ground. I will never complain about you ever again.

When I get to the bottom of the stairs, Royce takes my helmet, which I'm grateful the moment I see Rueben. He's standing off to the side, a big smile on his face, but there's something different about his eyes. They're intense, and maybe a little nervous as he watches me walk his way.

Rueben takes me in his arms and spins me around. When my feet hit the ground, his hands frame my face in that way I've come to love and expect, and he places his hips against mine. Then, before I even have a chance to kiss him back, he moves, kneeling in front of me.

What in the world?

My mouth opens to ask him if he's okay, but when he gazes up at me, something steals my breath. It's the look in his eye that tells me everything I need to know. I see his love for me, for our life we've made, and will continue to work on together. I see a little anxiety and a bit of tension. But I also see an anticipation. Question.

250

Holy shit!

Suddenly, it all starts to make sense.

The signs.

Will you marry me?

Holy shit, someone is proposing.

A gasp falls from my open lips as my hands cover my gaping mouth. I gaze down at him, a smile crossing his handsome face. "Cricket Hill, this past year has been the greatest of my life, and that's because of you. You make me a better man, and I can't think of a better way to spend my life than with you by my side, as my wife."

He pulls a ring from his jeans front pocket and holds it between his thumb and first finger. A cry slips past my lips as he grins up at me, takes my left hand in his and positions it at the tip of my finger. "The moment I saw this ring, I knew it was made for your finger. Just like you were made for me. I love you, Cricket Hill, and I want nothing more to than to marry you. Will you be my wife?"

I'm not sure I even wait until he's finished his question. "Yes! Yes!" I holler, my entire body shaking.

His grin could light up the night sky as he slips the ring on my finger and stands up, taking me in his arms once more. Our lips meet in a frenzy of urgency and celebration as applause rings out around us. When we pull away, I'm shocked to find a handful of employees of the zipline company there, as well as Royce, who just so happens to be using the camera on my helmet to tape our exchange.

"I love you, Crick," Rueben whispers, kissing my forehead

"And I love you, Ruby."

He growls and nips at my ear. "You're going to pay for that," he whispers.

Giving him a saucy grin, I reply, "I sure hope so."

The End

Don't miss a new release, reveal, or sale! Sign up for my newsletter at www.laceyblackbooks.com/newsletter

Acknowledgments

A huge thank you to everyone who had a hand in bringing this book to life!

Melissa Gill – Thank you for the wonderful cover.

Give Me Books – Thank you for your tireless work organizing the cover reveal and release.

Kara Hildebrand – Thank you for your editing expertise.

Sandra Shipman and Jo Thompson – Thank you for beta and alpha reading, and for your help in making the storyline consistent.

Kaylee Ryan – Thank you for always being just a text or phone call away.

Holly Collins – Thank you for always believing in me.

Brenda Wright, Formatting Done Wright – Thank you for another amazing format.

My ARC team – Thank you for the early reviews and for sharing the book with the world.

Lacey's Ladies – Thank you for your continual support and for making me laugh every day.

My family, husband, and kids – Thank you for always standing by my side.

Bloggers and Readers – Thank you, thank you, thank you!

About the Author

Lacey Black is a Midwestern girl with a passion for reading, writing, and shopping. She carries her e-reader with her everywhere she goes so she never misses an opportunity to read a few pages. Always looking for a happily ever after, Lacey is passionate about contemporary romance novels and enjoys it further when you mix in a little suspense. She resides in a small town in Illinois with her husband, two children, and a chocolate lab. Lacey loves watching NASCAR races, shooting guns, and should only consume one mixed drink because she's a lightweight.

Email: laceyblackwrites@gmail.com
Facebook: https://www.facebook.com/authorlaceyblack
Twitter: https://twitter.com/AuthLaceyBlack
Website: www.laceyblackbooks.com

Made in the USA
Monee, IL
14 September 2020